A HINT OF DARKNESS

MAGIC OF THE DAMNED

MCKENZIE HUNTER

This is a work of fiction. Names, characters, businesses, places, events, and incidents are either the products of the author's imagination or used in a fictitious manner. Any resemblance to actual persons, living or dead, or actual events is purely coincidental.

McKenzie Hunter

A Hint of Darkness

© 2022, McKenzie Hunter

McKenzieHunter@McKenzieHunter.com

ALL RIGHTS RESERVED. This book contains material protected under International and Federal Copyright Laws and Treaties. Any unauthorized reprint or use of this material is prohibited. No part of this book may be reproduced or transmitted in any form or by any means, electronic or mechanical, including photocopying, recording, or by any information storage and retrieval system without express written permission from the author/publisher.

Cover Artist: Orina Kafe

For notifications about new releases, *exclusive* contests and giveaways, and cover reveals, please sign up for my mailing list at mckenziehunter.com

ISBN: 978-1-946457-31-8

ACKNOWLEDGMENTS

When a book is completed, I am forever appreciative of the people who made it possible. Thanks to my friends and family for their endless support and encouragement, and for checking on me when I'm hunkered down in my writer's cave. I'm grateful for beta readers and editors who work so diligently helping me with my stories.

I appreciate the readers for choosing my books from the many available to you and following quirky Luna and broody Dominic's story.

1

Helena's piercing eyes seared into me. Her curiosity had warped into accusation. One moment they had Peter, the Dark Caster, imprisoned in a cell, and the ability to move freely between my world and the underworld. Moments later, they were the ones imprisoned in the underworld, Peter was gone, and I was left in his place. The only thing they knew was that I was the reason.

Despite my denials, Helena didn't seem convinced that I wasn't a co-conspirator. Her desperate need to learn the truth behind their imprisonment was clear in her graceful feline movements. Every time she moved, I did the same, cautiously, to keep her in my line of sight.

"Your human has caused a lot of problems," she said, snapping her eyes from me to Dominic. I could feel the collective weight of Dominic's and Anand's eyes on me, but I was too wary of Helena to risk looking at them. After all, she was the one who'd casually suggested taking off a finger and murdering me just on the mere possibility it would fix the problem and return the escaped prisoners. If I was the reason we were imprisoned in the underworld, and if she believed freedom could be gained by my death, there wasn't a shadow of doubt she would kill me.

"This is my problem to deal with," Dominic provided, his voice a grave command. Before she could respond, his hand braced around my wrist like a cuff and he was navigating me up the stairs. The more I struggled, the firmer his grip became.

The clench of his jaw made the muscles of his neck bulge. His silence was ominous.

"You know I had nothing to do with this," I explained as he marched me through the palatial home. The foreboding nature of his silence pricked at my survival instinct. I needed him to say something. Soothe my fears. Assure me that he knew I had no role in what had happened. Provide a plan of action. Something. Instead, he hauled me through the house as if I was a suspect. I hated that my mind kept going to his room of torture in his farmhouse. And the room at the entrance of the home, which he wouldn't allow me to fully see. My imagination went haywire.

"Dominic?"

Screw this. I'm not going any farther with him until I know where his head's at. Gripping my socked toes into the marble floor for traction didn't even slow him. It only reminded me of when he'd taken on a roomful of people in a macabre display of violence. At least his claws weren't out. Not yet.

I went limp. He wasn't going anywhere with dead weight. A flit of amusement curled his lips. In a flash of movement, he swooped me into a bundle and tossed me over his shoulder.

"Put me down right now!" I demanded.

After a few minutes, he did. After throwing open the door of a room, he lowered me to my feet. Unsteady, it took me a few moments to straighten to my full height. The several inches he had on me, I felt.

"Don't you ever do that again."

Banked fire raced across his eyes. They were dark amber, his eyes. They drank me in and he made his unspoken challenge, swallowing the space he'd allowed between us.

"Or what, Luna?" he asked, drawing out my name in a taunt.

"You know I had nothing to do with this, right?"

Canting his head, he studied me. In an attempt to keep space between us, I'd inadvertently backed myself into the wall. His arms caged me in.

"Do I?"

As a distraction from his intense gaze, I took a look around. The room was more spacious than the one they'd placed me in during my stay. Minimalist décor. A cognac-tan contemporary chesterfield sofa in front of the wall-to-ceiling window. Alabaster walls. Two slim dark wood bookcases in each corner. Bold scenic large art pieces on the walls that didn't distract from the view of the garden. Open French doors to his bedroom. I could only see the bed that stayed true to the simplistic style, but moodier. Dark steel-gray platform bed, larger than the typical king size. Fluffy duvet with contrasting darker coverlet. Three pillows lined across it. I assumed this was his living space. Everything about it was distinctly him.

"Luna," he said, coaxing my attention back to him.

"You do. Why would I do anything to lock myself in the underworld with your violence-positive sister and prisoners so heinous that they were sentenced to be here? I don't want to be here."

Still silent, his hand enclosed my neck. Not tight, yet I was fully aware of it and how easily that could change. His thumb ran lazily over the pulse in my neck that was pumping erratically. It wouldn't have been so frightening if he was more relaxed. Tension and wrath were in every slightest movement of his body. He was trapped in the underworld. A caged animal. He'd probably never been restricted.

"Tell me what happened again." He leaned in, his lips inches from mine and his thumb still languidly moving.

Rehashing everything that happened, I gave him minute detail, hoping he'd find answers where I couldn't. It wasn't like the incident when I'd unintentionally released the prisoners from the underworld. Then, it was apparent something had happened. One minute, I was perusing a weird book; the next, it pricked me, drew blood, and I was looking down at blank pages. This was entirely different, so he got the entire minute-by-minute replay of my mundane day. My day at work, details of what I ate for dinner, that I cleaned my apartment and had conversations with my brother and Emoni. The day had ended with me winding down with a cup of ginger tea and air-popped popcorn. Dominic knew in intricate detail the title of the rom-com I watched and that it had become my top choice over my previous favorite fantasy genre, having now had my fill of the supernatural world. Pushing down any form of embarrassment, I told him how apprehensive I now was about reading a book and how close I was to using my e-reader instead.

His eyes traveled over me. "Why did Peter choose you?" he inquired, but the question wasn't for me, just an internal speculation that he'd allowed me in on.

"I don't know," I said before his hand slipped from my neck and eased to my waist, under my shirt, the warmth of his touch slinking over me. Lavender filtered into the space, a somnolent feeling of peace fell over me, and I found myself relaxing into complacency.

No the hell I'm not. My hand shot out to punch him. He grabbed it and pushed it against the wall, then my other hand received the same treatment before I could make an attempt with it.

"Luna, Luna, Luna," he drawled, a sharp edge in his tone rounding off. "Why so violent?"

"Me? You just had your hand around my throat," I hissed.

His lips still curled. "Did you believe I was about to choke you?"

I wasn't confident enough in saying no to respond.

"If I wanted to choke you, I would have. I was just making sure you were telling me all I needed to know."

His thumb was back on the pulse of my neck.

"That's not how you take a person's pulse. You press two fingers to it." I demonstrated it for him. "And you could have just explained that."

"I'm not used to giving explanations." That wasn't an acceptable answer, but from his expression he clearly believed it was.

"And you were using magic to draw me to your will," I accused.

"I don't draw people to my will, I bend them to my desire."

Swallowing, I knew it was the truth. His way.

"You were agitated, and I was simply trying to calm you."

Helena had warned me that Dominic was ruthless when necessary but calculating in his execution. A tactician, a stark contrast to his sister who was ruled by impulsivity and violence-lust.

"I'm telling you the truth. I don't want to be locked in here any more than you do."

He leaned in closer, pressing a light kiss against my lips, his tongue brushing lightly against mine and causing me to immediately forget I was in the middle of an interrogation. Dominic's hand glided along the curve of my waist. The tentative kiss quickly became rough and hard. When he lifted me, my legs wrapped around his hips, pulling his impressive hardness against me.

He pulled away, his hands cupping my ass. "What am I missing about your family?" he requested, his lips resting against mine.

"What?" I exhaled in a rush of breath. *How did we get back here?*

"I don't believe the Dark Caster chose you randomly. There's a connection and I'm curious about it. Why choose you and not your brother, Forest?" A touch of humor was in his voice at the mention of my brother's name. Luna and Forest. People always found some amusement in it.

"Your parents met at a bar in Colorado, married six months later, and two years later you were born. They relocated a year after you were born because of a new opportunity for your father. He works as a bank manager and your mother as a stylist. Absolutely no connection to the magical world. Your brother is the least traditional of you all. If there is a familial connection, why not him over you?"

That was a polite way of saying Forest was a transient—or, to use his preferred definition—a 'discoverer of life' where he periodically attended college, moving from one calling to another, including being a barista, self-proclaimed events planner, writer, and social media influencer with a following that would allow him to influence a small classroom. In the past two years, he had trained to be an electrician and was currently working as an apprentice. It seemed to be something he enjoyed, although he'd comment it was just another *experience*. An experience I hoped would lead to a career he liked.

Dominic went on to list the various jobs and professions my brother has had since he was sixteen. Some, I wasn't even aware were part of his vitae.

"You seem to know everything. I'm not sure what more I can offer?"

The heat of his body was enveloping me everywhere his hands touched, his amber eyes as mesmeric as a dying flame.

"But there is more. He chose you and that wasn't by coincidence. Think. No detail is too small."

My life wasn't exactly exciting, and nothing stood out

that would remotely link me to the world of magic. My name inevitably led to people believing our parents were hippies. They couldn't be further from the truth. Our parents were so rigid in their beliefs that bringing up even the possibility of a supernatural world would have been quickly dismissed. The connection wouldn't have been through my family. So, I moved to my friends. Other than Reginald, the faux witch, I had no connections through my friends, past or present.

"I think it was coincidental," I admitted, acutely aware of Dominic nestled between my legs. "Wrong place at the wrong time. Maybe Peter watched me because I seemed likely to do what he wanted. How many people would find a strange book, take it home, and read it? The ring would have appealed to only some people, and he put himself in a position to be able to watch his plan unfold."

"Well this is an interesting interrogation technique. Will screwing her be part of the torture?" Helena said breezily, her blade-sharp glare traveling up my legs wrapped around Dominic's waist to his hands under my shirt and tantalizingly close to my breasts.

"Helena," Dominic ground out to his sister and her disapproving scowl.

"We're locked in here and you're busy playing with your human?"

"Anand and I are locked in here," he pointed out, a cruel reminder that without her magic, Helena lost her ability to travel between the underworld and my world. The loss of magic hadn't removed her depthless cold look that held its own diablerie.

"I don't need a reminder of your overreaction. If you value your human, you may rethink your stance on that," she said, approaching us slowly and extending her arms to expose the sigils on them that restricted her magic. Dominic released me and positioned himself between me and Helena.

"Should I remind you that I don't need magic to get rid of your Luna," she hissed.

Feeling belittled and also like a coward for letting Dominic be a bastion of safety, I thought about moving around him and presenting a brave front. And then what? Bravely get my ass kicked? Images of watching her destroy several supernaturals with minimal effort allowed me to reluctantly accept the protection.

"Oh Dominic. This is not a good look. You've allowed yourself to be brought low by a human. What is it about this creature?" Helena sneered.

Not a fan of that descriptor.

She gave me another appraisal. "I guess she is somewhat acceptable. Cute. Pint-size."

Nice insult, you giant. I pressed my lips together to keep the response from flying out.

"You've had better. Prettier. And sexier. If I didn't know any better, I'd think you were bespelled by *this* human."

Whether their speed was linked to their magic, or their very being possessed its own, she'd suddenly moved around her brother and locked her hand around my neck. I gasped out the final breath she let me take while I clawed at her hand.

"Let her go, Helena," Dominic said with the calmness of a person who was able to freaking breathe. "Now."

Several ticks of time passed as she scrutinized me and her brother. Then she released me with a shove and I gasped for breath, putting distance between us.

"Fuck your creature then do what needs to be done." She crossed her arms over her chest and stepped out of our pathway. What was she planning to do, watch? Dammit, I needed to get away from this weird family and their violent, voyeuristic nature.

"I need her. We need her. If we plan to ever get out of here."

"Dominic." The hostility had drained from her voice. "She is here and we are locked in. A temporalibus was done. She took Peter's place, but she is also keeping the spell active. He sees a weakness in you and is exploiting it. You have two choices. Play into his hands and let her live—or do your damn job." The latter was pushed through clenched teeth.

"That has always been the difference between us. You're impulsive. There's a reason behind him choosing her, and it is imperative that we find that reason. When we do, it will be used against him. I captured him once. You know it will happen again."

"Can't do it while imprisoned. Make no mistake, brother, we are as imprisoned as those in the dungeon. But ignore me if you must. It's not just you and Anand unable to freely roam between the worlds. It's Father, too. He will only tolerate captivity for so long. The problem will be fixed. Now you must determine on whose terms."

The slight clench of his jaw was the only response he granted her. It was enough to lift her mood. A smile spread across her face before she left the room.

The Lord of the Underworld. He'd handle the situation. That wasn't any comfort. Because *I* was the situation.

2

Turning to face me, Dominic's expression was indecipherable as he devoured the space between us. His finger traced the line of my jaw, down my neck, across my jugular. Silence.

Say something. Explain the situation. Ease the tension.

"Dominic," I whispered.

He remained withdrawn in his thoughts as his finger returned to the curve of my neck. I was fully aware that the fingers that lingered over the arteries in my neck could become claws in a matter of seconds. I swallowed when he pulled me to him, his hand twining around my hair. He yanked. Kneeling down at the threshold of the door, he laid the strands of hair across it.

"You have to ask before you do that," I snapped.

His head canted ever so slightly, the blaze of his eyes and his posture showing a raw resistance to my command. Clearly a man not used to letting people know what he's about to do.

"It's a simple request for courtesy."

"Or I could just not place the ward."

"Really." I frowned. "At my request for a basic display of

manners, you counter with leaving me vulnerable to your sister's whims?"

His crisp gaze lingered on me. Malice pulsed in his eyes and in a draw of breath, he was in front of me, his hand gently lacing through my hair. Heat from his body snaked around me. The intensity of his gaze as they held mine… a raging inferno lived in it. The previous strands of hair he'd taken from me were coiled around his finger.

"May I?" The heat in his voice seemed to be asking about more than just follicles for a spell.

"Yeah," I whispered in a low rasp.

"Thank you, Luna." The proximity of his body and primal sensuality that existed in any space he occupied made me think with my hormones instead of with the higher thinking that I desperately needed.

Luna, you're trying to make a point. Despite my victory, it felt hollow because he'd taken something from this interaction. It showed in his salacious smirk.

"Remember, once you cross it, the ward is disabled, allowing others to get in as well. Stay on this side of the door."

"This is where I'm staying?"

He nodded. "You'll be my guest here," he said. I preferred this politer version of 'my room is probably the only way to keep my sister from murdering you.'

During the first hour of Dominic's absence, I made myself familiar with my surroundings. Calling it a bedroom didn't begin to cover it. Bedrooms didn't have a kitchen, laundry, and two sitting rooms, one in the anteroom and the other in his bedroom. Sleep didn't come, so I curled up on the large circular chair in the bedroom with a book I'd found on the bookshelf. I'd perused several spellbooks; there was another that looked like a historical account of the supernatural world. I ignored the spellbooks. The night— No, the past few weeks had made me apprehensive about dealing with spellbooks. The account didn't offer anything more than what Dominic had already shared. It did give me a little more insight as to why Anand preferred living in the underworld to living among the others, which was that interspecies were often regarded poorly. If mixed with a human, they were viewed as a lesser being, their power diminished: for example, a human-shifter couldn't shift but retained some enhanced abilities. The few that were able to shift couldn't maintain the form long enough for it to be any use to them. They were never allowed to be part of a pack or pride. If the half-shifter was the result of the woman in the pack becoming pregnant, she was given the choice to abandon her child to the father or leave. The father was not given the option and was cast out.

Children who were human-witch combination were rare because witches valued protection of the strength of their magic over everything. Although a witch wasn't thrown out of their coven for the violation, their offspring was forbidden to mate with another witch. The diluted bloodline ended with their child. Because human-witch children only presented with a nominal level of magic, the magic line was quickly diluted.

Vampires couldn't have children, losing their ability to procreate once they were changed. The vampires they sired were considered their children.

Studying the book, I couldn't help but think of Anand, a hybrid therefore considered weak and a demonstration of a weakened bloodline. Inconsequential. I'd seen Anand's abilities. There wasn't anything weak or inconsequential about him. His stealth, ability to go undetected in any environment, heightened senses, and lightning-fast reflexes, which I was sure was attributed to his magic, were not what was generally believed.

What happened to supernaturals who contradicted established beliefs? Was it his choice to live in the underworld to seek refuge among those who wouldn't judge him or didn't care about those things? But whatever Anand's abilities were, I doubted they exceeded Helena's and Dominic's.

The historical accounts of the supernaturals in reality were a drastic contrast to the diluted fantastical view found in the *Discovery of Magic* that Reginald had given me. But anything could be viewed that way when the quest for power, cruelty, politics, and violence was removed.

I didn't need any reminders, but it was the nudge into action I needed. I didn't want to live in the underworld. It was an unlikely option anyway. If they didn't find a way to break the spell and free themselves and taking my life was the prevailing option, I wouldn't survive my stay.

How long did I have before their patience grew thin?

Despite fixating on the metaphorical ticking clock, I managed to fall asleep after setting aside the supernatural history book and attempting to read *Le Comte de Monte-Cristo*, putting my infrequently used French to use. Five pages in, I realized why it was infrequently used: I wasn't good at it. Trading it in for the English translation, *The Count of Monte Cristo*, I slipped into an uneasy sleep.

Startled awake by a hard knock on the door, I quickly came to my feet and answered the door, book clutched to my chest. Dominic, carrying two bags, was waiting.

"You need to let me in."

"Come in," I said, stepping aside.

His eyes dropped to the door. Rust and purple waves burst across the threshold before pushing him back. It was comforting to see the ward's effectiveness. When I stepped over the threshold, the pressure of the ward gripped my leg before releasing it. Dominic, now free to enter, came in and placed the bags on the trunk-style desk, which had become my favorite item in the room. Surrounded by clean lines, sterile neutral colors, and minimalist décor, I appreciated the whimsy of buckles on a desk. They worked and I was sure there was a story behind it that I was interested to learn.

"Clothing and essentials," he told me as he opened the larger bag, revealing its contents.

"Thank you. There are stores here?"

He shook his head. "We keep supplies for those who work here. And guests."

"How often do you all have guests?"

The underworld didn't seem like a popular trip destination. But before the transfer of duties, Dominic had been the arbiter of punishment for the supernatural world. A hostile situation instigated by his sister had required him to give up that power in order to protect her. The other people who resided in the underworld were those who'd struck a mutually beneficial deal to work there. Once the term of the contract was over, magic would be used to wipe their memories. They wouldn't remember the nice clothing they were given, the mansion where they resided, the prince they worked for, and all the peculiar things of the underworld that would make them compare and maybe appreciate their own world. Or recall the darkness of this world. A sun that never rose, a sky that was always dim, and a garden with the darkest of plants. No memories of the place devoid of greenery and sunlight so they'd appreciate those things even more upon their return.

I clawed my way from the despair that wanted to creep in and focused on what was in the bag.

Holding a button-down against my body, I looked at him.

Restrained laughter made his lips twitch.

I'd ask Dominic for a belt or scarf that I could tie around the waist so I could wear the shirt as a dress. Certain styles I avoided because they brought attention to my vertical challenges. This shirt wasn't one of them. Sorting through the various bits of clothing, I found several pairs of leggings, my preferred t-shirts both oversized and fitted, and jeans. There appeared to be enough to last me a little over a week. I hoped there wouldn't be a need for all of it and that I would soon be back home, coming up with believable excuses to explain my absence to everyone.

"Did you get anything from questioning Vadim, Celeste, and Roman?" I asked, refolding the clothes and stacking them on the desk.

His eyebrows rose and then his gaze followed mine to the bloodstain on his shirt. It was an educated guess, but he'd left like a man in desperate need of answers. I wanted some, too.

"Vadim and I are rarely civil when we interact." The shifter with magical abilities and immunity to silver. An anomaly among shifters.

I wondered if he managed to be civil with Roman, whose claws were poisonous to him. I distinctly remembered Rei, an Awakener, being excited to have Dominic come in contact with the vampire's claws. They were poisonous, causing a magic wielder to lose his magic until the poison was out of his system. Expecting vicious-looking claws like Helena's and Dominic's, I was surprised by Roman's slightly curved, seemingly innocuous nails. He was the worst of the worst, possessing an ability I hadn't seen with other vamps. A shudder of fear went through me at the thought of the third prisoner, Celeste, whose touch could kill.

"Did they know anything?"

He shook his head. "If they do, they're not revealing the information no matter what is done to them. Peter's freedom increased their chances of them getting their own, permanently."

"Can he release them again?"

"I don't think it's possible with you here. I'm still not convinced that him using you to release them the first time was a coincidence."

Once again, I was under his heavy gaze, but I didn't entertain comment because I felt differently. Me being locked in here now wasn't a coincidence, but I thought my initial entanglement was a crime of opportunity.

"If they are ever released and determine that they can't be returned to their prison, the chaos begins. A civil war where there will be no impunity for the victor."

"You'll do nothing about it?"

"I will."

I took his terse response, accepting being spared the details of the violence and death that would be needed to control the situation. And the inevitable firestorm he would face from other witches if he had to kill Celeste, whose magical link to the most powerful witches in existence meant that they would die as well.

Fear of what this meant for not just the supernaturals, but humans as well, brought new clarity. Everything I'd learned and experienced during my initial visit to the underworld raced through my mind.

"I might be able to leave," I rushed out, recalling the use of the Trapsen he'd given me before, which allowed me to travel between the two worlds. "And get help," I tacked on with zero confidence that was possible, because negotiation was why the responsibility of regulating the supernaturals had been taken from Dominic and returned to Demetrius. I had not made friends of the Awakeners, who wanted to expose the world to the existence of supernaturals, not as a courtesy to allow them to navigate a world where they were pawns between those who wanted to remain hidden and those who didn't, but because they felt that exposure would elevate the supernaturals to the top of the food chain, putting humans at the bottom where they would be treated in ways that would serve as a reminder of their lowly status. Things weren't much better with those who wanted to stay hidden, because if a human gained any knowledge of them, usually as a result of a supernatural's failure, humans paid. Magic was used on them to wipe their minds, or they were compelled by a vampire to believe what the supernaturals wanted them to believe.

Dominic pulled the triangular prism from his pocket and handed it to me. "I figured you'd want to try. I'm not hopeful that it will work." He flashed a small knife, which I'd need to draw blood and close around the Trapsen to activate it.

"It's worth a try," I said.

"If it does, then what?" His voice was neutral and his expression mild.

"I'll get Nailah to help me." Of the people I'd met, she'd exhibited the level of diplomacy that may yield the best results. "Have you tried it?"

He nodded.

"Give me Nailah's info and I'll contact her." Their Seer appeared to have a rapport with the Conventicle's representatives. Or at the very least, she didn't seem to antagonize them to the extent Anand and Dominic did.

I tucked away the piece of paper containing the various ways to contact her, including a spell, which I wasn't sure was useful to me.

"Ready?" Dominic asked.

I nodded and extended my hand to him. After a quick prick from the blade, I closed my fingers around the Trapsen, making sure it made contact with the welling blood. Closing my eyes, I imagined my small apartment. Home. Home. Home. How very *Wizard of Oz*. But I continued the silent chant with the entreat of a plea.

When I reopened them, Dominic had invaded the space between us, his expression expectant.

"Trapped here."

Maybe he had felt some hope for success, because anger and the promise of unspeakable revenge tinged his voice. He was putting a great deal of effort in subduing the raging beast who didn't appreciate being trapped.

After several minutes working for that control, he found

it. Exhaling a slow breath, he unbuttoned the cuffs of his shirt then the front buttons. When he shrugged off his shirt, my gaze moved from his face to the intricate sigils snaking around his body that made him immune to witch magic.

"Shower," he said, leaving the room.

To stop myself trailing after him, I returned to sorting through the remainder of the clothing. I found a few dresses, a pair of black heels, and flats, which surprisingly fit. Unzipping the smaller bag, I found underwear and socks. Warmth inched up my cheeks at the thought of him picking these items for me, then I wondered if he had chosen them or had someone else do it. There was a collection of cotton hipsters and briefs, lacy thongs, and cheeky panties. The same with the bras: comfortable-looking sports bras, balconette, satin and lace embroidered plunge ones, and even several sheer bras that served no other purpose than to be sexy. Even the assortment of footwear ranged from simple ankle socks to thick fluffy ones with hints of lavender permeating off them. Sleepwear consisted of oversized shirts and tanks with matching wide-leg pants, all nicer than anything I'd wear to sleep in. Barely there tank and matching shorts so cute there wouldn't be any sleeping, and an ultra-soft cami.

Thoughts of our sleeping arrangements were interrupted by Dominic calling me from the door. A towel was wrapped low around his waist, his hair was wet and messy, and the dimmed light cast a shadow that darkened his eyes.

"I'm out of the shower," he said. "It's free if you need it," he added, answering my expression of confusion.

"Where am I sleeping?" I asked, grabbing the cami and panties and following him into the room.

"Wherever you'd like." He moved to the bed, dropping the towel and giving me a glimpse of his ass before sliding on a pair of briefs and getting into the bed.

It was nearly impossible to enjoy the shower, the waterfall showerhead, the dark and jagged stacked stones surrounding me, and the soft lights designed to create a relaxing experience. I should have focused on all that, but my mind kept going to the sexy-as-sin prince just outside my door. Showered, I stacked my towel-dried hair into a messy bun and slipped on the clothes.

Dominic was sprawled on one side of the bed, the top sheet over the lower half of his body, the duvet rolled away. I had an unobstructed view of more sigils covering his back. I eased into the opposite side, which was larger than any king-size bed I'd ever seen. It was massive, which put to rest any worries of unintentional intimacy. If we neared each other for any reason, it would be intentional.

As it was when he moved, rolling toward me. Amber eyes a silhouette of a dying flame but with the raging intensity of a forest fire. Lightly brushing his lips against mine, softly at first, he then kissed me harder. Firm hands pressed into my back, kneading at my skin. The warmth of his body engulfed me. I wanted more. Needed more. When he pulled away, he was panting. Soft breath wisped across my lips. His fingers ran over the soft material at the front of the cami, making my nipples harden. His desire was palpable, along with his restraint.

"Why did you stop?" I whispered.

"We have a busy day tomorrow."

That was a BS answer if I ever heard one. He'd questioned the prisoners. They hadn't given him any answers about Peter, but maybe they'd disclosed something about me that left him unconvinced that me being in their lives wasn't coincidental.

"Goodnight," he whispered, turning his back to me. It was difficult to turn from him, ignore him, despite there being enough space to ignore the other's existence, or at least give it a gallant try. Dominic wasn't a presence that could be ignored. Eventually I turned my back to him.

"What's the worst-case scenario?" I asked.

My question was met with a contemplative silence.

"That you're more than you appear to be, a tool of chaos that needs to be handled," he admitted eventually. The prince wasn't one to coddle. I guessed I should appreciate that, for the second time today, he'd taken care with his wording. It might have been a verbal act of kindness, but it didn't chase away the knowledge of how the supernatural community 'handled' things.

I tried to wish him a good night, but the words were stuck. I settled into the uncomfortable silence.

3

Dominic had fallen asleep quickly. I couldn't begin to do the same. On my side, with my back to him, I was ever aware of the man next to me whose body radiated heat that couldn't even be tempered by the intentional distance he'd put between us. Frenetic energy permeated from him as if he couldn't rest even while sleeping.

In an attempt to find a position that would promote sleep, I moved to my back, then stomach, and finally to the opposite side, facing his back and quickly becoming distracted by how the subtlest of movements caused his defined muscles to contract and relax. The urge to trace my finger over the ink markings that covered them increased with each passing moment.

Before I could act on it, he turned to face me, groggy and seemingly aware of my thoughts. His slow, lazy half smile made me momentarily forget that we were trapped in the underworld, his role in both our worlds, and the power and brutality that accompanied that position. There was a gentleness to him, along with the ease of him moving closer to me. Tracing his finger along my jawline, he whispered something and a halo of warm, soft yellow lights shone above.

Tentatively, his fingers trailed from my jawline, along my neck and down my chest to the swell of my breasts. He held my eyes until dropping them to my breasts and, undoubtedly, the hardened peaks of my nipples. My breath caught when his finger ran lazily over them, and I exhaled a sigh of disappointment when he moved away.

"I'd like to satisfy my curiosity," he whispered in a low, rough voice.

"About what?"

His intense amber eyes held mine. "What's hidden on you that can't be seen with the naked eye," he admitted. I turned the question over, taking out the sexy lazy way he made his request. This involved magic. He wanted to use a spell to reveal things on me that he believed Peter had hidden.

"When Peter used you as a conduit before, he made the markings visible," he provided, his brow furrowed.

"You believe he changed his M.O.?" I asked as his hand slid under my shirt and curved around my waist, his thumb making languid circles over the exposed skin.

"No, I think I got to you before he could cloak it. I've been thinking about your last encounter with him. He had your hair and blood, enough for several spells. One possibly being a cloaking spell. May I?" he asked, inching his face closer to me. I inhaled his appealing scent. His lips brushing lightly against mine and the deep throaty question seemed like more than just a request for magic. The appeal came wrapped in a sensuous package. Fully aware I was being treated to the Prince of the Underworld's seduction, I allowed it with the excuse that it was done in an effort to break the spell imprisoning us and nothing at all to do with my desire to feel Dominic's expert touch as he searched for all the things he believed were hidden on me.

"Will it hurt?"

When Dominic thought I was a Dark Caster, he enclosed me in fire to force me to reveal myself and the spells that he then used to return the prisoners. It wasn't painless but I powered through it because it needed to be done. I'd do the same now but wanted to prepare myself for the worst possible scenario.

"No, but you will feel it. I promise I'll be gentle." A wolfish smirk skated over his lips.

It took a moment after him invoking the spell before I felt it envelop me like a weighted blanket. Each moment became lighter as the spell dispersed over my skin, slithering over every inch, trying to pull out the secrets it was called to reveal. Dominic eased me onto my back before pulling the sheet off me. He took his time, inching to my feet where he examined them, migrating to my legs and then thighs. His hand glided along with his eyes. Dark mischief flickered when he lifted them to meet mine. He moistened his lips, his eyes asking the silent question.

"You have to search," I encouraged. Dominic slipped off my panties. Exploring every part of me and rewarding me with his devious grin made me forget the main purpose of the search. I shuddered when he inched closer, nipping at my skin. A small moan escaped when his fingers slid over the sensitive parts between my legs, caressing and teasing the aroused area. I bit back the groan of disappointment when he ventured away. The touch promised more. I wanted more. A lot more. Dominic moved to my stomach, teasing me with warm soft kisses. He removed my cami, continuing to deliver the same attention to my nipples until they were painfully erect. Heat washed over me.

The Dark Prince who peddled in torture was subjecting me to a different form of it. I wanted to feel more than his tantalizing light touches, teasing, and erotic bites. Lacing my fingers through his hair, I pulled him to me in a kiss. His tongue explored mine, deep and hungry, and I felt his hardness between my legs as he settled between them. Wrapping my legs around him, I pulled him deeper against me. He taunted me with slight movements of his hips, pressing against me, smirking at my response.

I wanted the Dark Prince. Needed more of his lustful touches and ravenous kisses. The raw primal beast that peeked through made me want to unwrap the whole package.

A deep chuckle reverberated as he took my hands in his and held them over my head. His eyes twinkled with deviance as they held mine.

"Tsk, tsk, Luna. As much as I'm enjoying this, I also have work to do." The low rumble of his chastisement was contradicted by his soft panting and the ravenous way his fiery gaze took in my body. It made compliance difficult.

I took several breaths. "Okay," I huffed out between shallow pants. With a nod, he returned to his search, sensual mischief tugging at his lips.

In his typical sweeping grace of movement, he cradled my face. My breathing became sharp irregular bursts as his fingers sank into the crown of my hair. They ran along my ear, along the hairline, into the curve of my neck where he planted delicate kisses before moving me onto my side to continue his exploration. Delicate hands roamed over every inch of me, then slid between my legs to the delicate part between them, sensitive with arousal. The deep throaty way he said my name as he stroked me sent shivers up me. Moving my hips to meet each stroke, pleasure coursed over me, satisfying an ache I had denied too long. It built so much, I craved a release, expressed only in a low, wanton moan. Dominic's rough low urges had me giving in to the pleasure, seeking more of his touch. Masterful fingers were coaxing me toward a climax. I claimed more of his erotic caresses until I exploded, shuddering over the edge with a sound between a moan and a sigh. Content, I sank deeper into the softness of the bed. Dominic's body blanketed mine as he whispered in my ear.

"Is it safe to assume you're enjoying my search as much as I am?" Dark satisfaction draped over his words.

Probably more, but I couldn't offer him anything more than a feeble nod.

I was startled out of my relaxed pliability when Dominic's delicate touch turned clinical, pressing firmly against my lower back. The warm breezes of his breath held as tension radiated from him.

"This wasn't here yesterday," he said.

"What, my birthmark?" The muted sienna-color marking that looked like a poorly drawn infinity circle was located on the small of my back. At about two inches long, it was just big enough for me to consider tattooing over it, but small enough to escape notice most of the time, depending on what I was wearing.

"It wasn't there before, Luna."

My first impulse was to ask him if he was sure, but his rigid scowl and speculative look stopped me. He dressed, slipping on a t-shirt, underwear, and sweatpants so quickly that I didn't have time to sort through my thoughts. He headed out of the room while I lay there, my mouth slightly open, searching for the right question. The one that would yield the most informative response.

"Peter cloaked my birthmark?"

Dominic nodded. "You weren't chosen at random. It was a calculated decision, and now I need to figure out why."

I hauled myself out of the bed, searching for my discarded clothing.

"No. Go to sleep, Luna. You can't help me with this. I just need to search a few things." It might have been said in a suggestive tone, but it left no room for debate. He departed with a hurried "Goodnight."

Sleep didn't come easy. My mind was chaotic with thoughts and scenarios I couldn't make sense of. The first time Peter walked into our store, the peculiar man didn't seem to have any interest in me. Or in anyone. He was just the weird guy with an abundance of useless and useful knowledge who would undoubtedly give you an unrequested history lesson. But his views and words seemed to be skewed toward the loser, reminding anyone who'd bother to listen that history was written by the victors. Several times he'd said that the victors weren't necessarily the heroes.

As I tossed and turned, I wondered, what was my role in this?

4

When I did finally fall asleep, it was deeply. Dominic wasn't in the bed when I awoke. I wasn't sure if he'd gotten up early or hadn't returned.

"I'm here." Anand's voice rang through the door. I peeked out to find him seated near the bookshelf, flipping through a book. He lifted his eyes, scanned my clothing, and returned to his book. "Breakfast will be ready soon."

Was there caution in his eyes? Apprehension? Maybe I was reading too much into things because I couldn't let go of what we'd discovered last night and whether that was the reason Dominic hadn't returned. Forcing away all thoughts, I ducked back into the room and quickly showered and dressed. Returning to the sitting area, I found Anand now leaning against the door, legs crossed and waiting for me. I was sure his hearing gave him the advantage of knowing my progress as I got ready. The suite was large, but I was doubtful the size would impede his movements.

"Security?" I asked, sidling in next to him as he led me through the house to the kitchen.

"Just company."

And obviously a lie that he put no effort into making

sound convincing. But I didn't call him out on it because I enjoyed having him around. Seeing him was better than the unsettling camouflaging he did that made it creepy as hell when he allowed himself to be seen.

Prepared to grab something quick, like bread and fruit, I was pleasantly surprised by the vast selection of food in the kitchen. An array of berries, breakfast quiche, sausage, bacon, waffles, and scones was set on the island.

"Will this do, or would you like something else prepared?" a woman asked. I knew of the humans that worked in the underworld, but this was my first time encountering one or talking to any of the people who resided in and cared for the underworld's mansion. I'd been threatened by Dominic's security detail, who were human, but had had no other interaction with them.

"No, this is wonderful. Thank you," I said, curious if she was under some form of compelling spell. Did she not know she was working in the underworld? I studied her eyes more closely, looking for the glossiness that I'd seen in my ex when he was compelled by vampires. The royals possessed a magical equivalent. Instead, I was met with intelligent, knowing eyes. She was aware she was in the underworld, just blasé about it.

How does that transaction go? "Hey, want to work for me in the underworld?" "The underworld? Sure."

Some variation of that did in fact take place, along with them agreeing to have their minds altered once they left. What predicament would I need to be in to agree to such a thing? Perhaps it wasn't seen that way but rather as a new adventure.

The chef's eyes quickly matched the disconcerted expression she gave me. It had her hauling to what I guessed was another pantry, or maybe an area where they prepared the food. The kitchen was so tidy, it didn't appear as if a great deal of preparation took place there.

Despite the home's exquisite beauty, exorbitant décor, expensive art, luxurious natural stones, and beautiful library with its first-edition books casually displayed, the place never seemed pretentious. Even when guards greeted Dominic upon my initial arrival, it hadn't seemed ostentatious. A person dressed in a modern chef's coat, black pants, and hat seemed to take it to that level, putting the grandness of the home in perspective.

Once we had our plates, we sat at the kitchen table, where I had a view of the garden and the strange midnight-color flowers that managed to be both disturbing and intriguing.

Anand picked at his food, slowly looking over the room, his frenetic energy a distraction as I attempted to eat.

"Where's Dominic?"

"With his father." His curt tone was laced with finality of the topic, but my heightened curiosity had me ignoring it. There were too many questions that needed answers.

"Have you spoken with Dominic today?"

"Briefly."

It was becoming increasingly frustrating that I couldn't gather anything from Anand's expression or body language. An indecipherable slate. Did he know about what Dominic discovered? If he didn't, I didn't want to bring it up because I wasn't sure what it meant for me. No matter how I tried, I couldn't stop thinking of all the warnings Helena, out of spite, had revealed about Dominic. He was ruthless when he needed to be. He'd screw you and then kill you without a second thought. I remembered the look on her face when she revealed that. And that he hadn't denied it. I wanted to invalidate it because of the source, but Helena probably knew her brother better than anyone.

Fear crept over me.

"Will I meet..."

I let my words drift off, waiting for Anand to provide a title for Dominic's father. I'd given him the designation of

Lord of the Underworld in my mind but wanted confirmation. How would I address him? Dominic was the Prince of the Underworld, so it would be fitting that his father would be the king. Anand continued eating, ignoring the pointed opening for an answer.

"Anand." Tumultuous dark eyes, a stark contrast to his serene beauty, snapped up from his food to peer at me.

"Yes?"

"Will I meet the…"

"Lord." He sighed. "He is the Lord of the Underworld and I don't know if you'll meet him. If you do, it's doubtful it will be the pleasure you seem to think it will be."

His response made me fall into silence. I ate, my thoughts plunging into a darker place. Seated across from the enigmatic supernatural who was a miser with any information wasn't helping. I picked at some fruit, trying to calm myself so that I could think clearly. A spell got me here, so a spell would have to get me out. Not a binding or warding spell. I didn't know enough about the various spells to know which ones might help. Dominic said that Peter had enough body conduits to do various spells, and it wasn't sitting well with me that he'd hidden my birthmark. It was such an odd thing to do.

"Let's go for a walk," Anand suggested, breaking into my thoughts.

I jumped at the chance. I wanted to explore more of the underworld, but I also hoped it would help me focus, spark more ideas. Following him out the door, I had to double my steps to keep up. Noticing my struggle, he slowed. He usually moved with a fluid grace, long strides and quick movements. The challenge of having to change his rhythm was apparent, his gait becoming mechanical and lumbering. We walked past the garden, through a pathway of heavily populated poplars that nearly obscured everything behind it.

"Is it just the palace here?"

"Palace?"

Oh, are we pretending this isn't a mini palace? Okay, I'll play your game. "House. Is this the only home here? Are there others who reside in the underworld other than the humans and the guests downstairs?"

The question quirked his lips into a smile. "Guests. You mean unrepentant ruthless prisoners housed in the Perils," he corrected, amusement brightening his face.

The light sound of his laughter relaxed me. "The ruthless scallywags?"

"You are a peculiar human, aren't you?"

His head tilted toward me as if he expected an answer. How does one answer an inquiry about their weirdness?

"I'm just curious." I was also trying to be considerate of any feelings he may have, as he was the child of a person imprisoned in the Perils.

"This is the last stop for them. No hope for parole or reconsideration of their sentences."

"Consideration can't be given when the offenses are so terrible."

A knowing look crossed his face and I wondered how much he knew—especially about me.

"Have you spoken to Dominic today?" I asked again. I wasn't hopeful I'd get anything out of him, but it was worth a try.

"Yes."

"Did I come up in the conversation?"

"Yes."

Be more terse.

"That's not the question you really wanted to ask, is it?"

I wasn't sure if I could trust him, and would revealing Dominic's findings put me at risk with Anand? I'd seen his expression when he realized we were imprisoned. It was an easy link to make: If I died, the spell would be broken.

"I believe Dominic tells me everything. I'm a trusted confidante," he said.

"Dominic discovered my birthmark had been hidden. I have no idea what that means and he left before I could ask him. It haunts me that Peter using me isn't a coincidence and that he used me to release the prisoners and imprison you all here. I'm afraid that the only solution will be to kill me, and I don't want to die. Not like this, without at least knowing why I was the one chosen. I know so little about magic and this world and it's not fair. I know life isn't fair. It's like that for everyone, but it seems I'm beyond the typical luck of the draw."

My words spilled out without a filter, like a dam breaking, and I only stopped when Anand's eyes widened and he took an unsubtle step away from me. He was Dominic's confidante, not mine. But the words had demanded to be said. To give me clarity, to express my concerns, to acknowledge my fear. If I looked like I was handling things well, it was all a fraud.

His mouth opened, then closed.

Silence stretched as he looked at me with wary apprehension.

Great, I broke Anand.

"I shouldn't have unloaded on you like that," I finally said.

"It's fine." He looked over the surroundings, his lips beveled into a frown. When his attention returned to me, his expression was placid. "I guess it would be difficult being thrust into this world and trying to navigate it with limited knowledge. It is an unfortunate situation to be in."

Okay. A neutral response. No words of empathy or assurance that I was safe. The burden was heavy and made it difficult to follow him when he started to walk again. Noticing I wasn't with him, he turned and jerked his head, motioning for me to follow. It wasn't just his beauty that drew me, rather his many facets. It was the way the hardness of his eyes sometimes melted away when he looked at me, the effort he took at trying to accommodate me despite his conditioned ways, and his attentive commanding touches.

I couldn't move. My feet were planted to the ground by indecision and fear of the unknown. Anand was the unknown, along with everything surrounding me. My adventurous spirit had been silenced.

"Dominic is not impulsive. I don't know why, but he values your life. That will work in your favor."

That wasn't a ringing endorsement of my safety. It just meant that Dominic would try other options first.

"He's talented, resourceful, and arrogant. That arrogance won't allow him to choose the easy route just for the sake of ending a situation. He will need to find the reason and ensure it will never happen again. I don't always agree with his methods, but he has had far more successes than he's had failures. I respect that."

It was all I was going to get. No confirmation that I was entirely safe but that Dominic's arrogance worked in my favor.

I had no option but to accept that. Walking quickly to catch up, I fell in step as Anand slowed to accommodate me.

We made another turn that led us through a thicket of trees. Despite the dark coloring of the leaves, dark grays and deep currant, they gave off the same scent as normal trees. An earthy scent. The air was freshened by them. Woodlands and trees offered a comfort I was in desperate need of.

Anand led me to a section of the property that showed evidence of more life than suggested by the main house. There was a ranch-style building that I assumed was for storage. Several feet from it was a greenhouse. I wondered how successful it was without the sun but decided there must be magic involved.

Anand guided me farther away from the main house, bringing into sight two homes and a low-rise apartment building, which I assumed was where the humans who helped on the grounds resided. I wondered if the other homes were for guests and those who actually visited the underworld.

"That's where the caretakers of the underworld live." He pointed to the low-rise apartment, confirming my assumption. "Guest homes. Although very few visit, some request to stay in the guest home rather than in the main house. Nailah prefers to stay there." Turning away from the houses, he rushed out, as if it was inconsequential, "And the other home is where their mother stays when she visits."

His reveal had me rooted in place, blinking.

"What?"

Their mother's whereabouts had crossed my mind on more than one occasion, but I refrained from asking because her absence might have been rooted in a tragedy that they didn't want to share. That might still be the case, although the question spilled out before I could stop it.

"Mother?" I asked. "Why doesn't she live with the lord?"

"There is more than just one world like this," he told me after several moments of consideration. "Their mother lives in another. Their union is best described as—" He stopped abruptly as he searched for the right word. "Transactional."

Transactional? Was that the right word? Did anyone ever want that to be the case? Though, when power and influence was predicated on magical abilities, it made sense.

"Relationships like that aren't unusual. Dominic and Helena's father wanted heirs whose magic would match or be superior to his, so they could keep possession of this underworld. Lesser magical beings wouldn't be able to ward off the periodic attacks from those who want to dethrone him. This underworld is considered the most desirable because of its proximity to the human world and the supernaturals that exist in it. Those who wish to have this world because of its affiliations with the supernaturals of your world don't fully understand that it exists in a delicate—and strained—balance. It was cultivated over many years and with a great deal of effort. The ones who want to take this from Areleus—Lord of the Underworld," he clarified, responding to my look of confusion, "don't truly understand how precarious it is. Those who wish to overthrow us have numbers. Dominic, Helena, and their father have power. The power isn't omniscient, something that neither Helena nor her father have come to understand, but it has the potential to cause great damage to those who challenge them for this world, and even the supernaturals of your world."

Supernaturals of our world. He made it seem as if we had a harmonious and mutually respectful relationship. The supernaturals of my world lived in secret, using their magic to take advantage of humans and do whatever they pleased to us in order to remain concealed. The ones who wanted us to know of their existence wanted to subjugate us. I'd been able to negotiate some changes, when they needed me to return the most dangerous supernaturals to their prison. The underworld was now responsible for policing the supernaturals, making sure they stayed concealed and not at the expense of humans. If they violated the agreement, the Conventicle was no longer responsible for disciplining them —something they had proven to be feckless about, showing favoritism and leniency, especially when it came to supernaturals using humans or their magic against us. Although humans were in a better situation now, with regard to being the recipients of magic used against them, I couldn't discount how perilously close becoming casualties was the alternative option. A war was brewing between those who wanted to overthrow the Conventicle and the current Conventicle. The ones who wanted to replace the current Conventicle were more ruthless. I wasn't convinced they weren't the better option. They'd rule with an iron fist. The only reason I hadn't sided with them was because they wanted me dead. I was the problem, and they believed in ruthlessly eliminating all problems to maintain their anonymity.

Anand's teeth clenched his lip, giving me the impression he'd provided too much information, until out of my periphery, I saw the swirl of images around me. They took solid form then disappeared. I stiffened, responding to Anand who'd assumed an attack posture and was watching attentively.

Fading between solid and swirls of midnight smoke, one finally held its form, just inches from me. Its slitted coal eyes reminded me of a snake. The tall, coltish thing drew back its wings and circled me. Its round face, nub nose, and wide mouth gave it a docile look, which I knew was deceptive. Something was off about it. Clawed fingers reached for me then withdrew. More swirls of colors misted around me that formed winged creatures who crowded me, drawn to me like bees to honey.

Through a space between the crowd of creatures, I watched Anand who kept a careful eye on them, his brow furrowed. The first creature who approached me drew back his lips to reveal jagged double rows of teeth. A long-forked tongue darted in my direction. I shoved him away, my arms wildly moving to put distance between me and the creatures. In retaliation, his clawed hand sliced me.

Simultaneously, they let out high, pained screeches as they dissolved into mist and disappeared. Illuminated black tendrils fanned from Anand like wings, expanding and consuming the space. His eyes eclipsed to a dark abyss as stifling magic coursed through the air. I struggled for each breath.

His wings and magic receded as quickly as they had appeared, leaving him sagging into himself, where he stayed for several beats. He looked fatigued. I couldn't determine if it was from exertion or disuse. When he stood taller, ominous energy pulsed from him. A darkness clinging to him had me scuttling back to put distance between us. He advanced toward me but something in my face made him stop abruptly.

Holding his hand up, he said, "It's okay. They've gone."

It wasn't just them that bothered me, but it was a starting point.

"They being?" I asked in a shaky whisper.

"Shades. Bound here by magic, they're limited in their abilities. They live here but can't sustain a solid form." The "until now" remained unspoken. He blinked. "They typically can't maintain their solid form long enough to be any danger. They've never been a problem before. In your world, they don't have those limitations. There, they can fully use their magic in whichever unsuspecting human's body they take."

"It's your magic that keeps them here?" I asked.

He shook his head, moving toward. He abruptly stopped, waiting for my approval. Remnants of whatever drove his baleful magic still lingered in the air as the painful wails his magic pulled from those creatures replayed on a loop in my head. My attention was split between thinking of them and of his magic that drove them away.

Appreciative of the time he gave me, seconds became minutes before I gave him the nod to come closer.

I wanted to go home. Tears welling in my eyes, I looked down at the stain of blood forming on my shirt.

"I need to see it, Luna," he told me as he knelt and slowly rolled up my shirt. "It's not too bad. Dominic can advance the healing, but it will heal fine on its own. They're not poisonous."

Not poisonous, just shapeshifter creatures of the underworld who were impotent only there. Who were attracted to me and able to maintain form and harm me. No biggie. Nothing to see here.

I want to go home.

"What are you?" There was probably desperation in my voice because his steadfast countenance dropped and a flush ran along the bridge of his nose.

"My mother was a shifter-witch hybrid." I kept my face expressionless to not reveal that Dominic had told me that. "In my mother's animal form, her bite affected shifters and vampires. It suppressed the abilities of shifters, and vampires responded as if they'd been staked." Taking note that he used the past tense, I pondered what had happened to her, but his admission seemed to take so much from him that I refrained from asking.

Lifting his eyes to mine, he admitted in a low whisper, "My father's a Mors."

Witches with the ability to take a life with a spell and touch. But knowing that didn't enlighten me as to why the shades responded to him that way.

"My magic affects shades," he explained, standing up and running a hand through his hair, mussing it. A hollowness appeared in his hazel eyes. He nudged his chin in the direction we'd come from.

"Is that your only magic?" There wasn't any way his ability to navigate the world remaining virtually unseen was in my head and not part of his magic.

"I can cloak myself, a skill neither of my parents possessed. The magic world dislikes the mingling of species, not only to maintain the purity and strength of the line but because how mercurial the magic is in hybrids. The inability to fully understand and counter the magic of the unknown isn't handled well. If it's too complicated and becomes a cause for fear, they believe that for the safety of their existence, the entity must be removed."

His movements slipped back into a flowing ease but slowed by fatigue.

"I'm an enigma that would unsettle them. I chose to live here because knowledge of my lineage stays here. They speculate but nothing is ever confirmed. They just consider me a product of the underworld. It offers me a level of security and prevents challenges to force me to reveal my abilities, to be studied or judged whether I could be detrimental to them. This family are the only ones who know everything about me."

It could have been my imagination, but I heard hesitation. Perhaps they didn't know everything about him but rather what he wanted them to know. He turned to look at me. I knew that whether the family of the underworld knew everything or just a fraction of his ability, the information didn't need to go any further.

Giving him an understanding smile, I said, "It's already forgotten."

He exhaled, which I mistook as relief until his posture changed. His head swiveled to the right where Helena stepped into view. Her glacial eyes swept over Anand and moved to me. A knowing look overtook her expression.

"Helena," Anand said in a voice softened to a gentle lilt. A lilt that could soothe the most hostile of beasts, and there was no mistake, behind the low-heeled sandals with wounding leg straps, and the expensive-looking patterned t-shirt dress displaying her magic-restricting markings with contempt, and the flawless makeup, there lurked a beautiful beast.

Anand approached her but her eyes remained fixed on me. It wasn't until he was just a hair's breadth from her that she dragged her attention to him. Removing the expression from her face, she became a blank landscape.

"I saw it all," she said. "It needs to be addressed." The threat of violence was heavy in her voice. She lunged for me and he drew her closer to him, his fingers threading through the ends of her loose curls, his touch familiar but not intimate. There was an obvious connection that I couldn't quite put my finger on. I hoped I wasn't witnessing a budding relationship. *Anand, you can do better than the psycho-princess of the underworld.*

"Don't," he urged. "Your impulsivity hasn't worked to your advantage in the past." Releasing his hold on her hair, he gently gathered her hands in his and looked at the markings on her arms.

She looked at them as well. "Speak to my brother. Show him the errors of this."

My heart was pounding at the prospect of being confined with a Helena with access to her magic and claws.

He shook his head. "I won't because I agree with his decision," he admitted.

Helena's eyes sharpened to daggers. There wasn't any doubt that if she had access to her claws, he would have been introduced to them. Her lips drew back in a sneer and she yanked her hands from him, ripping away any tenderness that existed between them.

"I get things done!" she snapped.

"Yes, you get a lot of things done. You managed to get entire covens to turn against you because of your inability to choose any other option than violence when you feel the tiniest insult. You had the uncanny ability to leave a pack in shambles because you couldn't handle being cheated on. So, your over-the-top response was to kill anyone in that pack you suspected was the culprit. Do you understand the problem you caused with that tantrum? The situation should have been handled differently and left between you and the man you were involved with. I say this not out of cruelty but compassion. You have become your worst enemy because you've lived too long with impunity. This is just punishment. And if your magic is never returned to you, it is a punishment long overdue."

"I reacted to us having a fight. His response was an overreaction," she challenged.

"No, his response was holding you accountable and

letting you suffer the consequences. It only looks like an overreaction when you aren't used to being held to such things."

Turning away from her, he started back in my direction. It was a display of bravery I didn't possess. An angered Helena who hadn't gotten her wishes was a person I would want to keep an eye on. Jerking her sharp glare from Anand, she placed it on me, sending a shiver of fear up my spine. Straightening, I made a show of bravado that I didn't actually possess.

Helena shuddered with the effort to not react. She was reduced to seething with her hands clenched at her sides. Probably a first for her and a duplicitous attempt to demonstrate restraint and prove Anand wrong about her magic.

"You saw the way the shades responded to her," Helena called after him once we were heading toward the house.

He halted briefly but remained silent. He was just as concerned as she was.

"It will be addressed."

"With the exception of you, Father has no tolerance for magical anomalies," she threatened.

He'd surely learn about me being an anomaly. I was going to meet the Lord of the Underworld. I reined in the fear, but it became my single focus as I made my way back to the bedroom.

5

After removing the claw-ripped shirt, I discovered Anand hadn't been attempting to keep me from panicking by minimizing the severity of the cut. It really wasn't that bad. Once I applied pressure to stop the bleeding and cleaned it off, there was just a red line on my stomach. If Anand hadn't intervened, it could have been so much worse. I knew that. Thoughts of the danger were constant as I navigated through the house to the main library and the magic room, where I could review the spells. The only way to chase the thoughts away was to be proactive. I had to do something.

Despite my attempts to not think about the shades, I fixated on their enigmatic pull to me and what had them swarming around me, maintaining a form that they typically weren't able to maintain.

My belief that there was nothing magical about me was renewed by the ache from my injury. If magic existed in me, it would ease my pain, surely. But there was no use applying logic to an illogical world.

The shades were drawn to me for my lack of magic in the same way the magic room in the library repelled me. I felt the room's rejection as soon as I neared it. It was a nudge, shooing me away. For a moment, I considered taking the hint. I could stay in the main library and appreciate the many first editions, take in the beauty of the leatherbound books and peruse the vast selection, inhale the scent of vellum and run my fingers over the gilded emboss on some of the books I'd passed. But that wasn't going to get me out of the underworld.

Determined to be allowed entry, I pushed against the repelling magic until my hand reached the door handle. The handle turned, but the door wouldn't budge.

"Please," I whispered to the door. *That's about right. I'm pleading with a room to grant me entrance. Not weird at all.*

"I just want to go home," I pled, my voice low, aware of the dark-skinned man with low-cut hair and round-rim glasses that he moved to the tip of his nose in order to scrutinize me. His attire—crisp white shirt, blue herringbone vest with matching slacks—made me feel underdressed in my t-shirt and leggings. There was judgment in his look, which I ignored, going back to trying to get into the room, shoving my hip against the door to barge my way in. The room remained resolute in its denial.

When I added more force, it responded by tossing me back a few more feet. Once I regained my footing, I approached the door again and pressed my forehead against the cool wood. "I just want to look at your books. I will treat each book with the utmost respect, I promise."

A pledge that didn't cause it to waver.

"Oh, for fuck's sake. You know me. Let me in the damn room," I scolded through clenched teeth.

This was a new low. Fighting with a sentient room for entrance. The door remained closed. Removing the anger from my voice, I tried requesting again. It denied my request.

Closing my eyes, I kept my forehead pressed against the door. Maybe the room would have mercy or open just to have me fall flat on my face. I didn't care what manner the room let me in, just that it would.

Startled by the hand brushing past me and reaching for the handle, I was face to face with Dominic. As soon as we were in the room, he turned me toward him.

"Anand told me about your injury. I'd like to see it."

I nodded. Taking the same kneeling position Anand had, he lifted my shirt.

"It's not really an injury. Just a scrape," I said.

Scrape minimized it, but injury seemed to misrepresent it as well. The warmth of his deeply exhaled breaths breezed across my stomach. His fingers kneaded the skin of my back as he held me in place. If I shifted forward just an inch or so, his lips would be pressed against me. I pushed those thoughts away. Being distracted from my objective wasn't an option. Dominic blinked. Clearly, I wasn't the only one who'd let my thoughts go to naughtier places, although it was obvious our denial was for different reasons. It was in the tension of his fingers as they held me, the set of his jaw, and the deep contemplation in his eyes. It was obvious that what he'd discovered about me last night was with him.

His fingers moved across my stomach, leaving a menthol coolness in its wake. The scent of lavender permeated the room, and I eased into the peace that it offered. Dominic stood, taking with him the warmth of his body, which reminded me of the room's cool disapproval of my presence.

"Can you tell me which shade did this to you?" he asked, his deep eyes searching mine.

"No." It was the truth, but if I could have given him a better description, I wouldn't have. The thirst for violence and revenge laced his question. I knew nothing of the shades or whether they were like me, victims of circumstance and magic. I wouldn't sentence them to further violence. Anand's punishment was enough. I'd never forget their screams.

"I've heard Anand's version of what occurred. I'd like to hear yours."

I told him, taking out a lot of the commentary, especially the familiarity of the touch exchanged between Anand and Helena. I paid close attention to Dominic's reaction when I told him of Helena's comment about Areleus's intolerance for abnormalities, an opinion shared by the supernaturals in my world. Dominic's expression remained indecipherable. His eyes were intense with thought.

"They were able to maintain their solid forms around you?"

I nodded. "They were shadows until they were close. There were a lot of them. What are the shades?"

"The truly cursed. They're Sorcees. Their own race, best described as sorcerer-demon hybrids. It's much darker magic, stronger than anything witches possess. They were never given Strata designation because their magic fell into its own category. Like ours. They've existed longer than I have, forced to live in this underworld for their misdeeds in your world. They could take on less offensive forms than the ones you saw, allowing them to navigate through your world quite effectively. You saw them in their true form. They are agents of strife and cruelty."

Well, that decreased my desire to protect them, and the guilt I felt about Anand's response.

"Their loyalty lay with their kind only. They directed their cruelty, violence, and magic to everyone alike. My grandfather discovered a way to capture them and imprison them here in the underworld, where their lack of form gives them no power. Death would have been preferable, but that had proven very difficult. This was the quickest way to eliminate them. And with their history of hurting supernaturals, they quickly relinquished some of their authority to us because of that."

"That's why you were given the role of policing them," I surmised.

He nodded. "It was a dark archaic spell." From the rigidity of his voice, I knew he was holding something back.

My speculations ran rampant as I tried to piece together everything that had taken place over the past few weeks. "There's more to why you eliminated the Dark Casters, isn't there?" I asked.

Dominic took a long time to answer, perhaps deciding whether to give me the varnished version. I grappled with which version I wanted, as well.

"Dark Casters are the only ones who would be able to release the shades, and they made it their objective to do so. They are menace by nature. No peace or rules work for them. When that happens, clearing the slate is best."

Clearing the slate is best? Banal description for such a violent act. Killing off a whole group of supernaturals. My goal to leave the underworld refueled, I moved to the bookshelf, grabbing books in English and perusing them for spells. As I stacked the books I wanted to review more thoroughly, I could feel the weight of Dominic's evaluating stare.

Taking a seat across from my stack of books, he reclined in the chair, his fingers laced behind his head as he tracked my every movement as I removed books from shelves. The buzz of energy from the room's offence at my invasion continued. Something had changed since my last visit. Before, the room offered me wary acceptance, whereas now there was poorly repressed hostility.

"You believe I missed a spell," he stated.

I understood the humor in his voice and the implication that a novice would be able to discover something he hadn't. Plopping down in a chair across from him, I set several English spellbooks on the table.

"This has nothing to do with your capabilities. I need to *do* something. Be proactive. Is it unthinkable that something could have been overlooked?" Opening the books, I reviewed each spell and attempted, with my limited knowledge, to figure out how they could be used to free us.

After reading an unbinding spell, I looked up from it to find that I was still the target of Dominic's unwavering stare. His tongue swept languidly over his lips, moistening them.

"I've done every reversal and unbinding spell I know," he said. He quickly masked the frustration that eked through. "I have no idea what spell is being used on you to keep us here."

Dominic looked past me, pulled into his thoughts, his expression whetted by knowledge and experience of a world where I didn't belong. The rawness of his curiosity and dark magic pulsed frenetically, needing a target, only to be left unsatiated.

"You are quite the enigma," he mused softly with a touch of acute interest.

In a world of magic, being an enigma can't be good.

Dominic leaped to his feet and turned to the door. He sensed it moments before I did, and what I felt triggered me into the opposite response. He moved closer to the door as the torrent of strong, ominous magic swept into the room. Nor was he bothered by the turbulent energy that accompanied it. My self-protective response had me on my feet in a rush, shuffling back and pressing my body into the corner, wanting to shrink as far away from it as I could. Putting on a brave face wasn't an option. I wouldn't have been able to find one no matter how hard I tried. Dominic appeared to welcome it.

The door opened and a man approached us with an ethereal lithe movement. The room shuddered and then calmed to an eerie stillness, quieting at the presence of the man wearing a charcoal-gray shirt, stone-black slacks, and a scowl that was just as dark. Magic swarmed the room. The ominous change of energy that accompanied his presence was a trumpet announcing him and all the introduction I needed. I was in the company of the Lord of the Underworld.

With great effort, I pushed from the corner where I'd retreated and squared my shoulders to stand taller. Once he was in front of me, I managed to hold his depthless smoke-black eyes despite the panic racing through me. His pronounced features were sharpened to a blade's edge and accompanied by a wide full mouth and thick, short-cropped dark hair silvered at the temples with such precision and perfection I wondered if it had been professionally done. Perhaps to distinguish himself from his strikingly similar son. Looking between him, Dominic, and Helena, who trailed behind him, the minimal deviations in their appearance made me wonder what their mother's contribution to the gene pool had been.

Just an inch or two shorter than Dominic, the man had a similar build, equipped not only for immense power but speed, too. A deadly combination that I'd seen in action with Dominic.

What were their rules of etiquette? Were they the same as meeting the royal family? You're not supposed to touch the queen, but this guy's not a queen, he's Lord of the Underworld. A president of sorts. It's okay to touch the president, but do it unexpectedly, you'd probably be tackled to the ground. Or worse.

How do you greet him? Bow, like I was meeting a dictator? Nope, wasn't going to do that. Salute? Curtsy? A simple handshake? "What's up, Lord" definitely wasn't right. Fist bump definitely not a contender.

The Lord of the Underworld cocked his head and skewered me with a look.

"This is the problem?" he asked, his lips drawing into a tight line. His eyes trailed over me in scrutiny. Great, not a curtsey, bow, or handshake. I was really fighting giving him the finger. I mirrored his critical gaze that regarded me with cynical interest.

"Yes, she *is* the problem," Helena chimed in, confident that it would now be handled in the manner she wished.

His eyes flicked to Dominic. "I'm assuming you've checked for any new wards, binding spells, cloaks."

Dominic's head barely moved into a nod. Heat inched over my face at the reminder of his exploration.

"He did detection spells, checking our domain only. But nothing with her. We have no idea what his little pet is hiding. Or if there are any spells on her," Helena provided.

The lord took in the information, his attention sliding from Dominic and dropping back to me.

"She has been checked for any magical bindings, wards, and cloaked spells," Dominic refuted, shooting his sister a sharp look. I wouldn't meet the gaze she slid in my direction, hoping I wouldn't reveal my knowledge that Dominic was withholding information. I wasn't sure why he didn't disclose about my birthmark being hidden, but they wouldn't get that information from me.

"The problem needs to be eradicated." The lord looked at me, clearly identifying me as the *problem*. Problem, human, or human pet weren't names I was willing to accept while imprisoned here. Nor would I continue to allow them to speak about me as if I didn't exist.

"Hi, I'm Luna," I greeted, extending my hand to him and hoping that giving a face to the *problem* would make him soften his position. He regarded my hand for a few moments then ignored it, switching his attention back to Dominic and then to Helena, who had moved closer to him, treating Dominic to the same judging gaze given by their father.

"You've not found any new wards or bindings. It's safe to assume she's the conduit being used to block our travel. Why is she still alive?"

His satiny smooth tone was far too casual while inquiring why a person hadn't been murdered yet.

"Because Dominic would like to play detective and find out why she was chosen, opposed to fixing the problem," Helena piped in as her self-appointed role as Underworld Commentator.

The lord's mouth pinched in disapproval.

"Shall we get rid of the problem rather than finding the source of it, to prevent this from ever happening again?" Dominic challenged.

Without a moment of thought, he responded. "Yes. If it frees me from being trapped like an animal, then yes. Destroy anyone and anything responsible for it."

"Or I can prevent its reoccurrence. Since this is my responsibility, I chose that option."

Areleus cleared the distance between him and Dominic with a lightning strike of movement. Mere inches from each other, their looks were an unspoken challenge, one that seemed to perpetually exist when powerful people share each other's space. It was even more pronounced with them; similar magic and an obvious bitter history that could not be ignored.

"This doesn't need to be an issue, Father. Have I ever failed?"

The lord just offered a cocked brow in response. There was something hidden behind it.

"Don't create a fight when one isn't warranted," Dominic said.

A half smile curled the corners of the lord's lip. "Is it truly a fight if one is outmatched with no chance of winning?"

"Perhaps, but that's not the case with us, is it?" Dominic said.

I wasn't witnessing a dispute between a father and son, but a tumultuous relationship between a ruler and his successor. My attention bounced between the two, trying to determine how one ascended to their position. Does the lord retire or is he dethroned? I abandoned my thoughts to focus on the delighted smile on Helena's face. Violence, chaos, and strife was thick in the air, and it appealed to her no matter the source.

"I'm sure we can figure out a way to break the curse and let me live," I offered in a low, neutral voice, feeling like the slightest misstep would only add fodder to the volatile situation. My diplomacy induced an eyeroll from Helena.

Canting his head, the lord's brows arched but the ominous air remained. Dark amusement washed over his face, revealing a small smile as ominous as his presence. "What gives you such confidence, Luna?"

"Because we found a solution before when the prisoners were released. I'm confident it can be done again. No one will have to die." With a confidence level that was well under fifty percent, I gave him all the bravado and assurance of a person fighting for her life because, essentially, I was.

"I assure you, someone will die for this. Perhaps it won't be you. But someone will pay." He turned and headed toward the door, offering a temporary stay of execution. Helena's thrilled expression suggested that it wouldn't be for long.

Dominic kept a razor focus on his father's back and didn't appear surprised when his father stopped with his hand on the door.

"Remove Helena's restrictions," he demanded.

"Why don't you do it, Father? After all, your magic outmatches mine—or so you believe."

The lord looked over his shoulder, putting Dominic in his assassin's scope, but Dominic's comment had bothered him. It was obvious that he couldn't do it. A man who possessed limitless power wasn't used to being limited by magic or the threat of violence to get what he wanted.

"Because you restricted her magic, you need to be the one who makes her whole again." As he opened the door before closing it behind him, he tacked on, "It wasn't a request, it was an order."

Once Areleus was gone, Helena, beaming, presented her arms to Dominic.

He approached her, resolution in his expression. Her chin tilted in defiance as he took in her marks before returning his attention to her face.

"I'm not removing your restrictions," Dominic told her.

Helena's expression switched to fury. A wintry scowl skewed her features. She tensed, looking as if she was going to crumble under the self-imposed restraint. "It was an order," she hissed.

"You're no stranger to disobeying orders. What makes you think that I can't follow suit?"

She inched closer to him. "This has nothing to do with principle and everything to do with your pride. I refused to be controlled by you and your wounded ego."

Her selective memory was astonishing. His request for her not to kill me had led to her clawing his face and later putting a jagged wine glass to his throat. If that's her being controlled, what was she like unfettered?

"I've done worse."

What kind of defense was that? The 'I'm always terrible, why try to rein it in now?' strategy.

Despite my best effort, slight admiration seeped through my disdain. This woman had audacity to spare, and I was morbidly fascinated by it.

"You have. Far too many times. I have reached my limits with you." He'd taken her aggressive response well. Better than anyone else had, and I wasn't convinced he would have retaliated if she wasn't so dogmatic about going against his wishes and killing me.

Her docile look of regret and innocence was hard earned. I could see the effort she'd put into it. She thought her magic restriction was because she'd clawed him. "Granted, I have been…shall we say, a little overenthusiastic with my response to you chastising me. It was a regrettable act."

Great non-apology. And when has clawing a person's face been considered overenthusiastic? How would she describe murder? A guided escort to the afterlife?

Dominic's low chuckle held no humor. "I no longer have the patience or the forced diplomacy to make amends and excuses for your behavior. Nor do I wish to continue to clean up your messes. We have been placed at a disadvantage far too often because of it. When your magic is returned, you would have earned the privilege by your deeds. When you are no longer an anchor, your magic will be returned."

Her winged cheeks flushed, the coloring inching over the bridge of her nose as she took short, sharp inhales through her nose. She sounded like a bull readying to charge. She turned in a huff, her eyes raging with promised retaliation. "You've never had me as an enemy, brother. It is not something you want," she grounded out through clenched teeth.

"You've not had me as one, either. I can guarantee, you don't want me as one."

I can attest, you all need a family counselor.

As she angrily flounced away, Dominic returned to his chair in silence. I wanted to return to searching the books for possible spells, but I just couldn't do it. Were we supposed to behave as though that dysfunctional drama didn't need to be discussed? Did he consider that entire interaction normal?

I made a sincere effort to overlook it as I flipped through several pages and asked the correct questions only for him to inform me that the spell was inappropriate or had been attempted before. By the twentieth spell, my mind was so clouded with the interaction between his family that I had to give up.

"Your father's interesting," I cited, leaving an opening for more dialogue.

His fingers clasped behind his head, the languid way he

was sitting back in the chair, his slim-fit shirt pulled over his impressive form, and his eyes roving over the titles on the shelves behind me all gave the impression that his father being interesting wasn't a mutual belief.

"I take it you two don't get along," I probed.

Brow furrowed, he pulled his attention from the books to me. "What gives you that impression?"

What gives me that impression! Had we witnessed two different interactions? An incredulous blink was all I could muster. He had to be screwing with me.

"I don't think our interaction is any different than anyone else."

"I suppose. My dad has asked me to kill a bug or two, yours a person. Totally similar."

A smile coursed over his lips. But I persisted. I wouldn't be sidetracked by a sultry smile and an amused glint in his eyes.

"My brother and I have our share of disagreements, but he doesn't try to slice and dice my face when it happens, nor does he add me to his list of enemies. I'm positive his enemies list consists of whoever tries to price gouge when game consoles become scarce, and the inventor of oatmeal chocolate chip cookies. He really has it out for that person."

That pulled a chuckle from him, but it was strained.

"You didn't share the information about my birthmark being cloaked."

"I have no answers so there isn't anything to discuss."

"Finding that it was cloaked isn't worthy of discussion?"

He shook his head. "It could mean nothing." *That's a lie.* "Or it could mean everything. Does your brother have a birthmark like yours?"

"Not like mine. His looks like a—" I searched for the right way to describe a haphazard starburst enclosed in a circle. It was the best way to describe it, so that's what I provided to Dominic, who took in the information with a nod. He stood and approached the bookshelf at the opposite end of the room, unceremoniously putting an end to our conversation. But that wouldn't discourage me from continuing my questioning. I simply grabbed a notebook and pen from the middle of the table. On the paper, I wrote "Dark Caster" and "Imprisoned." The cause and the effect. And the line down the middle was to divide the spells that had been performed and the potential.

"You did ward and binding spells for the property," I said, "but Helena pointed out that you never did one on me. Maybe you should."

"I have," he admitted, taking a book from the shelf and flipping through it.

"What? When?"

"When I started questioning you about what had occurred before you ended up here."

I remembered the lull into complacency as the lavender-scented magic spun around me. I'd thought that was a tool to make me more pliant to his questioning. I didn't like it but at least I knew what had been done to me.

"You were distracted," he provided, answering my questioning look. No, *he* was distracting me. The questioning, the touching, the warmth that wrapped around me were spells being performed without my knowledge.

"Do not do spells on me without me giving approval," I said. "I get a say in it all."

His attention snapped in my direction. I got a fleeting glimpse of the man who'd taken on a bar full of people, killed assassins with minimal effort, and struck contempt and fear in powerful supernaturals. It was enough to make me cower. But I wouldn't.

"Do you?"

Squaring my shoulders, I stood from my seat. "Yes, I do." Not enough conviction in my voice to do anything more than amuse him.

"How do you plan to enforce that?" he asked in a neutral tone.

My heart pounded, my breath became shallow rasps, and the feeling of hopelessness washed over me. I was imprisoned with the very people the powerful feared. How did I enforce my agency with them?

"I guess I can't," I admitted, puncturing the quiet. My anger grew with his continued silence. I needed to get away from him. From the magic. From everything that reminded me of the absurdity, cruelty, malice, and dysfunction that existed in this magical world where I didn't belong.

Leaving the books where they were, I rushed out of the room, slamming the door behind me.

6

*L*eaving the library, I caught the attention of the man I saw earlier, his expression curious as I passed him. I could feel his eyes on me. I turned to find him fighting hard to resist the smile threatening to emerge. If I wasn't so determined to put distance between me and Dominic, I would have asked him what was so funny, but getting away from Dominic and everything he seemed to represent was a priority.

In the vast hallway, I was faced with the reality that I had nowhere to go. Roaming the house with an agitated Helena in it wasn't the wisest thing to do. With shades drawn to me and willing to attack me, going outside wasn't an option, either. My hand pressed against my injury.

"Anand," I called out, turning toward the west wing of the house where he told me he resided. At least, I hoped it was the west. At that point I was just guessing. Scanning the room and above, I saw him approach the railings of the second floor. He was wearing dark blue track pants and a tank. He watched me the entire time as he made his way to the stairs and down them.

"Yes?" he asked, approaching me. Closer, I could see he

not only had the scar on his face but also one on his right shoulder where he'd been clawed. He looked where my eyes had landed.

"Helena?" I blurted. It wasn't out of the realm of possibilities, although after seeing him fight, I couldn't imagine anyone being able to get close enough to inflict such injuries.

"No." His curt response didn't leave a lot of room for further questioning. I warred with my curiosity and courtesy. The latter won.

"Want some company?" I asked.

"Not particularly."

Well, I had to appreciate his honesty. He looked over toward the library. "I won't mind it too much if you want to accompany me."

Ignoring the 'too much' part, I happily followed as he led me from the library and down the corridor, where I passed more rooms with closed doors. Only one was open, and I thought it was a poorly lit office until I saw the collection of swords on the walls and the menacing masks on the wall and a gothic-looking dark chair. The high back was covered with emerald velvet, complementing the elaborate carvings that extended to the claw feet and arms. The Lord of the Underworld was sunk back in the chair, fingers curved over the edge of it, distorting the carved design. I stopped, feeling the full impact of his eyes—the glow of a dying flame that didn't waver. His lips parted as if he was about to say something but then closed. His study of me continued, leaving me to wonder if Helena had told him about the shades or about Dominic's refusal to remove the marks that bound her. Simply giving him a stiff wave, I hurried to catch up with Anand, who swung open a set of double doors to reveal an impressive gym divided by fitness equipment with a bike, treadmill, salmon ladder, bars, dumbbells, and weight plates.

"You're a shifter. Why do you need any of this?"

"The preternatural is inherent, and most feel that's enough. Not for me—for us."

So Dominic's carved physique wasn't just winning the genetic lottery but also physical work. It would be ridiculous to think that fighting skills were innate. Which explained the mat and heavy bag with a man's face and torso.

"It's a body opponent bag for precision strikes and punches," Anand explained.

My attention moved from the equipment to the collections of blades and swords on the wall and tables. There wasn't anything less dangerous to practice with, like training swords or blades. The sharp blades glinting under the bright lights showed me their sole purpose: to inflict a great deal of pain.

"We heal fast," he offered, when I picked up one of the blades from the table. That wasn't the answer I was expecting. *Sparring with razor-sharp blades is fine because they heal fast?* I wanted to return to my normal boring life where the answer wasn't 'you heal fast, let me stab you.'

"Is there anything you want to use to practice?" he asked.

The extent of my exercise was running, which I did only occasionally.

"I don't work out," I admitted, a little embarrassed by the confession. But if beings with preternatural strength and speed did, I could probably do a squat or pushup sometimes. Fighting—I'm just swinging my arms windmill-style and hoping one connects. I was confident I could throw a punch, kick a person in a soft spot that would ensure pain, but I wasn't confident I'd fare well in a fight.

"Other than assaulting my cheating ex's Good and Plenty's, I've never had a fight," I admitted.

"Explain?" he coaxed. Retelling the story of my boyfriend cheating on me and my reaction brought a smile to his lips. It was the first time he'd shown genuine interest. "Then let's start with the basics," he said.

After a few hours of him showing me beginner punches, it was undeniable that it wasn't just being the strongest and fastest that appealed to them but also the endorphin high. Each strike shot filled me with an intoxicating level of exhilaration. For that moment, the dark world fell away. It was a moment of clarity and peace, and I didn't even mind Anand's peal of laughter when I attempted, without any instruction from him, to duplicate a combination strike and kick he'd done on a heavy bag in the corner and ended flat on my ass. Where I stayed. Tired, I lay back on the floor and closed my eyes. They snapped open when I was nudged by a warm, wet nose. I couldn't see anything but knew it was one of Dominic's hellhounds. I assumed Zareb, who seemed to be Dominic's favorite.

"Hey, you," I greeted, sitting up. He revealed himself before plopping onto my lap where I stroked his fur. Between the workout and pet, my anger and frustration had eased. I was in a better place until Dominic appeared, abruptly signaled Anand to leave, and Zareb to do so, too, after Dominic jerked his head toward the door.

Standing up, I attempted to mirror his indecipherable expression, but the frustration and irritation had returned, making stoicism difficult.

"I'm not used to asking for permission when I use my magic on anyone. If I'm using it, I have an objective and it supersedes all things," he said softly. In a world of the powerful, perhaps consideration and kindness was viewed as weakness. After meeting his father, I wasn't sure if it was just about not showing weakness and being the biggest predator, but rather the nature vs. nurture situation. Helena had given over to that side, whereas Dominic seemed to have a tenuous grasp keeping him from falling into it.

Whatever role I played in this situation, I didn't want or belong in his world.

"I'm not asking you to be that way with everybody. Just me," I said.

He considered it for a moment, the reluctance apparent. He'd taken me out of the human category, so I was unwillingly an *other*.

"I don't belong here," I reminded him softly. He swallowed the distance between us, his gaze dropping to my lips.

I couldn't determine if the low growl was acceptance or simply acknowledgment.

"Luna, Luna, Luna." The smokey rasp coursed through me. Magic laced around me, tugging me closer to him. The warmth of his breath wisped over my lips.

I rolled my eyes. "More spells?"

Leaning in closer, his lips brushed lightly over mine, his tongue teasing my bottom lip. He looked around. "Let's go to the room," he suggested softly.

My libido had taken over, and the only thing I could think of was seeing Dominic's body again, his expert touch, and him. Even the possibility of more of his magic touching, the heat of it, ran through my mind. He offered none of it. Once the door closed, his appearance was grave.

"You're a Scaphium," he revealed in a somber whisper. "A vessel."

"What does that mean?"

"You're a vessel for magic."

"Human," I blurted in defense, clinging to it for all it was worth. That I wasn't just an inanimate object in a human shell, used as a vessel. I needed to have more. "I don't have magic," I continued, defending my human existence. "Nor can I hold it." I distinctly remembered the torturous feel of Madeline's magic when I borrowed it.

"Exactly, you are a vessel for magic. One of the Tenebras Obducit imbued you with their magic. Peter either knew already or discovered it, because he's been using you for your intended purpose. A well for their magic."

It all fell into place. Peter in the bookstore constantly, watching me, his seemingly innocuous questioning. He knew what I was and didn't want me out of his sight. Or maybe he suspected, and using me to release the prisoners was the confirmation he needed.

"So, what do I do now?" I asked.

Dominic looked as conflicted as I felt. I was the problem: a vessel being used by Peter. Get rid of me and the magic disappeared. The dilemma was clear on his face. I wasn't just imprisoning him, I was a well of magic that Peter could return to at his discretion. The quandary was heavy on Dominic's finely carved features.

"I need a shower," I rushed out, heading toward the bathroom to give us both a well-needed break. Although I had no idea what resolution I'd be met with when I returned.

Showered, I blow-dried my hair and took extra time putting curls in it using the curling wand left for me in the room. Along with a few glosses and three different types of liners and mascara. Ignoring the liners, I did give my lashes a few swipes with the applicator and opted for the lip butter instead of the glosses. An excuse for the time I'd spent in there trying to devise a plan. But in the end, all I had was the skill of coercion. They needed me alive to see what more I could be used for. Instead of a weapon being used against them, perhaps I could be of use to them. That's all I had, because escaping and hiding wasn't an option. Z had my scent and would find me without any problem. If I dared to go outside, what would the shades do to me? The last ten minutes in the bathroom were spent cursing the situation, Peter, and the Dark Caster who did this to me, for putting me in this situation.

I returned to the sitting area to find Dominic pacing the length of the sitting room.

"Feel better?"

My motives behind the shower weren't as clandestine as I thought.

"I feel clean." Better was no longer in my grasp.

Dominic gave me a long measuring look. "This world doesn't scare you, does it?" he asked, the echo of curiosity replaced by intrigue.

My bravado must be more convincing than I thought. "Everything about this world scares me. A place where everyone is a tactician so they can acquire more power just so they can live life without consequences. People speak openly about murdering me, and I don't seem to have an identity other than being 'your human.'"

Something salacious threaded through his smirk. He didn't have a problem with me being his human. He moistened his lips and I was reminded of last night.

"I'm not fearless. I have no option other than to do what is necessary to come out of this alive. And with everything you revealed, I am scared," I admitted.

"My position hasn't changed, Luna. I want to find the root of it. What your existence means. Could you be of use to me? One tool I'd love to have is the ability to weave spells. Could you be the answer to me doing it?"

"You're able to do so much with your magic, why is spell weaving something you need?"

"What I do is chip away at the various spells in a weave. It's complicated, time consuming, and not very efficient. Weaving spells would allow me to do more with a single spell." He was calculating the possibilities of becoming stronger than he was already. Maybe I wasn't scared of his world, just not able to be the person I needed to be to survive in it.

He inched in closer to me. "Besides, I don't like Peter

having any claim on you. None." The possession in his statement was apparent. His. I wasn't sure how I felt about that. He kissed me, fingers lacing through my hair, the other hand sliding under my shirt, kneading at my skin. His erection pressed against me. I tugged his shirt from his pants, quickly unbuttoning it. When there was a knock at the door, we ignored it. Dominic shrugged off the unbuttoned shirt, pulling away from me long enough to yank my shirt off. His lips trailed from mine down to my neck, the swell of my breasts. Slipping my bra off, he cupped them, his tongue languidly moving over my nipples that hardened at his attention. I wanted him. All of him. And I responded accordingly, a throaty moan escaping as he teased them.

The knocking persisted and we attempted to ignore it until the commanding booming voice said, "Dominic, play with your…Luna, later."

The pause I assumed was him deciding whether he'd give me a name or refer to me as 'his human.' We quickly redressed. I was smoothing out my hair when the lord entered. He gave me a sweeping dismissive glance before bringing it to his son. Even with a tight, polite smile, there was something adversarial in it.

"Dinner is in an hour. I'm expecting your and Luna's attendance," he said, turning on his heels. "Let's not have a repeat of the defiance you've shown with Helena, son." With that he left.

Dominic had given in to that insolence full throttle. He clearly had no intention of going. His kiss was hard and ravenous. When he attempted to return to where we'd left off, I stepped away.

"Dinner?" I reminded him.

He sighed, running his fingers through his hair. He expended a great deal of effort averting his attention from my lips.

"Fine, I need to get you appropriate clothing," he said

before leaving. Did they seriously dress for dinner? What's wrong with my jeans and button-down shirt? If this wasn't acceptable, they'd be downright offended by my home dinner wear of an oversized shirt, occasionally some pants, and fluffy socks.

Well, I'd play by their rules and *dress* for dinner despite knowing the dinner was a facade for something more. I was just as curious about the Lord of the Underworld as he was about me.

7

When Dominic returned, I took the dress bag he handed me. Unzipping it, I stared at the beautiful blush-taupe midi sheath dress with the dramatic draped neck. Dressy but not formal.

"It was Helena's suggestion," he admitted with a tight smile. I hope my face didn't reveal how off-putting I found the dynamics between him and his sister. It wasn't just their interaction I found complicated; it was her. One moment she was cheerfully insisting on my murder, the next she was selecting beautiful dresses for me. That suspicion had me eyeing the dress and forcing my imagination to resist going into hyperdrive determining the many ways she could use the dress to end me. Nothing feasible that didn't require a multimillion-dollar production budget came to mind, but in the world of magic, I was sure there were things possible beyond my imagination.

"She'll use this one act to prove she's changed." Dominic shrugged with a knowing frown. Even with my limited knowledge of the antics, I understood his frustration. I couldn't imagine years, probably decades, of dealing with it.

Dominic kept on his slim-cut steel-gray slacks and black

shirt that complemented his honed physique. He directed me to a different dining area with a beautiful spiral chandelier that added a modern touch to a formal dining room which held an ornate wood table that could seat twelve. Dark blue wainscoting made the vast and intimidating room more inviting. A section on the opposite side of the room had a lounging area complete with a bar. Like the dining room, it didn't appear to get much use.

Areleus looked at ease seated at the head of the table with his daughter to his right. He directed Dominic to take the one to his left. I sat next to him. Anand entered, dressed similarly to Dominic but in dark green pants and an alabaster shirt, his hair slightly mussed from him idly running his fingers through it, which he was doing from the moment he entered the room. Him taking a seat at the far end of the table drew the lord's attention.

"Anand, I appreciate you joining us. By joining, I'd hoped you would truly join us."

So, it wasn't just me he didn't want to be around. Anand wasn't a people person. With a heavy sigh, Anand stood and took the seat next to Helena and across from me. His interlocked fingers seemed to be more interesting than the people in the room.

With a personal invitation for dinner, I expected more than mundane chatter about the meal and the occasional request to pass the condiments. Once the plates were nearly empty, I became the recipient of Areleus's undivided attention as he interviewed me, asking about my childhood, where I attended school, my interests and hobbies. He didn't seem interested that I sketched and wrote poetry when I wasn't reading. He seemed unimpressed that some of it was used in songs written by my best friend, Emoni. The notebooks filled with my musings were shared only with her. She'd always been a safe space for that. Thinking about the way her face brightened when I finally built up the courage to show her sent a pang through me. Remembering her appreciation and how I felt when she asked for permission to add stanzas of them to her songs, I felt a real longing for her. I missed talking to her, our banter, her urging me to live by her mantra of being my authentic self, and even her wild plots to get revenge on Jackson after our breakup. My heart ached knowing that when I returned for good, I would have to lie to her.

"I've upset you?" Areleus asked. The deep-seated confusion in his tone snapped me from my drift into Emoni.

Offering a tight smile, I said, "Not at all. I was just wondering how I'll explain my absence to the people in my life once I return." I gave Dominic a look. "Without using magic against them."

The lord took a slow drink from his wine glass, his considering eyes turned in Dominic's direction. His stony countenance turned pleased. As if he'd solved a puzzle. "I see the fascination," he said. "Her optimism is contagious. How she'll 'explain' her absence," he repeated with a chuckle of dark amusement.

"Yes," Helena cooed with the venom of a viper and a flourish of movement drawing attention to her magic-restricting marks. "Of all the toys he's had and broken, she seems to be his favorite." Her voice was cloying in contrast to the dagger-sharp glare and cutting remark.

"Toy?" Dominic challenged.

"Your human," she scoffed. "She's your favorite little human—until she's not."

I could see Dominic's crude rebuttal brewing, but before he could comment I said, "I'm neither a toy nor 'his' human. I'm Luna. You can start by calling me that."

She smirked. "Your *Luna* seems to be your favorite of all the humans you've had over the years." Treating me to a critical once-over, she grimaced. "I struggle to see the root of it. *Your* intrigue has *me* intrigued."

It had been said so often, I was wondering the same. I was not one for self-deprecating thinking, but Helena's harping on it had me wondering what drew Dominic to me. It seemed more than just carnal lust.

Areleus looked from his daughter to his son. "Helena, how have you missed it? There's plenty to pique his interest. The human Luna"—Did he think that was better?—"restored our position of rule with the supernaturals. Reclaimed her power by refusing to be a pawn in the Tenebras game, and undid his wrong. And she is quite determined to undo his misdeeds again." He raised his glass to me. "Although Helena has missed how truly lovely you are, I appreciate it fully."

Reluctantly, I admitted that Lord Areleus's smile was enthralling. He gave it out so infrequently, it was otherworldly and enchanting. As I held his gaze, there was a hum, an allure, not the necessary fight or flight instinct. Jerking my eyes from him, I remembered that looking a vampire in the eyes was dangerous; it gave them the opportunity to compel. These people's magic had something similar. I wouldn't be lured into complacency, especially by him. Returning to my food, I put all my interest in finishing the last of it.

"Have you made any progress?" Areleus asked, pushing his plate away and refilling his wine glass. Once his attention was off me, I did the same and took a long appreciative drink of the full-bodied expensive wine that I wasn't likely to experience after I left.

"Not yet. I will need access to the *Book of Umbra*."

"That book of spells is restricted. Magic from it should always be a last resort," Areleus warned.

I stole a glance at Anand. He was watching the exchange with a casual interest, but it was obvious he was looking for an appropriate time to leave.

"It will be used as such. No spell is unbreakable. I just need more time."

The lord considered it. "Is time in our favor? Our position among the supernaturals has been restored, yet we are absent. A civil war is brewing and by the time we are free, will we be met with the results of a coup? You've said that there are things at work that will change the power brokers of the Conventicle," he noted.

I wasn't opposed to new leadership of the Conventicle. I had a problem with them wanting me dead. But I was no longer the reason the prisoners were loose, so I was indifferent about who led the Conventicle. I was team anti-Awakeners.

"Which is why I need the *Book of Umbra*. I need to weigh all possible options. At this point it's harm reduction. I realize spells from that book come at a cost—an irreparable imbalance. Although I'm not in a rush to compromise my magic, I will if it is necessary."

The lord nodded, easing the pinched frown. "And you shall have it."

Anand took that as the end of the discussion and as an indicator that dinner was complete. Placing his napkin on the plate, he stood to leave. Areleus tracked his progress until he disappeared through the double doors, then he let his disappointment peek through.

"At least he joined us. That is the most we can ask for."

The moment I completed my dinner, Dominic offered a rushed goodbye and rose to leave as well. I was reluctant to do so when the chef mentioned dessert. But no promise of a delectable cake was enough to make me stay alone with them. Despite Areleus's stiff smile he gave whenever I looked in his direction, Helena only offered me glares. Dominic's rush to leave showed his exhausted tolerance of his father. The forced amicability was obvious in every strained word they spoke when they attempted conversation.

As we departed, Areleus called Dominic's name. As he turned to respond, an illuminated ball hit him in the chest with a thud, sending him crashing into the door and ripping it from the hinges. Splintered wood scattered. Pulled back against a hard chest, I was secured by Areleus's hand around my throat, his claws held steady at my stomach. Dominic recovered, glaring at his father's hand that with a swipe could do unspeakable damage. Fear made tears brim in my eyes. I tried not to blink because they'd spill. I wouldn't give Helena, who I could see out of my peripheral, the satisfaction of that. Despite my intentions, I did blink, and tears slid down my face. Fire ignited in Dominic's hand and narrowed eyes studied his father. Behind the glare were calculations and defiance.

"Release Luna," Dominic demanded. He inched toward his father. I released a sharp gasp when Areleus's hold tightened.

"My commands are not to be ignored, Dominicus," Areleus told him. "You will release your sister's magic as I requested."

Dominic's response was to take slow steps toward us, his eyes sliding in the direction of his sister, who must have been gleeful at the magic and violence unfolding in front of her, and even more so that I was the recipient.

Dominic's insolence had taken full control. This battle extended beyond just me and seemed deeply rooted in something I knew nothing of.

"Have you grown so confident that you no longer understand your position? So foolish as to mistake my commands as suggestions?" Areleus bit out.

Energy peeled from the air, along with what felt like the removal of oxygen, making it even more difficult to breathe.

"Do I need to show you the penalty for your disobedience?" Areleus growled through clenched teeth. "You want her alive for an ill-conceived notion of preventing it happening again. I've granted that to you. You realize I don't care. One swipe and I free us."

"You've always been short-sighted. An ill-fated quality that Helena shares."

"Yet, despite your efforts, I still rule."

Dominic's jaw clenched so hard he could make diamonds from coal. If there was ever a debate over the existence of animosity between them, which Dominic had suppressed into amused disdain, there was no question now. A fiery rage was in his eyes. A thirst for violence that he planned to sate.

Areleus's cruel laugh broke the silence. "I can see the plans, son. Shall your second attempt to dethrone me be as ineffective as your first? It's been a century, perhaps the years have dulled your memory."

Dominic glared at him. "I forgot nothing, including what led me to do it. Release her, now."

The claws pressed into my skin, to let me know of their presence and what they could do, and the control he possessed with them. My head filled with ways to break his hold. How close was I to his sensitive crotch? If I clawed at his hand, would he retaliate? His hold tightened, blocking all my breath when I touched his hand. His hold was powerful, clipping my last breath.

"It's my son who values your life, not me," he pronounced in a breathy whisper near my ear. And then to Dominic, "Remove Helena's restriction, now."

Dominic didn't move, his chin tilted in an unspoken challenge. Anger flared in me at him using me to make a point. My heart pounded. How long would Areleus tolerate Dominic's insolence? His eyes were locked on his father, the restraint of fury a tendril nearly at its breaking point.

"You failed before. What skills have you acquired that you believe will lead to your success this time? I'm not as trusting of you as your sister is. And I would never put myself in a position to allow you to suppress my magic. You are aware that use of the magic in the *Book of Umbra* comes at a cost. Weakness of your magic. That will challenge your delusions of besting me, won't it? This is my final warning."

"Helena," Dominic called softly. She quickly made her way to him, her expression a sheet of innocence as if she wasn't the source of this altercation. Turning to face his sister, Dominic took hold of her arms. His mouth moved, but he spoke so low his words were inaudible. The marks on her arms became gilded before illuminating. They unraveled slowly from her arms before disappearing. She studied her brother during the spell, her lips twisted, seeing something in him that registered as concern in her face. Once the markings had disappeared, he pulled Helena to him and whispered something that made her face go pallid.

The second I was released I dashed out of the destroyed doorway, heading toward the bedroom but stopping in front of the library. I didn't want to be around Dominic, and Anand was clearly at his limit with peopling. Absently, I stood in the hallway, without a clear direction to go.

"You look like you could use some tea," said a melodic deep voice from the library entrance.

I turned to find the man who'd judged my clothes earlier leaning against the frame of the opened door, offering me a sympathetic half smile.

Nodding, I followed as he led me through the library, around the stacks, and down another hallway to a door. He opened it to reveal an oasis. A vibrant tall fiddleleaf plant in the corner offered the dose of greenery I hadn't realized I'd missed so much. On one of the shelves and on the corner of the desk were smaller verdant plants. The one with a hint of pale orange reminded me of a plant that Cameron, the owner of Books and Brew, had in her office. I sighed. I missed her, too. I could use her infectious optimism and vitality now.

"The only one that's real is that one." He pointed to the plant on a table next to a chaise at the opposite end of the room. "It doesn't require a lot of light so it can thrive with the light from the greenhouse. I take it out there occasionally for a dose. It's not the real sun, but it's serviceable."

I got the impression that the fake sun was as much for him as it was for the plants. The sage-gray walls… I exhaled at the peace they invoked. It felt like I had been holding my breath since I left the spectacle between Dominic—or rather, Dominicus—Areleus, their drama, and the threat of death. Pushing all thoughts of that from my head, I took in the oversized curved boucle sofa and the combination of traditional and deco art and furniture. It was a surprising design style for a man who wore a vest and speckle-rim glasses.

"I love your office," I said, making a huge assumption since the spacious room, except for the desk, didn't look like a typical office.

Pleased, he headed to a narrow, free-standing range in the kitchen nook. He added water to the gooseneck kettle.

"Relax and make yourself at home."

I headed for the chaise and settled back on it.

Within minutes of the kettle whistling, the aroma of chamomile and something I couldn't quite identify hit my senses. Inhaling the scent didn't make the incident from earlier disappear, but it was a comforting distraction. I crossed my legs, giving him room to sit on the end of the chaise, and extended my hand to the area, inviting him to join me. He was human, or human passing. It didn't matter. It was comforting. He was comforting. Hesitating, he studied my face before taking the seat.

"Thank you so much…" My words trailed as I waited for a name.

"Jasper," he provided.

"Thank you, Jasper. I'm—"

"Luna," he interjected. "You have been quite the talk as of late."

That was surprising to hear since my interaction with people was limited. "Really?"

"Maybe not the talk." He shrugged. "But you've piqued everyone's curiosity. No one knows why you're here. You don't seem to have a job here and Dominic has never brought a…" He searched for the right word. "Paramour here."

I applaud your search, Jasper, but that's definitely not the right word. That description made a relationship seem benevolent and simplistic and the opposite of what existed between Dominic and me.

"How long have you been here?" I asked, not ready to discuss Dominic, his violent family, or his paramours—or people he enjoyed fucking and betraying, if Helena's accounts were to be believed.

"Eight years. I've been here the longest. Usually, people stay a year or two. Chefs tend to stay a little longer, three to five years." He shrugged. "I'm not sure why."

"And the librarian stays the longest," I teased.

"It was what I did before I accepted the invitation to come here. It's easy and I'm surrounded by books. It's a good existence." He said it with a smile, but sadness crept into his voice and I debated whether to press for more information.

"You prefer being somewhere different?"

The pensive smile he worked at was achieved with a great deal of effort. "I prefer living in a place where there aren't any reminders of loss," he admitted. For a stretch of time, he was silent as we drank our tea. "My partner. He and I had many great years together, and when he died, it was a hollow existence. Here I have no reminder and I stay relatively busy."

How, I wondered.

He leaned in with a conspiratorial look. "I've never been in the other room." I figured he was referring to the magic room. "I spend a great deal of time trying to trick it into granting me entrance."

My laughter lifted the somber heaviness that had drifted

into the room and made him grin. I wanted to keep that grin there and him far from the morose mood I'd glimpsed when he spoke of his partner. I directed my attention to the cabinets where he'd taken out the tea. "This isn't just chamomile, is it?"

His face brightened. "My special blend." He escorted me to the cabinet and opened it to reveal canisters of various labeled herbal teas and blends. His love for it rivaled Emoni's love for coffee. That squashed my desire for them to meet. A love for tea and coffee wasn't the recipe for a budding friendship.

"There are a few books there." He jerked his chin toward the table. "You're welcome to stay here as long as you'd like."

I took a sip of tea, grimaced at the tepid temperature, and was about to rewarm it in the microwave when Jasper's eyes widened with disgust. *Okay, I'll drink cooled tea.* He offered to make me another and directed me to the chaise. Watching him prepare the tea, I was convinced he enjoyed the preparation as much as the tea.

Lifting the hardback of *Charlotte's Web*, I gave him a quizzical look.

"Sometimes a return to the books we loved as a child is what we desperately need."

I wasn't nostalgic enough to relive the bittersweet tears I'd shed reading it. Instead, I decided on falling into N. K. Jemisin's world of *The Broken Earth*. But sleep had other ideas.

8

I awoke, covered by a heavy blanket, the book next to me, and fully aware of Dominic's presence. It couldn't be ignored. He'd repositioned the desk chair just a few inches from me. His turbulent energy was chasing away the calmness of the room.

"You didn't come to bed last night."

The underworld's odd light didn't ebb in from the small window. The room was lit by the flicker of golden radiance from Dominic's magic and the transfixing glow that dwelled in his amber eyes in varying degrees. It was muted now, a hint, and they were intensely focused on me.

"I didn't want to be around you," I blurted before I could tamp down my curt admission. I kept being used as a pawn in his world, first by Peter and now by the Lord of the Underworld. Peter needed me alive. Areleus didn't.

He grunted. If my words bothered him, nothing about his expression hinted that it did.

"Your father was going to kill me," I said, my voice quivering. It was achingly difficult trying to ignore the phantom touch of the lord's claws pressed into my stomach, to not replay his cold venomous words over and over.

"That is who he is," he asserted, emotionless. I detected the undisclosed part as well. That's the way *they* are.

"Are you like that?" I asked, the need for real answers overriding my fear of knowing just how vicious he could be.

"Sometimes." Without any inflection in his voice, I couldn't determine if it was a source of shame or pride.

"Because it's necessary or you choose to be?"

"Violence and cruelty are necessary in this world, Luna. It is unfortunate that he sees you as a bargaining tool," he said.

"Unfortunate for you," I barked. I needed some form of emotion. His lack of passion infuriated and scared me. I was locked in the underworld with them, and it didn't seem like I had any allies. My chances of survival were whittling away if I didn't at least have Dominic.

"Do you want me to leave?" It seemed more like a challenge than a question.

"I don't know," I whispered. He closed his eyes and took away the magical ebbs of light, plunging the room into darkness.

"I need light," I told him. My request was left unanswered so we sat in darkness, the tension thick between us, the silence heavy with hostility.

"My father's right," he whispered, sparking an urge in me to run. The air changed, becoming heavy and uncomfortable. Toxic energy slithered over my skin, and I tried to determine if it was subtle magic or the obvious animosity between us.

"I could end this right now, break the vessel." His hand created a gentle gird around my neck that could easily become the death of me. His dagger claws could sever the vessels in my neck in an instant. My heart thrashed so hard, he had to have heard it. I stilled and closed my eyes. It wasn't as if I could see it coming. Do anything about it. Helplessness felt horrible. No part of me could let that define me or the situation, despite all evidence to the contrary. My fingers crawled toward the book that I'd fallen asleep with. Could I strike him hard enough to give me the advantage?

He whispered my name. It carried in the room, something desperate and conflicted in the strain of that one word.

A soft light glowed between us. Dominic looked contemplative as his hand rested on my neck. As if he was looking for the inspiration to perform the execution.

"Dominicus?" I whispered.

"Don't call me that," he demanded. A wrathful blaze ignited in his eyes, then faded into a depthless darkness. I swallowed at his palpable warring emotions.

Dominic's hands moved to my jawline. At a gentle rhythm, his thumb ran along it, then swept across my lips. As quickly as he was near me, he was gone, leaving me with even more questions.

I fumbled around the room, looking for a light. Once I found it, I turned it on, spilling much needed light into the room. I folded the blanket and returned the book to the table before reluctantly heading for Dominic's bedroom to get dressed. Staying away from him wasn't really an option, and I was so unsettled by not having a definitive answer. Could I trust Dominic with my life? That question dominated all the many thoughts, inquiries, and tactics in my mind.

Before I left the library, I found Jasper, who was busying himself dusting and wiping down books, probably as an excuse to distance himself from the mercurial Dominic. I waved goodbye to him and thanked him for his hospitality. Jasper responded with a nod and bringing his hand to his chest. I wasn't sure if it meant his pleasure or that he enjoyed my company, but it was a welcomed response.

Making my way to Dominic's room was a slog. I was on edge, fearful that I'd run into the lord or the magically restored Helena. Despite my determination to get more answers from Dominic, I wasn't enthusiastic about seeing him, either.

His struggle was real and so was his disappointment at his inability to choose the simplest resolution to their problem. Dominic's curiosity might be his Achilles heel and my guaranteed safety. Getting rid of me might prevent him from learning more about my purpose and what the vessel was capable of, but it would free them and prevent Peter from ever using me again.

As I eased the door open, I could see Dominic on the sofa, legs spread. Like his presence, taking up far too much space. Nothing about his mien felt approachable, nor did it feel like the time to talk. The conflict had placed a rigid crease between his brows. With each step I made toward the bedroom to get to the shower, I could feel his eyes on me. Hard and penetrating.

"I want you alive, Luna," he whispered. Was that all I was going to get from the embattled Dominic? I needed more, but nothing about him at that moment showed I'd get it.

I slipped past him without a word and headed for the bedroom where I grabbed some clothing and retreated to the bathroom, taking that moment of reprieve before I talked to Dominic. After, I was determined to get everything I needed from him: a promise that he'd do everything to ensure I left the underworld alive.

Clean, relaxed from the shower, and dressed in clothes that weren't a reminder of the previous day, I headed back to the seating area resolute and draped in faux bravado. I was getting answers and an oath of protection from him. But in the sitting area, I found Dominic gone and Anand in his place.

My bodyguard has returned. I probably needed one more than ever.

"Breakfast?" he asked, standing with a smirk, responding to my growling stomach. Worrying had proven to be a calorie-burning activity.

Stopping abruptly at the sight of Areleus seated in the

kitchen, a coffee in hand, and a croissant and fruit on a plate, I was shocked— No, I was fucking appalled by the audacity of him greeting me with a brilliant welcoming smile.

"Good morning, Luna." His voice was a deep purr of malevolence. "Would you like to join me?"

Was he fucking serious? I could see where Helena got her sociopathic gumption from. He was bathed in it.

"No," I gritted out. "Why would I ever want to have a meal with you?!"

His eerie speed of movement had him standing before me in a breath, looking down at me, darkly amused by whatever he saw.

"I do see the appeal," he admitted softly. "There's something quite alluring about you. I'd go as far as to say it is intoxicating. It has certainly left my son addled."

"You're exploiting it?"

"Why wouldn't I?"

Furtively, I looked around for the guards. I was confident the Lord of the Underworld was about to be kneed in his man berries and I needed to know how close the guards were. Because after the assault on them, I planned to get in as many punches as possible before the guards stopped me. It wasn't likely they'd side with me, but if they had any idea what was said, they might not handle me as roughly.

He moved closer. "What is it about you, Luna?" Another person with that gift of putting so much into my name. He moved around me. I followed. I would not let a poisonous viper out of my sights. It amused him. Areleus's eyes dipped to my lips, his leering obvious and gross. Areleus was a sociopath and I couldn't see past that, no matter how sinfully attractive he was.

"Anand, what is it?" he asked, keeping his eyes on me. I risked a glance in Anand's direction, but he seemed genuinely confused as well.

"I don't know," Anand finally admitted.

"Yes, it is quite the conundrum, isn't it?" Areleus's eyes narrowed. "He's not sharing information with me."

"What? He's not providing information after you attempted to murder his friend? The audacity," I spat out.

Areleus repeated my assertion of being Dominic's friend with the revulsion of a vile curse.

"*Anand* is Dominic's friend. I don't doubt that when he's with you, friendly thoughts are the furthest from his mind. You are a siren to him, and he's answered your call. Is it you, Luna, the peculiar little human, or is there more to you? Will I need to crack you open to see?"

Fear and adrenaline jetting through me, I drew taller and met his challenging eyes. These people were energized and provoked by fear, so I would deprive him of it. The seconds ticked by before he gave me another assessing once-over before departing. His threat lingered.

"I want to go home," I whispered.

As if saying it would bring it to fruition.

My interaction with Areleus didn't ruin my appetite. Anand had a scone and coffee while I devoured a lot of food in hope it would hold me for the day and decrease the chance of further encounters with Areleus or Helena.

My plan to head to the library for more research if the magical room allowed, or visit with Jasper, was squashed when Anand directed me to Dominic's office. It was the midnight-blue room where Dominic had showed me how to use the Trapsen to travel from the underworld. There wasn't a magical key required for entrance this time. Anand pushed the door open without so much as a knock. Dominic was eying several objects on the desk. Expectant eyes flicked to me and I quickly moved toward Anand.

"You want to practice more later today?" Anand asked.

"Practice what?"

He chuckled. "Your punches and"—his lips quivered from

obviously fighting the urge to laugh at the image of me attempting one of his combinations moves and landing on my butt—"kicks. Perhaps we can go over kicks."

"I'd like that."

He was headed out the door before I could get a time.

"Just call my name, I'll find you," he told me. *Yeah, because that's not creepy at all.*

Dominic's lips furled into a sneer at the door. I couldn't determine if Anand felt it or sensed it, but he turned back around. Their eyes locked. I couldn't see what was going on between them. Anand's lips pursed and the shake of his head was so imperceptible I questioned if it was my imagination. Dominic inhaled a deep breath, letting it ease out. Something substantial occurred during that exchange that was borne from knowing each other well and for a long time. No matter how minute, I hadn't missed it. With the tension in the room eased, Anand left, giving me a quick look and a heavy sigh. The wariness in it was palpable.

"What do you want?" I asked Dominic. All the warmth had drained from my voice. I had reached my limits with his hot and cold, indecisive, mercurial ways.

His fingers slithered over a large worn black book with gold edges. Gilded embossed words were on the cover in a language I didn't recognize.

"The *Book of Umbra*?" I asked.

He nodded. "It's a last resort. I don't know how many spells will be needed to undo the imprisonment. They will need to be stable and complementary to the others," he pondered.

Sight of the orb, the knife with sigils on the blade, and the glass bottle of ink on the table made me uneasy. As a distraction, I picked up the book and flipped through it. It served no purpose other than to make things more confusing, since I didn't understand the ominous-looking language. The sigils and strange markings in the book looked even more foreboding.

I turned when I felt the heat of his body behind me. He was close, too close. The smart thing was to put distance between us and stick with the single goal of getting the hell out of the underworld. He slipped the book from my hands and let it drop to the floor. Drawing me close, his fingers twined in my hair, his lips inches from mine, and the heat that radiated from him curled around me. His presence and touch were an intoxicating mix. It was impossible to deny his raw sexuality. The desire to see his entire body overwhelmed me. To feel his skin against mine and the masterful touch of his hands moving over me, caressing my skin in his dark, seductive way. I responded to his lips brushing lightly against me, his tongue teasing my lip with promise of more to come. The languid, commanding way his hand moved over me made it easy to forget about the previous days, but I forced them to the forefront. I wouldn't let my libido make me ignore his earlier behavior; the indecision and frustration that came over him at his inability to take the easy option. He wanted to but couldn't. Whatever kept him from doing it then may not exist in the future.

"No," I said, pulling away from him. "I can't do this. You're confusing me." Putting even more space between us, I crossed my arms over my chest.

"How?" he asked in a low and raspy breath.

"Have you dealt with a human woman before?" I asked, incredulous.

"I've dealt plenty with human women," he said, the devilish note in his words teasing me. I wouldn't be distracted by the salacious implications.

"I can't speak for others, but *this* human woman can't function with this volatility," I admitted.

"That's the problem, Luna," he said. "Are you really human? You were chosen as a vessel for Dark Caster magic. I can't help but wonder if your existence is solely to hold the magic. If that is the case, how much of you is actually human?"

The look he gave me earlier passed over his face. I was slipping in and out of categories and I didn't like it.

"I saw the way you looked at me earlier and I hated it. You were wondering if you should take the easy way out and destroy what's keeping you imprisoned. There was a struggle, and fortunately, I was on the winning side of it. *This time.* One moment, I feel safe around you, the next, I'm not so sure."

"I'm not sure, either."

Did he believe that response was praiseworthy? Helping this situation in any way? He won for *worst* response. I didn't attempt to hide my thoughts.

"Dominic, I need more than that. Can I trust you?"

The long, contemplative silence was worrisome.

"Dominic?"

"You don't understand how volatile the state of human existence and the maintenance of supernaturals' good behavior is. You live in a bubble of protection because of machinations you can't begin to understand. I doubt you truly know how close your kind is to being exterminated or forced into servitude." He didn't sound duly convinced of that last part. My kind. He wasn't thoroughly convinced I was human. And now neither was I. A shadow of humanity and peculiar duality of both worlds.

"Sacrifices must be made to maintain it. No one is precluded from it. I know you want more, and I wish I could give more. The only thing I can promise you is that I will do all within my power to keep you alive because I value your life. Know that my power is immense."

I didn't need the humble brag, but the tension that was clouding my mind and making it difficult to breathe eased.

"To determine whether you are truly a vessel for the

magic or you only exist to be a vessel of the magic, we need to take it."

"Then take it. Take the magic out of me. I don't need it and I don't want it," I blurted.

He moved to the window, his hands shoved in his pockets, his face pensive as he stared out into the grayness of the underworld. "Luna, I don't think you quite understand what needs to be determined. How much of your existence is predicated on the magic that dwells in you? If the magic is removed, will you continue to exist?"

"Is that the reason you haven't shared this with your father?" I asked, inching closer to him.

"No, it's none of his concern. As far as I'm concerned, his imprisonment is the only positive thing that has come out of this. He should relinquish his position as lord of this underworld."

"Why?"

"Vampires hang on to their humanity for the first century or so of their lives. It's as if they remember what it is to be human, so they act accordingly. Shifters and witches are the most human of the supernaturals and therefore show those qualities in their behavior and decisions. There's no part of me, Helena, or our father that is human. We must work to find that humanity, to ensure that we don't give in to our nature. As the years pass, it gets harder to care about such things. My father is at that point but doesn't possess the awareness to step down."

A vampire wanted to have a taste of me then attempted to coerce me into hurting myself, shifters stalked me, and the witches were 'Team Kill Luna.' It was hard to see them as being aligned with their humanity or occasionally tapping into it to find balance. Those judgmental opinions came to an abrupt stop once I considered the undiluted version of history, the cruelty of human existence, all the turmoil I saw in the news, and social media, which was a staunch reminder that humans weren't in any position to cast judgment.

"He's no longer discreet with his plans. He doesn't want supernaturals to exist—or rather, those who can challenge him. He wants servitude, and unchecked authority and power. His punishments are harsh even for the most minor infractions. He chooses to kill instead of imprison. It is my understanding that Anand told you of the tenuous balance we have with the supernaturals. Establishing a working relationship with them wasn't my father's doing, it was mine."

"They don't like you, either," I blurted. It could have been edited to be nicer, but this conversation demanded candor.

He smirked and shrugged. "I don't care if they like me. It's better if they don't, then they're not disappointed when I'm cruel. Make no mistake." His eyes darkened as he presented the minatory part of him, the part he managed to suppress when he was with me. But it was a blunt reminder of what and who he was and for me to never forget his capabilities.

"He is more powerful than I am and relies on the brute force of his power. My attempt to take the throne failed, but I will dethrone him because tactical maneuvering and patience are qualities and skills my father doesn't possess. If he did, he would have dethroned my grandfather through clever machination rather than waiting until my grandfather was weakened by the spell he used to capture the shades."

No wonder they were reluctant to use the magic from the *Book of Umbra*, if the cost was weakening them enough to leave them vulnerable.

"Taking the throne is?" Part of me knew what it meant to take the throne, and it definitely involved violence. I just wasn't sure if it was to the extent of murder. Was it acknowledging defeat and relinquishing the throne, or a darker variation?

"My grandfather was killed. It was warranted," Dominic

said matter of factly. Not a hint of mourning. "He didn't care that the shades were violent chaotic beings. He just wanted them to be *his* violent chaotic beings. If he had succeeded, the world you're aware of, where the supernaturals are in the shadows, wouldn't exist. They'd be gone and you all would be at the whims of my grandfather and his army of creatures. Despite there being only fifty shades, they can cause a great deal of trouble."

"If they take on human form—"

"Take a human body," he corrected. "They can't take on human form. What you saw is what they look like in your world, too. They are intelligent and pragmatic, which adds to their level of danger. In a human body, they wouldn't be perceived as the threat they are."

"What happens to the human?"

"They become a shell to host the shade. When they take a human's body, they're subjected to human frailty. They won't age, but they are easier to kill. With magic like theirs, getting to the point of killing them becomes harder. They're known to discard the shell to guarantee their survival. If my father figures out how to control them, he'll want the same. This world isn't enough for him. He wants yours, too. He'd use the shades and other supernatural sycophants to subjugate the ones with the highest population."

Dominic had told me of the numbers and how so many of the supernaturals had infiltrated a significant part of our world. I just wanted to go back to my simple life, but I feared there wasn't any going back to simple. Because now I knew too much.

I made no effort to hide how troubled I was, and Dominic took the cue. In his eerie strike of movement, he'd picked up the book he let fall to the floor and returned it to its position next to the others.

"Are you willing to let me attempt to take your magic away?"

"Is it safe?"

He gave me a wary half smile. "I think so."

I'd like more surety, but when it came to magic, that was impossible.

"Let's try."

He opened the book and flipped over a few pages until he got to the one with the worrying-looking sigils. He reviewed it. "This isn't one of the stronger spells, so it shouldn't leave my magic vulnerable." Taking my hand, he used the ink to mark my palms with identical markings from the book. When he picked up the knife, I sucked in a breath. The razor-sharp edge would ensure it would cut with the slightest touch to my skin.

"Can't we use a strand of hair?" I joked in an attempt to calm my nerves. It didn't help.

"It will be fine." He kissed the tip of my finger. When he nipped at it, a shudder ran through me. He knew the effect he had on me. He dropped my finger, moving closer, his unoccupied hand grazing my lips, sliding down my neck, easing over my collarbone, over my chest, and teasing my nipples. They responded to the languid featherlight touch. I started panting softly, and my eyes went to his lips, wanting to feel them over the delicate area. To tease, kiss them, and touch me the way he did when he'd searched my body for markings.

"Just one prick. I promise to be gentle," he told me in a low, sultry voice that promised more than gentle touches.

I jerked back with a sneer. "Stop doing that! You're making me associate magic with inappropriate things."

"Luna, I can assure you sex and magic is quite appropriate."

"Just do it," I pressed, trying to break the association he was trying to get me to make. Nope. Magic was complex, violent, powerful, and the root of most of my problems. I wouldn't let one source of it being wrapped in a sexy, dark, sensual package make me forget that.

Chuckling at the sheer determination I was displaying, he took my hand. I blurted, "No touches. No kisses. No rough breathy instructions with sexual innuendos. Let's just magic."

He moistened his lips. "Of course, Luna, let's magic," he said, breaking all the damn guidelines I'd just put in place. Pointing to the orb, he said, "This will hold the magic. It won't be able to be used but at least it'll be out of you."

"Why didn't you do this before when Peter used me to free the prisoners?"

"Peter is quite skilled at misdirection. Before, I thought it was the marking on your hand only and the spell. It would have slipped my notice if he hadn't cloaked your identifier."

"Birthmark."

He frowned. "I don't know if it's a birthmark. I've explored every inch of you," he said, giving me a look that probed at the memory of that, "and there's a lighter discoloration on your right thigh. I believe that's your birthmark."

I eyed the small orb. "If that gets broken, what happens to the magic?"

"It'll be released. I'd like to take it, but I'm not sure if I can hold it. Witches can't steal my magic. It's incompatible. The same happened with you. You thought you couldn't hold witch magic. That wasn't the case. The Tenebras magic was dormant and it was warring with the witch magic."

Growing silent, I contemplated trying the magic, seeing if I could wield it for my benefit, essentially. But doing so would undeniably catapult me into the world I desperately wanted to escape. Curiosity got the best of me.

"I want to try a spell—to see."

He nodded. Opening the drawer to his desk, he pulled out a book. "Let's try something simple," he suggested, pointing to a spell.

It didn't seem simple. To them, maybe. It appeared to be a transfer spell, moving an object from one place to another in the room.

"Does size matter?" I asked.

"I don't know, does it matter to you?" he teased.

I glared. "Remember the guidelines."

"Of course, Luna." The low rumble of his words told me he had no intention of complying.

"The object's size. Does something small require less effort?"

He shook his head. Magic, like anything, seemed easy when a person had mastered it. I decided to try something small. Moving the jar of ink. Looking at the spell, I said the words, then looked at my target, commanding its compliance to move to the other side of the table. It gave me the middle finger. After five more attempts, I gave up. I wasn't sure why Dominic had me attempt more spells, but in the end we discovered that I couldn't control elements, calm him or myself, or use defensive or offensive magic. I wasn't going to knock him down or pin him to the wall with magic. Nor could I protect myself from magic with a ward. We even dabbled in seeing whether I could grow claws. Nothing. My sole purpose for magic was to be a vessel, from where magic could be pulled by others to be used by them. That wasn't a good feeling, like a sordid violation.

"Now what?" I asked, plopping onto the luxurious pebble-color leather tuxedo sofa, which looked more comfortable than it felt. Rigid and practical like the rest of the minimalist room. There wasn't any décor on the walls. Not even a task light, but when you can call light at will, it wasn't necessary. His large, plain black desk was brought to life by the brass handles on the drawer. The console, on the other side of the room, was for storage. Nothing about this room was meant for comfort or solace.

"We do the spell to remove the magic. Peter won't have a well to pull from, and hopefully it will make the spell he's using to imprison us null."

And without me as a source of magic for him, I would no longer be any use to him.

9

The room held a steely silence as Dominic leaned against the desk, drawn into his thoughts and absently rolling up the sleeves of his shirt, drawing my attention to the ink markings on them. His spicy sandalwood scent permeated the room. Dominic's bemused eyes lifted to meet mine, and he flashed a smile, making me blink hard at the realization that I wasn't just looking, I was gawking. His merciless beauty was captivating.

"I think you're beautiful, too," he said in a low, smoky voice.

"What?" Panic raced through me. Could he read my thoughts? That would explain how he seemed to anticipate a lot of my actions. That had to be just anecdotal. I had plenty of thoughts that if he knew them would have definitely caused problems between us. There would be more hostility.

"You were staring," he noted. "Most women do…" After a moment of consideration, he amended. "Most people."

"Everyone thinks you're hot. How do you manage such a burden?"

"Not a burden at all. It has its advantages," he touted with a level of confidence that quite efficiently straddled the line between admirable and infuriating.

"But you possess something far more extraordinary," he admitted. A hint of reluctance was in his voice as he studied me with the intensity of looking at a specimen under a microscope. A strange specimen. "I encounter a large array of supernaturals and humans. They provide that hint of humanity that keeps me grounded in purpose. There's something quite alluring about you, Luna. It vexes me that I can't place it. Something I've never experienced in the centuries I've existed. What is it?" The latter was a speculative whisper. The desperation to find the answer lingered in his voice.

"Maybe it's as simple as you like me. Is there something wrong with that?"

The crease of his frown showed an internal battle that I couldn't quite understand until I remembered the way he had looked at me. His struggle with leaving the vessel be, when the most effective thing to do would be to break the vessel.

"Yes, there is," he admitted, turning away from me to gather the orb and knife and unceremoniously putting an end to the conversation. "Ready?" he asked, his back still to me.

Hauling to stand, I approached him, extending my hand much closer.

"Why haven't you used this on the Mors? Take away their ability to kill by touch?" I asked. This seemed like it would be the answer to all their problems. The threat of losing their magic was probably just as cruel as imprisonment.

"You'll see," he explained, taking my hand in his and pressing the knife against my skin while he waited for me to give approval.

Nodding, I sucked in a breath and waited for the blade to pierce my skin. Dominic exhaled a shuddering breath, hesitating before he pressed it into my skin. Placing the orb in my hand, he spoke the spell. That went on for a stretch of time. With all the spells I'd seen, this one had to be nearly four pages long. At any point, I could just drop the orb, end the spell. But I held on to it as Dominic spoke the final portion, magic slithering over every inch of me until it had bound me in an invisible cocoon. I forced out a wheeze as the magic poked and prodded with an aggressively intrusive touch. The pull became violent. Pain seized me. My body temperature rose to an inferno and I closed my eyes and clenched my teeth. Unable to steady myself, I collapsed to my knees, my fingers affixed to the orb. No matter what I did, I couldn't pry them away. I wanted it to stop. Needed it to stop. Pain so excruciating, tears streamed down my face. Focused on the pain, I was faintly aware of Dominic prying my fingers from the orb and the heavy thud of what might have been him tossing it aside.

He pulled me to him, chest to chest, my legs curled around his waist. He lifted me and carried me to the sofa where he plopped down on it. The low, gentle brusque of him calling my name, soothingly rubbing my back, and telling me everything would be okay was fades of noise. I was too far gone.

Another sharp lash of words as he called my name. Cradling my face in his hands, he patted my face. It was so aggressively hard, I reared back to escape it.

"What are you doing? Stop that!" I snapped.

"There she is," he breathed out in relief, pulling me to him, my face resting in the crook of his neck. After several beats had passed, I leaned back and asked, "Why did you stop the spell?"

His thumb was making rhythmic circles at my side. He scoffed, his mouth forming a slight O before pulling into a rigid line. His finger tangled in my hair as he drew me closer. "It needed to be stopped, Luna. I needed to stop it."

"I was handling it." That was an interesting retelling. But I would have handled it if it meant I'd be freed.

"You didn't appear to be handling it."

"I'm dramatic sometimes." I managed a half smile, an unconvincing attempt at a joke. He saw it for the tactic it was, making light of a situation so I could better deal with it.

"There are other options to explore," he said. I couldn't determine if that was the truth or conciliation. His expression revealed nothing. When he dropped his hand from me and sank deeper into the sofa to look at the celling, I attempted to dismount. He quickly held me closer to him.

"I like you here," he whispered.

So did I. I shifted, pressing against the generous bulge that showed his pleasure with my position. He was ruining magic for me. I'd struggle not to have a Pavlovian response. Magic meant touches, kisses, sexy straddling, and the naughty way he looked at my lips as if he was always moments from covering them and tasting me.

Driving in the point of me conflating magic with him, his hand slipped under my shirt, running a delicious path over my body. Nails edging over my skin sent pleasure through me. He yanked off my shirt, a deep rumble reverberating in his chest as his eyes drank me in. Unclasping my bra and freeing my breasts, he palmed them, his thumb teasing them to hardened pebbles before taking one into his mouth. Laving over it with moist lazy circles as the familiarity of his magic caressed my skin, pulling a deep, throaty whimper from me. Fisting his hair, tugging him away until we were face to face, I glared at the devilish glint in his eyes.

"You're doing it again. When I conflate sex with magic, it will be your fault."

"I'll wear that blame with pride," he growled, drawing me to him in a ravenous kiss, his tongue exploring my mouth. Tasting me in a kiss so intense it left me panting softly when he ended. He trailed lazy kisses over my neck, collarbone, before returning his attention to my breast. Giving it the same treatment. Slow languid sweeps of kisses and laves had me arching into him, desiring more. With a deep groan, Dominic shifted me onto my back, tugging my pants off, hungry eyes devouring me, sweeping over my form in just my panties. A quick jerk ripped them from me, and he discarded the torn material on the floor. He traveled up my body with kisses and hedonistic licks, demanding a sexual submission that I gave in to when he settled between my legs, his hard bulge resting between them, taunting me. The throaty way he said my name, replete with an unsated need. He shifted into me. I yearned for him and needed every inch of him in me. My desperate fingers clawed at his shirt, pulling him to me.

"Luna, close your eyes," he demanded.

I obeyed. He repositioned, pulling me to him and wrapping his arms around me. Coolness breezed over me before swirling. I opened my eyes. When the clouding in my head eased, he lowered me onto his bed. Dominic gave me only a few seconds to take in our new location before devouring me with a kiss, hard and deep. A torrent of powered emotion. I was acutely aware of his raw masculinity and the command he had over it. He gave hard and still managed to leave me wanting more. Needing more. Aching to take everything he had to give.

Withdrawing one of the hands that fisted his hair, I used it to tug up his shirt. For a fleeting moment, I was aware that I was seeking sex instead of the answers we needed. It was a bad idea and I didn't care. Dominic was a delicious distraction, and I was eager to let his all-consuming sexuality and presence be that disruption.

Dominic broke the kiss to help me with my clumsy attempts to remove his shirt. His lusty appetite matching mine, he shifted back, tearing away the shirt. Buttons rained onto the floor. I wanted to trace the cut muscles of his abs, the V that formed along the crest of his hips, graze my nails over his warm skin. He disrupted my intention when he removed his pants and underwear, revealing his hard, thick length. A smirk tugged at his lips when I bit down on mine.

A sharp moan escaped from me when he took my nipples in his mouth, teasing them before traveling to my stomach, hips, and inner thighs. His tongue nestled in my mound as he moved between the folds, caressing the area with his tongue. His thumb thrummed over my swollen nub and my body was begging for a release. The dark amused fire in his eyes at my moans had me writhing from his erotic touches. Stroking earned an orgasmic shudder. I threaded my fingers through his hair and pulled him to me in a kiss as I urged him to his side so I could give in to my earlier desires, running my hand along his chest to his stomach. Edging back to plant ravenous kisses and nips along the same path. Nudging him to his back, I straddled him. Slithering down his body, tasting his skin and inhaling his scent. With each touch and kiss, his cock grew harder. Just touching him did nothing to satiate my need. Continuing my exploration, I slid down until I was face to face with his hardness. Taking hold of it, I stroked the length of it. Hot need burned in his eyes. He hissed a groan as my tongue ran over it. Taking him into my mouth, caressing him with my tongue. Stroking the remainder at a slow rhythm that had the Prince of the Underworld in an undeniable conflict: close his eyes and enjoy it or watch me. Biting down on his lips, he gave in to the latter, holding my gaze with his hungry eyes, showing his great pleasure with my attentions. His low groans filled the silence of the room before he twined his fingers into my hair, urging me up. When I was positioned over him, with his erection settled between my legs, I grinded against it.

He cursed before pulling me to him and rolling me to my back, taking me in a demanding, wanton kiss that became increasingly fervent and commanding. My body became pliant to his carnal, possessing touch.

I could feel his reluctance when he pulled away and opened the nightstand drawer. Pulling out a condom, he unwrapped it and rolled it on with efficient deftness while my eyes traveled over the length of it.

"Human women are far more fertile than we are," he whispered in my ear, the heat of his body blanketing me as he settled between my legs. I thought briefly about mentioning I was on the pill, but the thought was obliterated as he slowly entered me, meeting a slight resistance as I accommodated his thickness. He slid deeper into me and I moaned with shock and pleasure. Moving at a fast rhythm, I wrapped my legs around him, meeting his unfettered thrusts. Our movements were hard, frenetic, desperate. It suffused over me like a wildfire. My fingers curled into his back as I climaxed with a shudder. His breath battered against my lips as his strokes came harder, more intense until he, too, shuddered from the pleasure. Sinking deeper into the bed, he rolled from me, discarded the condom. Nudging me to my side, he wrapped his arms around me.

He nipped at my shoulder and neck, the caress of magic gently skittering over my skin. I'd become quite sensitive to it.

"Stop it. No mixing magic with sex."

His deep chuckle vibrated in his chest. "I believe it's too late for that," he teased into my hair. "But this may have backfired. How will I resist the urge to touch you"—his hands wandered between my legs, slipping into the wet folds—"to see how you respond whenever I perform magic?"

"Here's the dilemma. Will I respond like that to just *your* magic?" I teased. He stiffened behind me, his touch possessive.

"Mine. Just mine." The claim was in his words, along with the edge of something else. Contentment. I felt it in his nuzzling me.

His. The Prince of the Underworld.

10

When Dominic sat up, so did I. We'd had our sexy distraction; now work needed to be done. His hand running through his mussed hair, disheveling it more, was a reminder of the shambolic situation.

He got out of bed and snatched up his underwear and put them on. I did a quick scan of the room for my discarded clothing before remembering some were somewhere in his office.

"There has to be another way to nullify that magic. Pulling it from you to do so needs to be the last resort," he said, holding up his hand to stop my response. "I know you said you could handle it, and if there aren't any other options, then we will try it again. But if it felt as torturous as you looked during the spell, I question how likely you are to survive it. Those spells always come at a cost and often they're not worth the benefit. We have no idea how entwined the magic is to your existence, so finding an alternative is best."

The thought that I might die had crossed my mind as the spell ravaged through me, but I thought the pain had made things seem worse than they were. Dominic was looking at me again, with a strange, considering probe. "How did you go unnoticed for so long?" he mused.

He knew the answer to that; the question he really wanted answered was how did Peter resist using me for that long? I could only speculate that all the times I considered Peter just a peculiar, observant patron, he was watching me to see if I was the type of person who'd unwittingly help him. Knowing that my predictability aided him was annoying. If I'd left the ring or never picked up the book. Ignored him at Wine Down Thursdays. Or at the very least known to check the ring for things or body conduits, then I could have stopped this. But Peter likely had plenty of backup plans.

"He's doing this because he feels wronged. You 'got rid of them.'" Their innocuous-sounding word for hunting down and destroying a population. "This is him retaliating."

"They were destroyed because they were ruthless, violent, powerful, and unable to be reasoned with. Their demise was inevitable," Dominic said with a brutal edge in his voice.

"And could he say the same of you?"

He didn't give my question a lot of consideration before answering. "Perhaps. If I'm driven by violence and ruthlessness without the ability to see reason. Or become so single sighted in my thirst for power that I need to be handled. So be it. That will be my fall."

Should I be impressed or repulsed by his candor? I was mostly confused by the welcoming acceptance of violence and death. The only thing I could do was make sure their casual use of it remained in the confines of the supernaturals' world and didn't spill into ours—and we become victims of it. I felt that was my duty, despite the revelation that had me oscillating between human and other. It was a precarious place to be.

"You aren't concerned about my relationship to the shades?" I asked, trying to get more information about my otherness, especially since Dominic hadn't taken his probing eyes off me.

He shook his head. "The attack was to see if your magic could be used to free them. In their shadow form, they are ineffectual." That anger he demonstrated when he demanded to know the assailant of the attack resurfaced, forcing his lips into a rigid frown. "To prevent them making another attempt to free themselves. You'll stay away from them from now on, and on your return visits, we'll have to erect a ward."

Return visits? I had no intention of returning to the underworld like it was a vacation destination. Vessel or not, I would divest myself of this world. I just didn't know how to do that and keep Dominic in my life. But that was a discussion for another time. Despite the heaviness of the topic, it wasn't chasing away my post-sex calm. My body pliant, mood somnolent.

Dominic headed for the bathroom, and I lay back on the bed, giving in to all the thoughts that came racing back into my mind.

"Now that he's fucked you, I hope it has assuaged whatever drew him to you. Hopefully he can see what I've known all along. There's nothing exceptional about you and absolutely no reason to continue to protect you," Helena sneered from the bedroom door. I shot up with a start, securing the comforter to me, in time to see her toss my panties and bra in my direction, landing them next to the bed.

My eyes went to her exposed claws as they tapped lightly against her leg. She approached me slowly, each step measured and intentional. A predator assessing a prey, as a wrathful frown bracketed her mouth. Her turbulent emotions stifling the air had my chest pounding.

"Helena," I said in a voice soft and nonthreatening while I scanned the room for a weapon I could get to quickly. The bedside lamp was an option. Warily, I watched her approach.

If I was going to defend myself, I had one shot. I'd use the lamp to pummel her and then go for the eyes.

"Dominic and I protect each other," she said in a hushed, rough voice. "I won't deny that the protection has been one-sided in my favor more often. In the end, we protect our family and, indirectly, you trivial, ignorant humans with your blatant and nauseating unearned confidence and self-importance. You're all so unaware of how quickly we could bend you to our will. Wipe you out if we chose to do so." Her advance swallowed the distance between us. I'd have to react soon.

Despite none of the spells I'd tried earlier working, I was frantically whispering them, hoping for a fluke that would lead to one working. Toss her on her ass where I wanted her. Nothing.

"He always forgives me, covers for me. He gets irritated about it, but I'm *always forgiven*," she said with a smirk.

"Seems like he's pretty damn tired of forgiving your bad behavior and wants you to take accountability. After all, it took you running to Daddy to get your magic back," I snipped, foolishly poking the Princess of the Underworld.

For a moment, her beautiful features were twisted into a disfiguring scowl. The reality of her fading impunity for her actions lingered in her expression and the tense curl of her fingers at her side, the lift of her chin, and the darkening of her eyes. My comment had landed. Landed hard. More effective than any punch I could have delivered.

Her head snapped to the bathroom door where Dominic stood with a towel draped haphazardly around his waist, water dripping on the floor, his hair wet and messy.

Pools of amber submerged the flames, but there was still heat in his glare. It bored into her. Helena directed all her attention to her brother. His expression was indecipherable.

"What are you going to do, kill her?" he asked.

"You'd like that, wouldn't you? Make me the villain because you don't want to break your little human toy."

"My decision is sound. If I handle this, us being in captivity like this will never be something we have to worry about again. You kill Luna, what happens then, Helena?"

She blinked but didn't offer a plan. It was highly unlikely she had one other than killing me: the short-term solution. Although I wasn't sure how much I could offer toward a long-term solution.

"You want to imprison me in the Perils," she whispered, pain and disbelief heavy in her accusation.

"No. I said once this is over, you will be held accountable for all that you've done. The Conventicle will be given a say in what they feel are appropriate consequences for your acts. To keep it unbiased. After all, you are my sister. I have done a lot to protect you."

Disgust at the suggestion she'd be judged by lesser beings curled her lip. She needed to bottle this confidence because it was second-level arrogance.

"Would you have them judge you?" she countered with a sneer.

"If I'd done a fraction of what you have, then yes. You know I don't shy away from violence or doing what would be viewed as reprehensible, when necessary. Far too often, it has been your first choice. Your only choice. It has to stop."

Her accusing glare slipped in my direction as if I was the facilitator of this and not her bad behavior and clawing his face. As if this wasn't a response to her extrajudicial killings, violent tantrums, unstable and poorly thought-out reactions —or rather, overreactions—to anything.

"You know they'll want me imprisoned."

"No, they'd want you sentenced to death. I will persuade them to sentence you to prison."

"Or we do as we've done in the past, ignore their desires?"

"No, that's what you have done. Until..." His indecipherable expression broke, his brow cocked, a gentle reminder of why they had to surrender their judicial position to the Conventicle. Her violent rampage.

There was a long contemplative silence. "You've shown weakness too often. Father has noticed as well. I'll leave him to handle things." Her disappointment showed when she didn't get any other response than his stoicism. Helena's departure was just as quick and unobtrusive as her arrival.

"I have to worry about her, don't I?"

He shook his head, although I had no idea where that confidence came from. "My sister is a lot of things. Even at her most impulsive and cruel, she still manages to be as calculating and tactical as she's accused me of being. We aren't very different. She's trying to determine the manner in which I'll take the throne. If Areleus relinquishes it to me on amicable terms, then with respect for his previous rule and gift, I'll take his counsel into consideration. She'll remain loyal to my father, because he can be of use. If I take the throne forcibly, she'll snatch her loyalty from him. Because I will be making all the decisions of the underworld. All. Ultimately be the sole decider of her fate." He sighed. "She's my sister."

He loved her, but I remained unconvinced he liked her.

"Do you think you'll obtain the throne amicably?" Nothing about his interaction with his father showed amicability was an option.

"I love my father."

His shifty response only left me with more questions. Did he really love his father? I saw hints of his struggle dealing with his sister. Compassion fatigue, frustration, and disappointment. None of those emotions were present when he dealt with his father. Was it comparable to the way we're instructed to love that odd cousin who shows up for the family reunion every five years? You love them because of the familial link and societal indoctrination. Love your family, your entire family. They're blood. Even if you have no more connection or knowledge of them than of a stranger sitting near you in a restaurant.

"If it can't be handled amicably?"

"Then I have to kill my father," he tossed out before returning to the bathroom.

After we'd both showered and dressed, I expected to have a new perspective and not be bothered by Dominic's admission of possible patricide. In need of something to take my mind off that, I was more than happy when Dominic said he had to study the spellbooks without distraction. Since I couldn't read the language of any of them to be of any help, I gladly accepted his suggestion to call for Anand. So much so that it didn't bother me that he showed up in front of Dominic's office door just moments after I called him.

Moving in double-time to keep in step with him as he headed for the gym, I asked, "So you live in the west wing of the house?" Anand's secretive nature made me want to know things about him that I'd never care about with anyone else.

"Yes." He smirked at my frustration.

"You and Dominic are friends, so why do you stay so far from him?"

"How close do you live to your friends?"

"A twenty-minute drive."

He grunted.

"That has to do with finances. I'd love to live closer but there wasn't anything in my price range when I was looking."

A look passed over his face. Obviously, they never experienced any limitations due to money. What a peculiar way to live.

"I like my privacy," he said.

"Really, you mean the man who answers questions like

he's protecting government secrets likes privacy. I never would have suspected it," I teased.

He stopped. Head canted to the side, he gave me an evaluating look that lasted long enough for me to feel the weight of his scrutiny. "I get it," he announced finally. "It's not just you being the puzzle Dominic needs to solve, you're the mascot for humanity that makes it easy to fight for their existence."

"Mascot." I frowned.

"Not in a bad way. You're caring, adaptable, a champion for your people—not just the ones you know but those you don't—and you're seemingly innocuous."

"Innocuous as in weak." I sighed at the thinly veiled insult.

"Not at all. One of the problems with our world is that there aren't many facets of strength."

I never got the impression that any of them wanted to be human or even respected humans, but apparently there were aspects of being human that they did want. I suspected very few aspects, but the desire existed, nonetheless.

He gave me a half smile. "The human mascot should live," he said. They had a thousand books in the library, worn from use, and he was probably responsible for some of the wear, yet 'human mascot' was the best he could do. It didn't bother me. I launched at him and gave him a hug, which shocked both of us. The stress was getting to me.

Stumbling back, I covered my mouth. "Sorry. Cabin fever."

"No worries. I don't like being locked in here, either."

That was an obvious understatement. He was buckling under it, and all the time he spent in the gym was an attempt to stave it off. As was wanting to train with me. It was a distraction. Still, he knew that killing me would free him, and yet he wanted me alive.

My time with Anand was more enjoyable than I would have expected. He was still a miser with information and words. Most of the questions I posed went unanswered or given the tersest response imaginable. He managed to stay stolid and a focused instructor until we transitioned to learning kicks. I followed his demonstration, and he seemed as surprised as I was that I needed less demonstration with them than I did with punches and strikes. There seemed to be more skill needed to execute them and prevent injury.

His stolid demeanor was being challenged as his lip twitched in an effort to refrain from laughing.

"Yes, I just kicked him in his imaginary berries," I touted proudly. "Your instructions were to make it hurt. I did. I can tell you from experience, kicking someone in their man giblets hurts. And it makes the exact point I need to make."

He tossed his head back in a howl of laughter. A hoarse strained sound. I was convinced he didn't do it often. "Now, do it with punches," he said. "Jabs and uppercuts."

So I did. After two lessons, I knew I'd never be able to hold my own with the likes of Anand or anyone else, but it was a confidence booster. Adrenaline and determination to do the best I could chased away all thoughts of Dominic not giving me the opportunity to quiz him about patricide being an option. A very real option.

Plus, what were Dominic's thoughts about me? Did I exist only for the magic? When did that happen? My mother gave birth to me, I knew that. There were pictures. My dad had a ton of stories about the pregnancy. And my brother. Was he a vessel, too? Could *he* be in danger? Before I could stop it, I was spiraling. My strikes hit harder into the body opponent bag, and when I placed a haphazard kick in its chest, ignoring all Anand's teachings, he placed a hand on my shoulder.

"Take a break," he said and handed me a bottle of water. Taking it, I plopped on the mat and every emotion I had been suppressing rushed in with a vengeance. Flooded with a sense of despair, I drew my knees up and tried to breathe. Ease the morbid feeling of impending death. Wishing I could do it all over again and leave the book where it was and never give it an opportunity to use me as a conduit. Deny Peter the gift of finding me. I wouldn't have met Dominic, but what would I have missed? Great sex, flirting with a handsome man who gives me hot and cold messages. Right now it's hot. He wants me alive. Claims he'll do whatever he can to protect me. But will that promise stand if there aren't any options? Even so, I stay here in the underworld until when? I die. They are immortal, but I'm not.

Panting uncontrollably, my hand shook too much to hold the water. Anand was next to me, taking it from me and capping it.

"Magic is entropic. It has always been and is the reason supernaturals don't like interspecies breeding." He flashed a wayward smirk at my response to his clinical description of having children. "The same with spells. Even people skilled at magic weaving make mistakes, because creating a spell from others can be like making a bomb with unstable ingredients. It's the reason tried-and-true spells are usually used. People don't use the archaic spells as much because there's always the question of what will be lost in translation. I've seen spells go bad with deadly consequences. And I've witnessed miraculous results from spells that many were too afraid to try. Those, mostly with Dominic. He's not feared for the things he's capable of but because he's resourceful and he rarely fails. I've known him all my life and I'm fully aware of what he's capable of."

"I was there when he entered the Conventicle's meeting. They don't just fear him. They don't seem to like him."

Anand shrugged. "That's because he's also an asshole."

"They didn't seem to like you, either," I pointed out with a teasing nudge.

"I'm one, too." The audacity. I needed just a tenth of it, I thought as I wiped away the tears that streamed down my face. Some from laughter but most from relief.

I gave Anand an appreciative smile as I stood up. "Ready."

"Yes, but don't kick my body opponent bag in his nonexistent—" He stopped for a moment. "Good and Plenty's," he added.

Nodding, I tossed my water in the corner. "Why? You having sympathy pains from hearing about it?"

"Definitely." He started toward the body opponent bag, then his head jerked and he turned his head toward the door, alerted to a sound that I definitely couldn't hear. Maybe the wind or something. When he sprinted out the door, I was feet behind him, unable to keep pace with his preternatural speed. I only caught up when he stopped at the entryway of the home where Nailah, the Seer, stood.

11

Nailah's unexpected presence had Dominic, Helena, Areleus, and his guards with their weapons drawn rushing toward her. Areleus halted the guards' approach with a slight wave of his hand, then quickly dismissed them in response to her annoyance at their presence.

"Areleus, when was the last time you've had an invasion attempt from the other realms? Forty, fifty years? Are the guards really still necessary?"

His narrowed eyes fixed on her, and he lifted his chin in defiant hauteur.

With noticeable effort, her tightly pressed lips formed an insincere smile. "My apologies, *Lord Areleus*," she pushed out in a stiff voice.

The mien of discontent faded, replaced by his brand of cool arrogance as he closed the distance between them. Nailah placed the small overnighter tote clutched to her chest on the floor and shrugged off the oversized jacket to reveal layers of clothing. A sweater over a button-down shirt, slim-fitted jeans, and boots. With a sigh, she pulled the hair tie from her bun and let her braids cascade over her shoulders.

"I've never traveled to the underworld alone and wasn't sure I'd end up in the right place on my first attempt. So, I needed to be prepared for any destination," she explained. "My vision saw me here, but navigating travel isn't where my magic lies."

Seer abilities were subject to the butterfly effect, as was everything in life. Anything could have happened during her transport to change the outcome. Her transporting to the underworld wasn't part of her magical abilities, confirmed by the curious looks she was getting from everyone.

"I made it." She exhaled a deep sigh, her tension disappearing.

Areleus's smile seemed to be a genuine display of appreciation at seeing her relaxed and safe. Her genial personality swept through the room in a manner that felt mystical. I suspected the sense of comfort came from being in a room with a person who possessed the ability to warn you of potential danger.

"How did you get here?" he asked.

Opening her hand, she revealed the Trapsen. It conjured identical looks of betrayal from Areleus and Dominic.

"You said that Madeline's grandmother had the last one," Dominic challenged.

"No, I said you had all that you needed *collected*," she countered softly, ignoring his sharp look of disapproval.

"A lie of omission," Dominic said.

"A necessary misdirection." The underworld's royalty didn't seem satisfied with the answer.

"Shall we argue over my dishonesty or discuss what brings me here?" Nailah asked, breaking the tense silence.

The rigid expressions made it obvious her lie of omission was the topic they wanted to discuss, but the need to satisfy their curiosity took precedence. At least, it did for Helena and Dominic. Lord Areleus's lips drew back in a sneer. Poorly suppressed anger flooded the room. Magic thickened the air and he straightened with the need to exact punishment for dissatisfaction. My dislike of him was dipping into hate territory.

Nailah's arrival gave me hope. If she was able to get into the underworld, there was a possibility of us getting out.

Lord Areleus inhaled a long breath, keeping his eyes on Nailah. She pulled her shoulders back and, giving as much illusion of height her diminutive stature would allow, inched toward him, removing the small space that separated them. Her expression unyielding, she paid careful attention to him when he cast a glance in my direction. They exchanged a look, expressing ideas that I couldn't figure out. The fiery menace that dwelled in Lord Areleus's eyes couldn't be denied.

"What you are thinking of doing, don't," she whispered.

His lips pulled into a thin taut line. "Are we forgetting our roles again?" he challenged.

"That is something you'd never let me forget. Do I need to remind you how important I am to you?" Despite her assertion, her tone was gentle and entreating. He considered her but his attention kept slipping in my direction. What was she pleading with him not to do to me?

Her tone was still hushed, but in the silence it was hard to keep the conversation between just them. "I was with the Conventicle when I had visions of Madeline and members of her coven dying. The lives of several shifters snuffed out and vampires destroyed. It was carnage." She started to lean into him to whisper something in his ear, but changed course. Her eyes swiveled to find Dominic. "If Luna is killed, a lot of supernaturals will die." She turned to me, her eyes showing confusion and concern. She was aware of the connection between me, Peter, and unspeakable violence but couldn't determine what it was. As the tension thickened, I knew the speculations were a windfall. Helena and Anand knew the shades were drawn to me. Areleus was aware that Dominic was keeping secrets about me.

Whether or not they were choosing to ignore it, I couldn't ignore her hands clenched at her sides, the glow over her face, and her glistening eyes. It had to be difficult to see clips of events and try to make sense of them, envision futures and potential deaths and try to coordinate the right activities to prevent them happening. To witness the world on fire and try to determine where to direct the hose to save the most lives and minimize the damage.

Feeling secondhand distress for her, I stepped in her direction to comfort her, feeling the weight of Dominic's scrutiny as I did.

"Nailah, let's have a drink," Dominic suggested with a half smile. "We have a bottle of Louis Latour Corton-Charlemagne Grand for you."

A smile eased onto her face. "A glass would be nice."

I, too, wanted to ease what troubled her, but day drinking and problem-solving with a tipsy Seer seemed like a bad idea.

Nailah grabbed the overnighter and kept a nervous hold on it as we navigated to the kitchen. Dominic went to the cellar and returned with wine and Cognac. Anand retrieved the glasses and Helena remained on the outskirts of the room, watching everyone with a cool indifference that I was sure hadn't fooled anyone.

Dominic pointed at the bottles for me to indicate which one I would like, the wine or the Cognac. I declined both. In a room with a person who suggested killing me or at the very least cutting off my finger, and another who'd held me hostage with claws at my stomach, I wouldn't risk having my senses dulled by liquor. The rest settled on Cognac, leaving the wine for Nailah. Dominic placed the bottle on the table where she'd taken a seat, then perched on a stool at the island, next to Areleus. It was easy for me to study the many similarities between them. The same dark aura of power that couldn't be dampened. The stamp of ruthlessness that could be accessed at any time. The command of the room and the warring hostility that marked their mood when they were in the same room. Their palpable contention made me wary as I slid onto the chair one seat over from Nailah, from where I could keep a careful eye on everyone. I speculated that was the reason she chose her seat. She might have been part of the supernatural world, but she had to be acutely aware that she was surrounded by predators. And when you're not the predator, you default to prey.

Helena maintained her distance, calculating and staying in her spot even after Anand offered her a snifter of Cognac and invited her to have a seat. When she declined, it didn't slip my notice that he stayed at her side.

Nailah took a draw from the glass, appreciating the first taste of the wine with a sigh. Placing the glass on the table, her gaze drifted to the peculiar midnight-color flowers in the garden. It couldn't have been her first time seeing them, but she looked at them with the curiosity of someone seeing them for the first time.

She took another long drink. "I don't know what the connection is between Luna and the Dark Caster but there definitely is one. I fear that her death will cause irreparable harm," she disclosed, giving Areleus a pointed look.

The wheels of speculation were turning, and there was a part of me that wanted to give her the answer in hopes that the information would help her come up with a solution. Fear of Areleus's and Helena's reactions kept me from doing so. I trusted her and made a plan to get a moment alone to tell her. I'd give her the missing piece to the puzzle.

"That may be so, but her existence has caused just as much harm, including our imprisonment. Either way, we are affected, so I prefer the option that leads to our freedom."

Areleus took a sip from his glass, savoring the amber liquid before his foreboding eyes were cast in my direction. Disgusted by how flippant he was with discussing my life and death, I wished I had taken a glass of wine for no other reason than to have a weapon if he decided to act on it.

Nailah stood up and moved closer to him. Placing her hands over his, her delicate touch showed a familiarity between them that had me questioning whether their relationship had always been professional. What had transpired between them that led to her staying in the guest house during her visits? Perhaps her gentle nature created an unintentional bond and the perception of intimacy.

"Areleus." Tenderness laced her whisper. At that moment, he didn't take issue with her dropping his title. "As of late, patience has not been your strength. It is essential that you find it. Make it your best asset because it is crucial that you do." Her soft melodious voice lulling, Areleus appeared to be taking in her request. The distinct change in his coldness made me question whether there was more to her Seer magic. Did it also possess some form of compulsion? She'd brought me comfort when I first met her. The only off-putting things about her were her glowing violet eyes and the stifling magic that took away the solace that usually accompanied her presence.

"So, what do you propose we do?" he inquired.

"Wait. I've spoken with Madeline and she is confident that she can break the spell," she asserted, renewing hope that had dwindled during the course of her visit.

No one in the room held that same level of confidence and they made it known with their derisive scoffs.

"Madeline?" Areleus drawled with hints of skepticism.

"It was she and her coven who discovered a way to punish Helena," Dominic pointed out.

Helena's cool guise dropped momentarily, revealing her disgust that an inferior had punished her. They'd performed a curse to remove Helena's magic. It took ten years for Dominic to find a way to counter it, and along the way he found a way to keep witches from performing magic on him. It took several minutes for Helena to gain control over her anger and replace it with the mask of indifference. Dominic's eyes held a deviant spark from her reaction. His pettiness was a little humanizing. A sibling taunt.

"Even more reason for our presence to be known and for us to make displays of ruthlessness for those who wrong us. This is our time to make a statement, and if Dominicus wasn't so distracted playing with his human toy, he'd see it as I do," Helena hissed. The glimmer from his taunt was snuffed away and replaced with contention and ire. Her eyes flicked from him to her father. "Break Dominic's little toy, leave here, and find Peter. Kill him in the most violent and torturous way possible. Make it a spectacle and a statement that we are *never* to be wronged, captured like animals, or subjected to their petty reprisals. We must be in accord with this. Unified. No faltering nor negotiations. Brother,"—her eyes were fiery slits—"compromise is never the answer. *Never.*"

I glanced at Areleus, who was clearly on board with her dictum, nodding with a dark regality as if reclaiming a position he'd momentarily deserted. Violence seemed to be his primary strategy for dealing with anything.

"I suspect the few challenges you've encountered in your life would have benefited from you demonstrating some skills of negotiation, or at the very least some restraint. Maybe you should consider behaving as an adult sometime," Dominic said, his tone blistering with disapproval.

"And you need to stop fucking humans!" Helena cut her eyes at him.

"I will if you do."

"There is clearly a difference in how we view them. I see them for what they are—entertainment. To be used to satisfy a carnal need. Nothing more." She directed her dissatisfaction in my direction. "They have, and always have been, there for our pleasure." She frowned. "Just like their existence, our dealings with them should be fleeting. It is foolish to value their lives over even our mildest discomfort."

I jumped to my feet. "You're an asshole," I snapped. "And you can go straight to hell. And I don't mean whatever this damn place is. I would like you to be engulfed in flames and to feel the sort of pain that only a person like you deserves." I turned to her father. "And the same goes for you." Stealing a glance in Dominic's direction and seeing the disdain from his sister's comment still on his face was the only reason I wasn't inviting him to do the same. Fuming, my emotions were difficult to sort out. "I've sat here, trying to be empathetic about how it must feel for powerful people to be rendered powerless, but you're all a horribly clear example of why some people don't deserve power or authority. I'm not an insect to be squashed under your shoe. I'm a person. With a life, friends, family, dreams, and humanity, and you keep viewing me as inconsequential."

"But you are. For some reason you've been led to believe you aren't. If it was our will, do you understand how quickly you could be squashed? So yes, you are inconsequential, as is the rest of your ilk," Helena said.

I swallowed my fear despite her looking as if she wanted to demonstrate my inconsequentiality.

"Along with going to hell, I'm going to invite you to shut the fuck up, too. Great power means you have responsibility to not be the biggest pile of shit in existence. Something you're demonstrably failing at. I had no choice in any of this, and if I had, believe me, meeting you would be the last thing I'd ever have wanted. You're all such unrepenting megalomaniacs and you can't see past your overinflated egos to fix this without resorting to violence." I gave Areleus a censuring look in case he thought he was excluded.

"I have no idea what Peter's endgame is, but I'm sure that if he fails, he's given others a lot of ideas. You're not an island. Dominic seems to be the only one who understands that. Stop being so casual and dismissive about killing me and work together to prevent this situation happening again. Get the other supernaturals to want to work with you because they see that your aligned interest makes it better for everyone. And stop underestimating humans. We're far more resilient than you will ever know. And I'm no one's plaything." I shot Dominic a look, drilling in the point in case for a fraction of a second he thought otherwise.

Helena was looking smug and Areleus peered at me down his nose as if he'd just watched a child throw a tantrum.

"We're aware that humans are resilient and that their lives have meaning, Luna," Dominic offered. I could see the unspoken part in the slight smile he gave me. *My* life had meaning, a sentiment not shared by his father and sister. At this point, I'd have been happy with anything from Anand. He was definitely the person in a room of chaos whom you could never use as the barometer of how bad the situation was.

"She isn't wrong," Nailah provided, taking Areleus's free hand into hers, redirecting his attention from me to her. My words were lost on him because it seemed he was more disgusted by my chastisement of him and his profoundly terrible daughter than by the criticisms lobbed at them.

I hated this world so much and knew without any doubt that I couldn't exist in both. The human world was where I needed to be. The smidgen of desire to exist in both was gone.

"We are to place our hopes in Madeline and her coven, without even you there to work on our behalf?" Areleus asked, gearing Helena up for another argument in defense of my death for the greater good and she was just the hero to do it.

"I wouldn't do such a thing. Glimpses of your captivity came to me, but I couldn't make much sense of it. But Peter met with the Conventicle, informing them that he'd freed them from your rule. Thanks to him, they're now able to move throughout the world freely and with impunity. I knew you all were in danger, somehow locked in here. Although he was coy about it, the implication was that Peter"—she rolled her eyes, leading me to believe it was a name he chose and not the name he was usually known as—"or rather, Ansel, was looking for a place in the Conventicle."

So I was right about his name. I hoped she shared my other reservation, which was that the reason he wanted to be part of the Conventicle was to launch a takeover. Likely a hostile takeover.

"Madeline doesn't trust him. After all, he and his kind have a history that can't be ignored. They choose to deal with the devil they know, one they know can be reasoned with." She gave Areleus a meaningful look to drive in the point before slipping an air of assurance in Dominic's direction. The acknowledgment brought a sneer to the lord's face. Contempt for his son or maybe what he represented: a minuscule amount of humanity.

"Madeline appears to be confident that she and her coven can figure out a way to lift the spell or circumvent it," Nailah added.

"Confident and sure are two very different things," Areleus pointed out.

Dominic's eyes settled on his father for a moment before he snapped his focus back to Nailah. "What will be the cost of this help?" he asked.

She frowned. "Removal. They believe you are no longer of use. They remove the spell and all ties between you and the supernaturals are severed." She returned to the table, reached down for the bag she'd placed next to her, and pulled out a roll of vellum. Opening it, the yellow glow of magic illuminated the words and below it her blood signature. Areleus took the paper, reading slowly over it, Helena easing in next to him to look at the terms. Once they were finished, they handed it to Dominic who gave it a long viewing. After he finished, he exhaled a ragged breath.

"What exactly do you expect us to do with our time?" Helena snapped.

Nailah kept a reserved demeanor, irritation flaring only momentarily in her cedar-brown eyes. "I'm sure you'll find other ways to entertain yourselves. The question remains, what is your freedom worth?"

"Everything," Areleus said. Despite being aware of their deadly speed and imperceptible movement, I wasn't prepared. The sphere of magic slammed into my chest. I soared back and slammed into the wall. My breath huffed out, making it difficult to take another.

Get out of the way, I scolded myself. Unable to get to my feet in time, I rolled to keep the next sphere from hitting me in the same place. It smashed into my leg with an explosion of pain. Sure that my leg was broken, I prepared for another surge of pain and scrambled to my feet. It didn't seem to be broken, but pain bolted through me.

With his claws exposed, Areleus lunged at me, but a burst of Dominic's magic smashed into his upper chest. Another arrow-shaped illumination hit the middle of his forehead, snapping his head back. In his falling, a chaotic turbulence of magic: a cyclone of fire, furniture flying throughout the room. I tried to follow Nailah as she dashed out of the room, Anand blocking the furniture careening in my direction leaving me to dodge the ones he missed. Again, I was slammed to the ground. Wincing and gritting my teeth through the pain, I yanked out the large shard of glass from my leg, tossed it aside, and forced myself to stand.

Areleus was on his feet, his attention split between me and Dominic. Fire blazed in Dominic's and Areleus's eyes as they locked on each other. Their magic came to an unsettling halt, as if an implicit decision had been made not to use it. Claws bared, they lunged at each other. Colliding, Areleus's claws retracted and he landed a hard punch on Dominic's chin. And with the other hand, which remained clawed, he slashed Dominic across the shoulder. As they fought, it was apparent that Areleus had a better command of his claws than Dominic. No restraint was shown as the fight devolved into a brutal exchange of flashes of movement, dodging, blows to face and body, and blocking slashes of claws to the neck. A powerful strike to Dominic's chest sent him soaring through the air, smashing into the stove and denting it. He recovered and plowed into his father, his claws scraping into his chest, shredding his clothing and making superficial gashes.

Helena looked perplexed. Immense calculation was in her eyes as she watched the fight.

My heart pounded hard when she directed her attention to me. Limping back, I eyed the stairs where I planned to retreat. Helena would have come for me if it wasn't for the shades taking the limited form they could, beating against the glass in an attempt to get in. Blood. I'd spilled blood and they were after me. Areleus's lips parted as he risked a glimpse over his shoulder at the shades' desperate attempts. Speculation on his face was quickly replaced with understanding. Ignoring Dominic, he rushed toward me. He got within inches of me before Dominic sank his claws into his stomach. Areleus dropped to his knees, eyes widening at Dominic whispering a spell. Magic thrummed the air with force. Areleus dropped his eyes to the small portion of skin exposed by his ripped shirt, where he could now see the markings that once covered his daughter, on him.

"Get her out of here," Dominic commanded Anand. I should have moved. Wanted to move. But found myself rooted, unable to rip my attention from witnessing Dominic murdering his father. If Areleus didn't have magic, he couldn't heal.

My breaths were coming too fast. I wasn't going to get any oxygen. I had to breathe. It was justified. He would have killed me. Those things replayed in my head as Anand ushered me away. Or rather dragged me away until he noticed my limp. Against my weak protests, he scooped me up, and the last thing I heard was Dominic's grave voice telling his father to look at him, and the shades' urgent attempts to get into the house.

12

Anand deposited me on the sofa in Dominic's bedroom and took a position of sentry at the door, as if there was a plausible threat of me escaping. If I could, what would I see: the fall of the lord at the hands of his son? Two siblings fighting over patricide? Helena pressing Dominic for more information about me? Or her plotting to complete what her father had started?

This had to end. I had to end it. I wouldn't be safe in the underworld until we were free.

"I have to go to Dominic's office. I know how to fix this," I blurted.

Anand's face was more emotive than I'd ever seen it. Pure. Undeniable. Doubt. He topped it off with a derisive smirk. He had every right to his misgivings, but I hated that he saw me as inconsequential. I wasn't and he needed to know that.

Anand was of the few people I felt comfortable telling everything about me. So, I did. As I told him about Dominic's discovery of me being a source for magic, the marking being concealed, and how my body responded to the magic being removed, Anand's derision became genuine concern, proving to me that Dominic hadn't shared the information with anyone, even Anand.

How dangerous was this information that Dominic hid it from his friend? It led to more questions that I wasn't sure could be answered. Was Dominic protecting him? What was the root of Anand's concern: me or the situation?

"That's why he's been able to use you so easily. Your magic is his magic." He wiped his hand over his face and sighed, a grim edge to his voice. "You're not just an innocuous human."

Fear slithered over me at the dark, considering look he gave me. It reminded me that the other supernaturals feared him, too. He wouldn't have survived being so close to the royals if he wasn't a force himself.

"I have magic but can't use it. Somewhat human." A tool that could be used for dangerous things.

How did the vessel of Tenebras Obducit magic fare in my world? Would Peter's demise really bring me safety and peace? Would my life be marked by the supernaturals trying to discover the link between me and him? If it was ever discovered, what would happen then? As a tool of powerful magic, I would never be left alone. My hope was to use the orb to remove the magic and render my connection to Peter moot.

"I'd like to try the spell again and remove the magic from me. If that can be done, then we'll be free. At least that's one problem I could solve. We could solve."

Assuming he could do the spell. I needed him or someone who could. Anand was an anomaly, a shifter who couldn't shift but had specific magic. I hoped that he could at least invoke the spell.

After several moments of contemplation, he gave me an unenthusiastic nod. Soon he was next to me, lifting me with that unsettling shifter's grace and power.

"I can walk," I told him with far more bravado and confidence than I felt. All the pains had merged to aches throughout my body with the mildest movement.

I should have taken the shifter-carry ride. My legs were giving my pride the finger and rightfully so. Nothing was broken, I was pretty sure of that. But I had suffered a strain or sprain. Each step sent a shock of agony through me. Determination fueled my journey to Dominic's office where I breathed a sigh of relief when it opened without the need for magic. My discarded clothing had been put away, but the orb and knife remained on the desk. I went to the bookcases and scanned the books. When I didn't find the spellbook Dominic used, I frantically searched the drawers, ignoring Anand repeatedly calling my name to get my attention. I was sure that I looked unhinged, because that was exactly how I felt. The mantra 'get the hell out of the underworld' cycled on repeat in my head. The mission was clear and I had no intention of being sidetracked.

"Luna!" Anand's powerful boom filled the room. My head snapped up. His cherubic looks were darkened by his sharp, savage eyes and scowl. Gulping a sigh, I plopped onto the desk chair, folded my arms on the table, and rested my face in the crook of it. Despite Dominic not being here, his scent wafted throughout the room. There was the tinge of magical energy drifting from either the orb or knife. They were all reminders of Dominic and the violence I had witnessed and that I had no means of escaping from. Tense silence stretched along with my patience. I was desperate to go home.

"He killed his father," I whispered, my words muffled. Dominic saying he would, and Dominic actually doing it were entirely different and difficult for me to comprehend. Murder was an abstract idea in my mind. How many times are idle threats of murder made? "You took the last piece of cake, I'm going to kill you." "She spilled wine on my white shirt, I wanted to kill her." "My dad's an inhumane monster of the underworld and I'm going to kill him and take his position." He said it and did it.

"He's not dead," Anand assured me. My head snapped up. Blatant lies from the lips of the seraphic man who was brutally honest was something else to add to the long list of things that were terribly wrong with this world.

I scoffed. "Have my eyes deceived me? I didn't see him stab his father in the stomach with his claws and perform a spell to prevent Areleus healing himself? How will he survive that?"

"I saw the same thing. I've seen their fights many times."

"I'm sure it was nothing like this," I asserted. No one could live with each other and show any semblance of decorum after engaging in such a ruthless battle. Not people like them. I distinctly remembered Areleus saying he'd never fall prey to Dominic restricting his magic in the manner that Helena had because he knew it would be his demise.

"Not quite," he admitted. His honey-laden voice felt like a trap, lulling me into complacency or acceptance of customs that no ordinary person should accept, but I refused be lured.

"Explain?" I asked, fatigue and doubt heavy in my voice.

He shoved his fingers into his hair, drawing my attention to his scar and his hazel eyes with the hues of green and secrets. With a look of introspection, he took an exceptionally long time before speaking.

"Sometimes, Dominic's softness is his weakness."

Great, we're just throwing away definitions to words now. Why not? Webster is now allowing 'irregardless' to be an acceptable way of saying 'regardless' and 'softness' can mean whatever the hell we want it to mean. A small smile flitted over his lips. He was definitely getting an idea of what was going through my mind because I wasn't making any effort to hide it.

"I know it's hard to understand. Yes, Dominic can be cruel and ruthless when necessary. He has no qualms about making a lasting statement—for an advantage. Luna, it is pertinent that you understand when it comes to dealing with his father and people like him, there's no alternative method. He must present his worst self. Nothing else will do. Areleus is his father, despite Dominic's dislike of him. With all his abilities to be pitiless, he's yet to pull from that well of cruelty and untethered violence to dethrone him. He says he will when it is crucial. It's been crucial for a while."

"He did today."

He shook his head. "He won't let him die. This was a statement. He's proven to his father that he is capable of taking the throne. He's allowing him the dignity of relinquishing it."

Dominic entered the room. Anand didn't seem surprised by his presence, although I was. Disheveled hair, shirt splattered with blood, and a vestige of unbridled violence-lust fueling his movements, nothing about this man hinted at kindness that would allow clemency.

"He lives?" Anand posed it as a question, but it had the undercurrent of a statement.

Dominic's head barely moved into the nod as he kept an unwavering eye on me.

"I need to change clothes," Dominic announced, backing out of the room. He stopped at the threshold. "Luna?" An invitation I ignored. His brow hitched, eyes smoldering and dark. He called my name with even more command.

"Go change then?"

His jaw worked from side to side and there was a glint of amusement in his eyes. No, a challenge.

I stood, meeting the challenge. The weight on my leg sent a shot of pain through me. I was getting less convinced it was a strain.

"Now, Luna." His request was clipped, cutting his demand off abruptly. A reminder of him saying that he wasn't used to asking for permission to use his magic. He wasn't accustomed to being challenged often, either. He inhaled a breath. "I'm assuming you are here to do the spell. If we end up at your home or seen by others, is this the appearance you wish them to see?"

Looking down, I saw that my appearance definitely mirrored the shambled way I felt. Blood was smeared on my shirt and arms everywhere I'd touched after pulling the glass from my leg. Nodding in agreement, I sucked in a breath to prepare for the pain of walking. My gut clenched with each step and I could no longer hide the signs of pain as I made my way to him. He held my gaze as he lowered to kneel, his finger gliding over my leg. A menthol coolness laced me, chasing away the sharp ache in my leg and ankle. Tissue felt like it was meshing in healing while I was being ensorcelled by the comforting scent of lavender and giving in to the soothing effect of his magic.

"Ready?" he asked, standing. I didn't miss the reluctant anguish in his voice. He wasn't as apathetic about what happened between him and his father as he wanted us to believe.

Removing his clothing as soon as he crossed the threshold, naked, he carried the bundle to the bathroom. The shower started to run moments later. He returned to the doorway and my eyes took in every inch of him, especially his impressive length that invoked a need to feel him inside me.

"Will you be joining me?" He gave me a sensual look that promised more than just a shower but an escape from reality as he explored my body and sated those rampant emotions that brewed in him. It showed in his face, his stance, and the way he looked at me.

"I should decline," I said, finding that miniscule amount of pragmatism that remained.

"Are you going to?"

Not at all. Following his example, I slipped off my clothing. Grabbing the armful of tattered and stained clothing, I dropped them on top of his pile of clothes and followed him to the steamy shower. He pulled me into the stall, pressing me against the wall, using the excuse of bathing me to lather me, trailing over each part of my body where the water hit with kisses and laves of his tongue. His fingers slipped into me to gather the wetness between my legs, stroking and teasing me till I reached a shuddering climax. His tongue speared my mouth with a ravenous longing. I took his silky hardness into my hand, husky ragged breaths filling the space as I stroked him. Going to my knees, I ran my hands up the length of him, stroking him as I teased him with my mouth and tongue. His breaths became uncontrollably ragged, his fingers twining through my hair, tensing with pleasure. I could feel the restraint and the tension in his legs as he denied himself the pleasure. Gathering me in his arms, he lifted me and retreated to the bedroom. When he sheathed himself, I opened to him. A hungry desperation had him gyrating hard into me. I met his powerful greedy strokes with a shared frenzy to replace all the events of today with pleasure. Raw, untamed heat drove his movements. I felt a need that barely tolerated the absence of his cock when he rolled me to my stomach and reentered me. Positioning me to half kneel, he palmed my breast, teasing my nipple while his teeth nipped at my ear. Unspent chaotic magic curled around me in sync with his strokes. A beast prowled in Dominic that needed to be sated. I felt every primal part of him with every grind of his hips. My desperate moans increased as he caressed my breasts, tweaking the hardened nipples, and pressed hot kisses over my body. I felt devoured by each delicious stroke that ended with a shared explosion of satisfaction. I collapsed onto my stomach, his warm body covering mine.

He slipped out of me and I rolled to my side to face him. My body tingled with the memory of his touch. My finger traced over the sharp edges of his face, along the contours of his jawline, and his lips. He pressed a kiss to each finger and closed his eyes. Both of us were reluctant to move.

"Better?" he asked softly. Relaxed and sated, the tension had left my body, but my mind couldn't ignore all the occurrences of the day.

"A little."

He waited for me to elaborate. Searching for the words that didn't come easily, I finally said. "Your father? I need to know what happened to him."

"He's alive," he whispered.

"Barely?"

"His magic is gone but I healed him enough that he shouldn't be in a lot of pain, nor should he succumb to his injuries." 'For now' lingered in the heaviness of the room. "I was not kind to him after you left."

Please don't go into detail, I pleaded silently. I couldn't stop the cruelty and violence, but I didn't have to be given explicit details of it, either.

As if he heard my silent entreaty, he left it at that. "It will be my sister's hand to determine if he lives. If she doesn't continue to heal him, then eventually he will die."

It was more complex than that. Dominic was testing loyalties.

Dominic and I showered separately and dressed. As we made our way to the office, the acute pain from my previous injuries gave me an appreciation for its absence. I renewed my focus on the problem at hand and not Dominic's touch in his bedroom. When faced with his raw intensity, muscled contours, and erotic touch, it was easy to forget the perilous state we were in and become dismissive, if not accepting, of his propensity for violence, and his willful—no, his proud acceptance of being an asshole.

He had become a physical weakness for me, and I didn't like that. Entering his office, the reality hit me that if I didn't put some distance between us, I would be forever linked to this world, the magic, and everything it embodied. I was determined to keep my involvement with the Prince of the Underworld exactly where it belonged—in the underworld. Once I was home, it and he would have to be a thing of the past. I just had to figure out a way to do it. What I did know was that we had to get rid of the one person who knew what I was.

With purpose, I breezed past Anand seated on the sofa and went to the orb and knife.

"We need the spell book," I told Dominic. Dark amusement moved over his face as he sauntered to the desk and whispered a spell to reveal the book, which had been on the desk the entire time. The markings around it illuminated a hazy bronze before pulling from the table and disappearing into the ether. His command of magic was remarkable, or maybe it was just exceptional to a person who didn't possess such skills. Anand seemed unimpressed by the display, but that was probably a result of having been exposed to it all his life. It was imprinted into his existence.

"We're going to do the spell to completion," I instructed Dominic. I turned my attention to Anand who was looking down at his hand, his dark curtain of hair covering his face. He lifted it to peer at me when I called his name, his hair moving from his face as if it had been instructed to do so. If magical hair was a thing, I was going to ignore it. His brows hitched up.

"No matter what happens to me during the spell, it must continue," I directed. Dominic had stopped the spell before, and he couldn't be allowed to do it again.

Their lips pinched. They were two people used to giving

orders rather than receiving them. Their expressions demonstrated that their compliance was clearly by choice and that they were finding entertainment in being on the receiving end of my directives. They gave me a look they might give a child discovering the world and trying to take command of the decision-making process with their limited knowledge and experience.

It earned them both a glare as they approached me, the humor still playing in their faces.

"Of course. The spell will continue to completion, as commanded by Luna," Anand piped in.

"Then what happens, Luna?" Dominic asked. His question lacked true curiosity.

"I go back to my normal life, and you handle Peter." Inhaling a deep breath, I closed my eyes for a moment before blowing out. "And deal with him." I gave in to the unavoidable fact that Peter needed to be handled. He was a menace, and any order and rule enforcement in the supernatural world was predicated on Peter not being there to cause havoc. I held on to the hope that with the magic removed from me, I would be of no use to him, and freed. I could then proceed with repairing the damage of my tattered life.

Dominic looked pensive as he gave me a tight half smile. Breaks of worry shone in his eyes. I knew it was because he hadn't confirmed if I existed only because of the magic. He didn't function well in the unknown. Once it was removed, would I cease to exist? It was a risk I had to take because it was highly unlikely I'd continue to survive in the underworld. With Areleus still alive, given enough time he could convince Helena to finish what was started. If he fully healed, it wouldn't be his last attempt on my life.

We hadn't found any other option, and based on before, it was just painful. I could handle the pain if it meant I'd be free.

Dominic took my hand and brought the tips of my

fingers to his lips. His warm breath breezed over my fingertips. He nipped at one of the fingers, sending a shiver through me and sparking a devilish glint in his eyes.

"Stop," I whispered. "I will not conflate the two."

But it was hard not to blend the splendor of his powerful and dark magical abilities and the allure of his raw primal sexuality. They merged into the essence of Dominic. Undeniably Dominic. Those qualities consumed my thoughts as he pierced my finger and handed me the orb to hold. I secured the magical object to me while Dominic read the spell. Magic curled around me, painful but bearable. It quickly augmented, violently ravaging through me, yanking and tugging as it stripped the magic from me. Tears welled in my eyes, the pain siphoning all my energy away until I collapsed to the floor, curled into a ball and gripping the orb to me, refusing to let it be taken from me or to roll away. I'd come too far, endured too much to let it end… Each moment became more of a challenge to hold on to it. I gulped down the shriek of agony as magic pierced every aspect of my being, pulling the dark magic that shouldn't be in me. Becoming light-headed as the minutes ticked by, I felt like I was being ripped in two.

The darkness was a welcome escape.

13

Soft melon-color light eked through the closed slits of the blinds as my eyes fluttered open. Acutely aware that the sheets weren't as soft and luxurious as the ones I'd slept on over the past few days, I stretched out on the bed, which wasn't the soft sturdiness of Dominic's bed.

I was home. In my bed.

It worked.

Bolting upright, I scanned the room and landed on Dominic's imposing frame standing in the corner. His hands were shoved in the pockets of his dark gray slacks. The crisp, slim-fitted shirt bound to the contours of his body. The Prince of the Underworld's lips were stretched into a severe line as his clinically assessing eyes took me in.

"You're finally awake," he noted in a whisper.

Running my fingers through the tangles of my hair, I made an unsuccessful attempt to smooth out the strands. "Yeah. How long have I been…asleep?"

Was I asleep? Unconscious? In a state of comatose shock from unbearable pain?

"Almost two days."

"It worked!" I preened, ignoring the part about losing

nearly forty-eight hours of my life. We were out of the underworld, and if the cost was lost hours and pain, it was worth it.

He nodded, although the blank canvas of his expression was worrying.

"What's wrong?"

My eyes followed his to my dresser where the orb was placed. The luminous lively green colors that filled it as it pulled the magic from me were gone. Reading Dominic's etched frown, the magic had returned from where it came.

In me.

His hands rubbed over the rough shadow of hair on his face and he blew out a breath. My heart pounded in anticipation of the bad news he was about to deliver. His face may not have betrayed him, but his tense posturing did.

"You're the vessel," he said, strained. "Taking the magic from you broke the spell, but it returned to you. You can't be without the magic."

One of the many questions had been answered. Removing the magic did nothing. I was still bound to the supernatural world—to Peter. I existed as a tool of malice for him.

"I need a shower," I blurted abruptly, scuttling out of bed and stumbling when I put weight on my legs. They felt like rubber. My initial steps were as awkward as a fawn learning to walk. My body felt off and unusually weak. A moment of reprieve and time to gather my thoughts was what I needed.

Steam from the shower filled the room, I supported myself on the vanity, looking at my steam-clouded expression, expecting to see something other than the woman who had stared back at me hundreds of times before. I was the same Luna and I desperately wanted the same life. But it wasn't the same and the sooner I accepted it, the more time I could dedicate to doing what was necessary to obtain a new version of Luna's normal. Taking the magic from me wasn't an option, so the next best step would be to make it unusable. If I couldn't get rid of the machine, I'd break it. I was going to take my life back.

The hard water battering against my skin brought a smile to my face. How quickly I'd gotten used to the comforts of the underworld's estate. *This* was my home. I lathered my body with fruity-scented shower gel, rinsing away the suds and any lingering defeatist thoughts. After washing my hair, blow-drying it, and securing it in a loose ponytail, I emerged from the bathroom to find Dominic gone and Emoni's strained voice making a poor attempt at hiding her frustration and concern as she asked for me. Rushing to dress, I threw on an oversized button-down shirt and leggings, and opened the door to find Dominic and Anand standing in front of her, preventing her from moving any farther.

The way Emoni clutched the oversized beige slouch purse she was carrying, it was likely she was moments from using it to whack her way through. The potency of her glare lost some heat with her more youthful appearance created by her thick coils of hair being gathered into a puffy bun, leaving the back loose. Frustration had placed a glow along the bridge of her nose and her cheeks. Where her features had softened to the point she seemed innocuous, she placed a blade edge in her voice at the sight of me.

"Out of my way," she demanded, tacking on a disingenuous "please" as she shoved past them. Tossing her bag aside, she gathered me into a hug so tight it pushed the breath out of me.

She whispered, "Where have you been? I've been calling you nonstop for four days."

Once she released me, I saw the entirety of her concern. It looked as if she hadn't slept in those four days. There were bags under her eyes and her emotive, lively eyes were dull. She retrieved the slouch purse and pulled it to her like a security blanket.

"Cameron is..." She searched for the words, but they didn't come immediately. "Disappointed," she finally provided. That hurt more than if she'd told me that she was angry. Our relationship with the owner of Books and Brew had been an odd tacit agreement different from the typical employer-employee arrangement. Having been with the company since the beginning, our roles weren't typical. Cameron took our ideas into consideration, allowing us to take an influential part in the bookstore and café's business. She gave us impressive holiday bonuses and a livable wage. The small, committed staff allowed us to become a work family and one of the reasons the business thrived. It was difficult hearing that Cameron was disappointed and believed I'd taken advantage of her kindness. We helped each other out and last-minute callouts were often filled by employees without a problem. But I hadn't shown up for several days. No-call, no-show. What could she think? And Emoni didn't have an explanation to give her. Cameron had to run her business and I was a no-show for work. I needed to make things right.

"I'll go in tomorrow and talk to her," I assured Emoni. Hopefully, I could convince Cameron to allow me to keep my job. But with my life the way it was, could I give her the consistency she needed? I had to. I wouldn't let Peter take that from me. He'd already messed up so many things in my life.

"Luna." Emoni's low, tentative plea pulled me out of my reverie and snatched me from spiraling into desolation. She nudged her chin in the direction of my bedroom for some privacy.

The desperation and confusion in her face made the decision I'd been grappling with since I'd seen her, much easier. I wouldn't leave her in the dark, nor would she be subjected to their magic to keep their secrets. Emoni could be trusted. She would be trusted.

"No, I think we should stay here. I have a lot to tell you and they should be here as well. They can fill in whatever information I may not have a complete grasp of."

Dominic's lips pinched into a line of apprehension. Shaking my head, I gave him a look that I hoped relayed how I felt. *She has to know.*

"Okay," she said slowly, easing to my small living room. "Coffee first, okay?"

It was close to noon. I had slept or been in a state of unaware for nearly forty-eight hours. Coffee was definitely what I needed. Or maybe something stronger. But I needed food, too.

I nodded and followed her to my kitchen, taking out the supplies to make pour-over coffee. Cameron had gifted us each with a Chemex and gooseneck kettle, and filters in celebration of the store's anniversary. Mine was only used when Emoni visited. I was content with the coffee from a drip coffeemaker. Emoni pulled a metal container of ground coffee from her bag.

"It was just ground today," she supplied, but the only person who cared about beans being ground within hours of use was her. I didn't know if Dominic and Anand were as finicky about coffee as she was. While she prepared the coffee, I went to the fridge to scavenge for food. At the sight of the stocked fridge, I shot Dominic an appreciative smile. At least he was optimistic that I'd wake up. I made a sandwich and ate it quickly while standing, scanning the room for something else to eat when I was finished. It wasn't until I'd consumed the food that I realized how hungry I was. Anand and Dominic declined my offer of food and looked amused as I finished off a bag of chips, an apple, a croissant, and the premade salad I found. Emoni halted preparing the coffee and watched with concern as I ate as if I feared the food would disappear.

Feeling full and fueled helped, though my body still felt

odd. The rubbery feeling had gone but I ached and felt an uneasiness, as if I hadn't completely settled into this world, a disconnect I couldn't quite describe. Grabbing a handful of chocolates that reminded me of the rich and decadent ones I had in the underworld, I handed Emoni a few. Her expression mirrored the way I felt, nibbling on one. Taking another bite, she savored it the way she did dark roast coffee.

I nodded and took a seat. Emoni finished the chocolate, which I quickly realized she'd been using as a temporary distraction. There had to be some part of her that knew things were about to get strange. Dominic and Anand took the coffee she offered, and once she'd gotten a cup for herself, she stood against the kitchen nook with it in hand.

"What's been going on, Luna?" she breathed out. The touch of desperation in her words made my heart ache for the betrayal she had to feel. She was my best friend, and despite my desire to protect her, I didn't think I'd done the right thing by keeping this from her.

Taking a deep breath, I looked to Dominic who had taken a seat next to me on the sofa, and to Anand who was seated in the kitchen a few feet from where Emoni stood, a small smile of appreciation for the coffee on his face. Emoni grinned in his direction, the interest piqued when she'd met him in the café now renewed. Being coffee snobs seemed like a poor foundation for any attraction, but I'd seen weirder.

I started by telling her about Peter. She didn't seem the least bit surprised that he turned out to be a horrific magic wielder. Peculiarly, she was taking the influx of information well.

"He has very strong magic and he used me to release prisoners from the underworld," I repeated with emphasis, expecting more emotion than her slowly nodding her head and sipping from her cup. The only departure from her head nodding was her shifting to change position against the nook. She clutched the counter for support when I told her about a vampire compelling her to deliver me to Peter. She paled when she learned of Peter doing the illegal necri spell that essentially sentenced her to death. I told her that Dominic had saved her life, although I left out the bit about him being reluctant to do so because it prevented him going after Peter. She faltered when I explained that her memories had been altered to forget the entire incident.

Anand's cup was on the counter and he was next to her in a matter of seconds, giving her a firsthand example of his preternatural speed. Grimacing at the display and his presence next, she closed her eyes and took in several long, measured breaths. The silence extended from beats to minutes as she struggled with that information.

I gravitated to her side and placed a hand over hers. She felt cool and her stance became stiff. She was going to pass out.

"Emoni," I whispered.

"I'm fine," she assured me. She wasn't fine. There were noticeable cracks in the brave face she was putting forward. It was only a matter of time before it shattered.

"I'm sorry I brought you into this," I said.

She shook her head before her gaze drifted to Anand, who was still standing close to her as if he was waiting for her to lose it. Despite the heaviness of the situation and her clearly being affected by it, she seemed to determine to not give Mr. Supernatural a reason to rescue her. A small snort of laughter burst from me before I could control it. Her pettiness was endearing and reminded me of her getting Jackson's order wrong every time he came into the café after our breakup, or writing 'cheating asshole' on his cups. It was Emoni in protective mode, and now she was showing that we had this, that we could deal with whatever was thrown our way. Her resolute personality always emboldened me.

She turned, addressing Anand. "What type of magical creature are you? Vampire?"

He sneered.

"I don't think he likes vampires," I whispered.

She looked confused, understandably so. I'm sure she'd done what I had and formed a division between human and not human. It was easy to do when you didn't understand the nuances, history, politics, and motives. A lot of it was still confusing to me.

"I'm a shifter. Wolf shifter."

Her disconcert became intrigue. "Can I see it?"

"I can't change."

Confusion swept over her face again and she looked to me for answers.

"It's a long story," I said. "Let me finish telling you everything."

Whatever resolve remained in her, she shored up to get through the rest. Her gaze continued to drift to Anand with a fierce curiosity. A seraphic-looking shifter who couldn't change, lived in the underworld, and refused to offer her any more information than that. I debated whether she needed to know the entirety of his history. Her interest would lead to more questions once we were alone, that much I knew, but his story wasn't mine to tell. I hoped she could respect that. Knowing her as I did, she'd respect my boundaries but wouldn't be afraid to ask the source. There was going to be an interview.

Her acceptance of this strange new world wavered at Dominic's role as Prince of the Underworld and dissolved when I told her about me being a vessel and being used to imprison us in the underworld, and what was done to escape. Dominic took over the retelling of breaking the spell that had imprisoned us, filling in the blanks in the story that I was missing.

The new information lingered in the silence as she rummaged through my cabinets and pulled out a nearly full bottle of peach-flavored vodka we'd opened a few weeks ago during our movie night: an excuse to drink, chat, eat snacks and food with zero nutritional value, under the guise of binge-watching TV. She poured out her coffee, rinsed the cup, filled it with vodka, and then took a long drink.

"You're the underworld's prince? What's your designation? Vampire, witch, a nonchanging shifter?" She flashed a playful grin in Anand's direction.

"None of the above," he said. His ethereal movement had him inches from her, claws exposed with the ease of showing her his nails. She took it in with a shuddering breath.

"That's the only thing that changes?" she asked, then took another long drink.

He nodded. "I can perform magic and spells, but it has its limitations, as with anyone. Whereas vampires can compel, I can manipulate memories. But I don't survive on blood. I'm immortal and very difficult to kill."

"So, if I staked you?" she challenged.

"It would anger and hurt me." After another long drink, her gaze dropped to his chest. A stake through the heart would *just* hurt.

"And you?" She directed her question to Anand.

"Shifters are harder to kill because we heal extremely fast," Anand offered.

I suspected he was even more difficult to kill because of the magic he possessed along with his shifter abilities.

Emoni's lips formed a tremulous line as she attempted to make sense of this new information and world that coexisted along with hers.

"Are you immortal?" she asked me tentatively, again displaying cracks in the courageous mask she presented.

"I don't think so."

"How do you know? You're a magical source. Are you considered"—she frowned, took in a deep breath, and held it before releasing it—"human? How are you different than a vampire, witch, or shifter?"

Dominic answered her. "No one is definitely immortal. We all can succumb to death. Witches and shifters live longer than average humans, but they will die from old age. Vampires can be killed, but their appearance stays as it was when they were changed. The same for me. I can be killed. It is quite difficult, but it can be done."

Dominic's clarification on immortality didn't clear up things much. Vampires didn't age and were hard to kill. That says immortal to me. Shifters and witches weren't immortal.

"What is longer than human?"

Emoni got to the question before I could.

"Witches can live to around two hundred years, shifters three," Dominic said. It may not be immortality, but they outlived the humans they would encounter in life. The risk of magical dilution kept them from mating with humans, but I suspected having to watch them die was another reason.

"I don't know if Luna is immortal," Dominic admitted.

My mouth opened but the questions didn't come out. Nothing. A flood of questions came to mind but I was speechless.

"She exists to hold Tenebras Obducit magic. Dark and powerful magic. Take it from her and she dies. I haven't been able to establish whether Peter drawing magic from the well takes away from her life." He held my gaze and with a great deal of effort my mouth closed and I desperately attempted to appear stoic, a task I failed on a massive scale.

As he moved closer to me, all emotion fell from his face, perhaps to offer me comfort. It served as a distraction as I focused on him—him alone.

"I attempted to bring you back but I couldn't until the spell was reversed." Pulling his eyes from me, he looked at Emoni then back to me. "You can die. You did. Briefly."

The cost of me leaving the underworld was more severe than I initially thought. Whether brief or not, that was the result. Death.

There wasn't any coffee in my cup and I didn't bother rinsing it out before dumping vodka in mine and taking a long drink.

"I was going to tell you earlier but you fled to the bathroom before I could."

Because I had to deal with not being able to remove the magic, not that I only existed to serve as some source of it.

"How did Peter find out what she was?" Emoni asked, giving me a small smile. "I can't imagine he did it himself."

"No, he's quite powerful. It had to be done by another Caster and Peter learned of it. We've made it our mission over the years to rid the world of them. She"—Dominic shifted to peek in my direction—"was a contingency plan. Their main goal was always to cause havoc and unchecked destruction. I'm one of the few whose magic and abilities rival theirs."

"Rival? He imprisoned you." Emoni was in protective mode and she was struggling to temper her words and frustrations.

"Yes, with the use of magic he pulled from her. He wouldn't have been able to do it otherwise. Which is why everything needs to be done to keep him from accessing the magic she holds." Dominic's tight-lipped smile mirrored Emoni's. A slight narrowing of his eyes showed his dilemma: admiration for her fierce loyalty and protective mode and annoyance that her enmity was directed toward him.

"What does this mean for Luna?" Emoni asked. "You're free. You have your weird job of supernatural enforcer back and, well, you need to do something about Peter, but that doesn't have anything to do with Luna. Lock him up, do a better job than you did the first time, and let her have her life back." She clearly meant a life without Dominic having any part in it. "You two"—she jabbed her finger at each of them—"are the only ones who know about her. Forget that information and move on."

"Peter will be handled. I have every intention of finding him and making sure he never has access to Luna. As far as I know, he's the only one, besides us, who is aware that she's a vessel of dark magic. That should keep her safe."

The ominous promise left nothing to the imagination. The room became quiet. I continued to sip my drink, watching Emoni deal fairly well with the overt admission that Peter would be killed.

"Forest," Emoni sighed, breaking the silence with my brother's name. She put the cup on the counter, eyes widened on me. "Is he like you? Maybe he's always known, which is why he's had problems finding his footing in this world."

Dominic shook his head. "I don't believe so."

I wasn't convinced. His 'explorer of the world' may have been a reaction to finding out that he was just housing for magic. He could know more. Could have known all along that his existence was to be a magical source. The realization of that being what I was became acid burning in my chest.

I wanted to be brave. Display bravado that I didn't possess. It was too difficult. My head pounded and I couldn't get my mental bearings. It was all too much. I needed a moment to process it. Figure out a plan. With two reminders of the crapshow my life had become, I needed a few moments of reprieve. I excused myself to my bedroom.

14

Taking a seat on my bed, I picked up my phone off the nightstand and distracted myself by scrolling through notifications. There were the expected missed calls from Cameron, plus from three other employees, including Lilith. Even Reginald, the tarot reader who'd confided in me that he was a witch and had relegated me to being suspicious at best. When I tried to get him to remember what he'd experienced in my home, he couldn't because Dominic had manipulated his mind. Reginald could no longer recall being present while we stood in shocked confusion watching magic remove wording from a book.

There were calls from my mother and father wanting to know why I'd missed our monthly dinner. There were multiple texts from Forest reminding me of the dinner to make sure I'd be the buffer between him and my parents' incessant questioning. His texts came at increasingly closer intervals, including one telling me to open my door because he was outside my apartment. When I was a no-show for dinner, his voice messages and texts became more and more agitated because my parents continued to ask him where I was. "I'm not your babysitter. Do better," he chastised in his first message. A day later, his voice was entreating and heavy with worry. Not text, his preferred form of communication. A phone call. Even admitting he needed to hear me say I was okay.

I frowned at the messages from Jackson requesting we meet for dinner, drinks, or coffee including silly emojis and using Lulu, his nickname for me, in an attempt to come off as endearing. Even in his attempts to reconcile he was inconsiderate and arrogant. He knew I hated being called Lulu; I'd told him enough times. His response was to try to convince me that him saying it would miraculously change my feelings about it. With the rose-colored glasses of love removed, all the signs that the relationship should have ended sooner was a hard pill to swallow. At least he was the one situation I didn't need to fix. I wanted him to stay away.

I needed to start mitigating the damage in my life immediately.

"How are you going to deal with this?" Emoni asked softly from the doorway.

"I don't know," I admitted, my hand covering my face. There wasn't a concrete plan, but I knew it would involve lying. Lots and lots of lying and the worst kind: lies of omission.

Emoni's lips were drawn tight, eyes full of sympathy that extended beyond just me having to mend my life. I was an *other* and there was no way around it.

"This changes nothing between us, Luna. You're my Luna. Luna with the questionable taste in men," she said, taking a seat next to me and wrapping her arms around my shoulders. She had no idea how much that meant to me, although it wasn't the truth. I wasn't *her* Luna anymore. So long as things wouldn't change in our friendship, I felt like I could figure out a way to handle everything else.

Pressing her head to mine, she said, "We have this."

"My taste isn't that questionable," I joked. "Dominic's not that bad."

"An immortal man who lives in the underworld and has no qualms about telling me—a stranger—that he's going to kill Peter isn't that bad?" Her brows rose. "How good is the sex?"

Snorting a laugh, I made a poor attempt at looking shocked and appalled by her assumptions.

"Drop the act. You two have definitely done the lusty dance more than once. The way he looks at you— The only thing stopping him doing it again is me and Anand being here. There were several times I don't think even that would have stopped him."

"He's quite interesting, but his family dynamics are even more interesting. No, that's not the right word. Daunting. Scary. Horrific. Those are the right descriptors," I admitted.

Which led me to giving her a windfall of information. I revealed everything, from my initial meeting with Helena, her terrorizations, Areleus threatening me, and Dominic leaving his father for dead. Her mouth formed variations of shocked and disturbed O's that remained throughout the detailing.

When the retelling was over, she released a weary sigh. "I don't know what you want from him. If you want more, maybe an occasional visit from him to…" She shot a lewd look in my direction. "Because I know it was good. Because you're guilty of looking at him like you want to do naughty things to him, too. Maybe it's more than sex—he may be a decent person… No, wait, thing? Immortal being. Whatever. But if you want to clean up your life, I think it's best to do it without him in it. Once Peter has been dealt with, don't get pulled back into that world—the supernatural world—his world. You don't belong there. I don't see things getting better in that regard. You'll always be used as a pawn if you stay in his life."

I already knew that.

Emoni's expression became shrewd as she tried to develop a plan to safely get me out of my situation.

"You should find out if Forest has anything to worry about. And your parents, could they be…whatever you are? What should I call you? Because Scaphium is a mouthful, and magic vessel…seems too generic? What are you, a magicless wonder?"

"Sounds like a terrible superhero," I shot back, but I agreed. Dominic was convinced I was the only one, but I wanted assurance.

When I called for him, he was in the doorway to my room before his complete name had fallen from my lips. Emoni and I exchanged a look. His quick reaction confirmed my suspicion that he may not have possessed Anand's preternatural hearing, but it was sharper than a typical human's.

After I voiced my concerns about Forest and maybe my parents as well, he frowned.

"It is doubtful. But I can check," he suggested.

"Check? Like you did with me? No, I'll ask. They don't mind talking about peculiar things on their bodies."

A bruise on my mother's thigh was a week-long conversation. I could easily find out whether they had any magic marks. The mystery remained of when I got mine. I'd had the marking all my life, or for as long as I could remember. At what point had I come in contact with the person who'd sentenced me to such a fate? The sooner I found that out, the sooner I could figure out what to do about it.

"I need to call my parents," I told them. With a nod, they both left my room.

My mother answered the phone in a rushed, soothing voice that sent daggers through me. I hated that she was worried about me. "Luna. Are you okay? You missed dinner. No call, no text. Nothing." Irritation thrummed along with the concern. "What's going on?"

"I'm fine." My voice was preemptively drying for the falsehoods to follow. I wasn't good at lying to my family. "I just needed some time, so I took a mini vacation."

"Oh honey, is it Jackson?"

Not at all. My mother was aware of the seismic changes my life underwent after discovering Jackson had cheated. Our breakup wasn't the uncomplicated type of separation where two people just decide the relationship isn't working out and end it, giving those involved the chance to slowly accept and deal with their significant other no longer being in their lives. Allowing a person some time to pack and find a new living space. No, it wasn't as civilized as that. It was abrupt, emotional, and tumultuous, forcing me to pack up, stay with Emoni, and make a performance of living a normal life while dealing with a broken heart. If I'd stayed, he'd have hounded me for forgiveness even more.

"I know it still hurts." Since whispering wasn't a skill my mother had mastered, she stage-whispered to my dad. "Our Luna is still brokenhearted," she told him. "It was her first love and you know how those things are." Jackson wasn't my first love, but in my mother's mind, high school romances didn't count. "Poor thing."

"Mom, I'm fine," I assured her. "I just needed a break. It's been a long time since I had a vacation, so I took one."

"I invited you on vacation with us," she touted. Assured that I was safe and not pining over my broken relationship, my mother was free to be her normal self. "We wanted you to go."

"It was a vacation to celebrate your anniversary. Why would I agree to go on that? You realize that's weird, right?"

"How is it weird?" No explanation would convince her otherwise. *Why not take your children on your thirtieth wedding anniversary cruise? Cuddling with your adult children, normal as the sun rising and setting. Not seeing a problem sharing intimate moments with the results of it sitting across from you.*

"I miss seeing you," I told her. That was the most truthful thing I'd disclosed in this conversation, and I felt a twinge of guilt because of it. The monthly dinners were something I appreciated and had taken for granted. Hearing my mother's voice made the void seem wider.

"We miss you, too," my father said over the speakerphone my mother had placed me on. A video call from my father interrupted the call. I answered to find their faces next to each other.

"You look good," my mother piped out, surprise in her voice as if she'd been expecting a bedraggled mess. "I'd say the vacation did you well."

I looked better than I felt.

"Thanks?"

"Where did you go?" my dad asked.

I told them I rented a cottage Airbnb where I did nature walks, read, and went kayaking.

"Good. And Jackson? Where do things stand with you two?"

During our relationship, he'd managed to burrow his way into my parents' hearts. They'd expected us to get married. But they weren't so blinded by his charm to approve of me continuing the relationship after his betrayal. My father, being a pragmatist in all things, understood it was a possibility. Love made people more forgiving and less rational at times. After learning of the reason behind our breakup, he simply said, "We'll support any decision you make without judgment." The last part was a complete embellishment that he could barely push out without voicing his true opinion. My mother was tight-lipped during his speech, her eyes widening from the effort to restrain from commenting and be in accord with my dad. I knew what she desperately wanted to say: He cheated. Work to get over him and move on.

"There's no Jackson." And further conversation about him

wasn't necessary. With everything else going on in my life, he was the last thing I wanted to discuss. "Can we have dinner tomorrow?" I asked, bringing a smile to their faces.

"Invite your brother," they instructed before getting off the phone. I had planned to because I wanted everyone present during my questioning. As soon as I ended the call, I called my brother. The heaviness in his greeting immediately lifted once he heard my voice. Relief flooded his voice when he spoke.

"Glad this call isn't a hostage negotiation," he teased. Forest hated phone calls and preferred the succinct communication afforded by text messages. He remained convinced that phone calls were reserved for parents, grandparents, scams, and probably hostage negotiations.

"How many negotiations have you handled?" I teased.

"None so far, but the way Cliff and Nancy were acting, you'd have thought we were just minutes from getting one about you," he said. "Don't go MIA again, sis."

"It was last minute and the only thing on my mind was getting away," I said, continuing with the lie.

"You let that pretty boy stress you like that? Don't."

"Pretty boy?" I teased, a description often used for my brother and one he hated, even though most people would be flattered by it, perhaps even trade on it. Coltish and tall, Forest had a slim build that gave the impression he worked out. We shared similar red hair, but his hues leaned closer to copper. The last time I saw him, it was darkened with azure woven through it, complementing the colorful sleeve of tattoos up one of his arms. Despite our contrasting appearances and personalities, we shared a lot of characteristics. His face was a definitive oval shape, with wide brows and lips fuller than mine. I cringed when Emoni described them as 'kissable,' which quickly forced a repulsed plea from me: "Don't kiss my brother." I had a feeling he'd hate me if he knew it was a promise I urged her to make. All his flirting and banter with her was in vain.

"Good for you. Take all the vacations you need but don't get back with that loser." Why was Jackson the topic of everyone's conversation? Were they able to see the real pain and my struggle through the façade I put forward? "If you talk to him again, tell him to lose my number." Disgust rang in his demand. "If I'm not responding to his messages and answering his calls, take the hint, asshole."

I laughed. Forest was an unflappable supporter of relationships. Period. If he's my boyfriend, he's a cool guy. Break up, then you quickly downgrade to asshole.

"So, you're coming to dinner?"

"No," he whined. "I had dinner with them when you were a no-show. I just can't with them."

"Please. I want to see you too," I pleaded.

"Fine," he conceded with a groan. "But tell Nancy and Cliff I don't want to hear it about my new career."

"Keep calling them Nancy and Cliff and you won't have to worry about them discussing your career. They're going to spend the evening ripping into you about calling them that."

Forest's passive-aggressive show of defiance was calling them by their names. Initially, they pretended it didn't bother them, thinking it would discourage him. It became a challenge for Forest to make sure it did.

I swallowed all my questions about his new career. I guessed he'd moved on from being an apprentice electrician. Curiosity burned in me, but I pushed it aside, deciding to get answers when my parents ultimately examined him about his new *journey*. Despite my brother's claims he hadn't missed me that much, he didn't immediately get off the phone. When our conversation ended a half hour later, I was surprised by the rumbling of my stomach in response to the smell of pizza wafting into the room. I must have been recovering from the days without food.

Cutting my reprieve short and returning to the living room, I found Anand and Dominic on the sofa and two large pizzas stacked on the nook being ignored. Emoni padded the length of the room, taking sips from her vodka-filled coffee cup between pressing the bridge of her nose.

"What's the worst that would happen if you all became known? It would give us autonomy and not allow you all to perform magic on us without us knowing?" Emoni asked, Dominic's intense eyes watching her carefully as if deciding whether to answer her. I was sure she'd been peppering him with questions since she'd left my side.

"How would you enforce that abnegation, human woman?"

We both glared at the tone of superiority and derision that drifted over the word 'human.'

"I think you've underestimated us," Emoni countered.

"I believe you've overestimated them," he said in response. "Once they are no longer required to remain secret, they'll have license to do whatever they feel is necessary to survive, which would mean decreasing your numbers. Shifters have infiltrated your military and law enforcement; they thrive on that structure. The numbers won't be any use if you're dealing with preternatural speed and access to tech-witches who can disrupt all your technology, and witches who can do spells to manipulate human minds or whatever they please to do to them."

Emoni frowned, reminded of what had been done to her.

"Vampires with preternatural speed and the ability to compel. There's no defense against that. It only takes a look for them to enthrall you. If humans rose up against the supernaturals, what would prevent them compelling humans to turn on each other? *And*, it doesn't take long for them to sire humans to vampires. The vampire bond formed between the sire and sired means they will ally with their creator. All human connections are forgotten with their vampire rebirth.

Yes, you have the numbers, which is a benefit, but seeing the division and discord that exists between humans, how likely is it that those numbers would benefit you?"

We had numbers in our quiver, but that wasn't the advantage we believed it would be. Emoni was taking the news worse than I had. She looked defeated. Dominic's confidence that even in the middle of a potential civil war among the supernaturals, they would put that aside to subjugate humans only added to her troubled frown. She'd finished her cup and had refilled it.

"Now that it's your job to uphold the secrecy of supernaturals, you must reinforce it, and they have to know that the onus falls on them if it's violated," I interjected. My assertion sounded more pleading than intended. The mocking amusement fell from his expression, his depthless amber eyes turning sincere.

"I will." A satisfying promise in his simple words.

Perceptive as usual, Emoni hadn't missed the exchange between us. Although she hadn't fully warmed up to either Anand or Dominic, her demeanor had relaxed significantly.

Nothing about the current situation was innocuous, but everyone seemed okay with moving on to me figuring out if my family were vessels of Tenebras Obducit magic, too.

I filled a glass with water instead of more alcohol. Tomorrow morning I planned on speaking with Cameron and didn't want to do so while dealing with a hangover.

With the exception of the dinner with Dominic's family, I'd never seen him eat, and watching him eat pizza fascinated me in a way it shouldn't have. Emoni, who kept her distance from everyone, stayed near the nook, taking small bites of pizza, her brows drawn in with thought.

"I don't really understand you. You're a wolf shifter who doesn't shift. But if you were a real wolf, you'd need to hunt for food," she asserted, pulling a piece of pepperoni from the pizza and eating it. "You have to desire raw meat at some point, right? I'm sure if I gave a lion a steak medium rare, he wouldn't eat it."

Of all the things revealed to her, she found shifter magic the most intriguing. Or maybe it was Anand, because he was a defunct shifter.

"If that's all he had to eat, he would," he countered with a smirk.

She considered it. "I don't think that's true." She looked at him. "Can you eat? Do you eat? Do you sustain life just by magic?"

I went to the kitchen and got my friend some water. Her consumption of nearly half a bottle of vodka was showing in her boundless curiosity and lack of filter. Taking it with a grateful nod, she gulped it and didn't stop until it was nearly empty.

"I don't like this," she eventually admitted to the room. Liquid brown eyes showed a disturbing level of sorrow and angst that I'd never seen on her before. Intrigue had eked from her expression, leaving behind a solemn troubled look.

"The situation or us?" Dominic scrutinized her, not as a threat but as the reflection of what would happen if they were to reveal themselves.

"Both," she acknowledged. "I don't like feeling helpless. And knowing that you all live among us and we just don't know, how do I go to work tomorrow, with customers moving throughout the café, and not suspect at least some of them are creatures of magic?"

If she was calling them that in her head, of course the situation would spiral.

"Supernaturals have always walked among us, Emoni," I said in an attempt to comfort her.

"What about the Broad Street wiccans?" she blurted, referring to the people who could be seen dressed like they were about to attend a Renaissance fair or Steampunk festival. "Or the People of the Night?" They were just as flamboyant as our Broad Street wiccans with their theatrical midnight-black or platinum-white hair and dark clothing, depicting the vampire noir look from old films.

Emoni had been dismissive when I told her about one of my contacts with Dominic when he'd accused me of being a witch. She'd considered it quirky. The abstract thought of the supernatural wasn't that scary, but when the curtains were pulled back and it was revealed that they could control your life, making you a marionette in their puppet show, things got darker. Being faced with the violence, politics, and instability of the house of cards was anxiety inducing.

"The people who dress up in their little costumes to stand out in the most ostentatious way?" Domonic inquired.

Emoni nodded.

"They are not creatures of magic." His lips twitched with an emotion I couldn't place. "Creatures of magic prefer to blend into the background. Go unnoticed among the unremarkable. Shows of magic and power are often used to intimidate. There's no need to intimidate or put on displays for the l—" He stopped abruptly before he could finish saying 'lesser.' "Humans," he amended. We both cut our eyes at him.

That could change in a blink of an eye if the Awakeners got their way and supernaturals were revealed to the world. There would be demonstrations of power and violence to intimidate us into subjugation. My heart began to race at the idea and the thud of it jerked Anand's head from Emoni's direction to mine.

"Worrying about it won't change anything," Anand said.

Great, the King of Comfort has spoken.

Dominic had sat back, hands clasped behind his head, in anticipation of further interrogation by Emoni.

"Find comfort that there are more people who want to stay hidden than there are who want to be revealed," Anand added, leaving out the part that two sects existed to do just that. The current Conventicle and the Conventicle-in-waiting that was plotting a hostile takeover. Their objectives aligned but not their means of enforcement. The Conventicle-in-waiting was more violent, choosing to deal lethally with any threats to exposure. The current Conventicle tended to coddle more, allowing threats of exposure to be handled at the expense of humans. The awaiting Conventicle wasn't opposed to that, but there would be dire consequences if that were to happen. My preference was a takeover; however, their extreme nature wasn't limited to their kind and they saw me as a threat and wanted me dead.

Anand's head whipped to the door. Several beats later, there was a knock. With the discussion of the Conventicles, Peter, and the Awakeners, I was tentative about answering the door. Perhaps I hadn't been convincing enough to my brother and he was stopping by to visit. I peered through the peephole.

My breath caught.

Areleus and Helena.

15

I hesitated to let them in.

"Luna," Areleus's voice called from the other side. His urging served as a warning and likely the only one I'd receive. The only reason I heeded it was from fear of what they'd do to gain entrance if I refused.

Once I opened the door, my eyes dropped to Areleus's arms, searching for the tell-tale marks of his magic restrictions. They were gone. Moving with his signature lethal grace, he slipped by me, taking command of the room. Midnight-blue slim shirt and cobalt pants showed a fit body that belied his presented age. A shrewd malice lingered in his eyes as they landed on me before moving to his son. Helena's outfit of white pants, jacket, and a terracotta midriff shirt, along with the elaborate twists in her hair that formed a crown of her head, gave a deceptive impression. A fashionable menace. I glanced at Emoni, looking for any signs that she was falling for the false presentation.

"Why are you here?" Dominic asked, his tone icy, narrowed eyes piercing them.

"If you weren't in such a rush to return to your"—Areleus frowned—"*Luna*, you'd have noticed the shades are gone." I knew he'd wanted to say 'human toy.' Using my name made me real and not just an animation that could be dismissed. Presenting me as more than a plaything that they didn't understand.

Anand's and Dominic's sudden intake of breath filled the room.

"All of them?" Anand asked.

Areleus nodded, looking at Emoni who crept away to the farthest corner, correctly reading the danger they posed. Her easing away was interrupted by Helena rushing over to her.

"I see you've acquired another one," Helena whispered, her eyes trailing the length of Emoni's body with a pleased smile. She reached out to touch the spiral of curls that had pulled from her tie. Emoni blocked her hand. When she made another attempt, Emoni knocked her hand away.

"Don't touch me," Emoni demanded.

"But I want to." In Helena's world that was all that mattered.

"That sounds like a 'you' problem," Emoni snapped back.

Undeterred, Helena made another attempt. Emoni pushed her hand away. "I'm being polite. You won't like it very much if I stop."

I think she would. A woman who suggested taking off my finger then invited me to dinner probably saw this as flirting.

"I like this one. I see the interest." She flashed a dubious brow arch in her brother's direction.

"She's not mine," Dominic said, and Emoni and I both skewered him with a look. I wanted to take his tight-lipped smile as an apology, but I had no idea what to make of it. How long would it take for him not to see humans as trinkets to be collected, used, and discarded when their interest waned?

"We have to find them," Anand said, standing, his odd magic roiling from him. It was noticeably dark, ominous, and dangerous, and for the first time Emoni openly showed a desire to be away from this mess. I didn't blame her. I wanted the same.

"Centuries they have been imprisoned and now they are free," Areleus mused. The look he lobbed in my direction showed his accusation, although he managed to keep it out of his voice. Snatching away the distance between us, he bent until we were face to face.

"What are you?" he inquired. "What secrets has my son kept from me?"

"None," I blurted. Even to me, I sounded unconvincing. I definitely needed to get better at lying. Not a skill I really wanted, but my new life required it.

"Nailah has set up a meeting with the Conventicle." Helena settled her attention casually on Emoni, but with wariness of having this discussion with her present. I assumed she decided Dominic would handle it, so she returned her attention to him. "She still sees the same deaths as she saw before."

Dominic's eyes narrowed to slits on his sister, studying her. "And what are you leaving out, Helena?" he asked.

"And ours," she admitted.

Emoni didn't require any encouragement to leave. Anand's mere mention that she should go home had her quickly gathering her things and readying to leave. Her dedication to my safety was the only thing that caused her to linger. She insisted I join her and refused to leave until I promised her, with a level of assurance I didn't truly feel, that I would be okay. That moment of hesitation cost her and Helena was quick to stop her exit.

"She's allowed to leave without consequence?" she asked, shocked. They had openly discussed information about the Conventicle in front of Emoni, which meant that information needed to be protected. Magical manipulation would leave her without any of the information.

Emoni attempted to sidestep past Helena. Moving with liquid grace and strikingly fast movement, Helena's hand was around Emoni's throat. She hoisted her into the air.

"Put her down, now," I hissed. Anger raced through me like an inferno, igniting all my protective urges. Grabbing the marble coaster from the counter, I used it to add heft to my strike to her head. Her mouth gaped in surprise. It was shock more than pain that caused her to release my friend.

"Don't you *ever* touch her."

Sheer awe at my retaliation had stunned Helena into momentary silence. The prey attacking the predator. Uncomfortable silence filled the air as we watched Helena's contemplation of how I'd pay. Her eyes were murderous, her claws extended, and thunderous magic rippled off her so violently it felt as if the building would eventually come down.

"Helena." Dominic's tone managed to be cajoling yet firm. The confidence with which he dealt with an enraged Helena seemed well practiced. "You will not retaliate."

She was past retaliation. The world needed to be set on fire to display her displeasure. It was extremely unsettling to remember that she was responsible for protecting humans and keeping the other supernaturals in check.

"If Luna trusts her, then she is to be trusted." Dominic looked to Emoni who had recovered and was standing a few feet away with pepper spray she'd retrieved from the contents of her bag aimed in Helena's direction.

"We can trust that everything revealed to you will be kept secret?" Dominic confirmed.

Without taking her eyes off her target, Emoni nodded.

"Just her word?" Helena barked. "No magical binding or oaths? We're taking the word of *humans* now."

Emoni split her attention between looking at the objects

on the floor as she returned them to her purse and Helena, while keeping the pepper spray extended toward her.

"She will be allowed to leave. No magic and she will not be touched," Dominic asserted, directing the demand to his father who looked similarly disgusted.

"I don't recognize you anymore, brother." The disappointment in Helena's voice made him flinch. He recovered from the insult quickly and appeared to be considering her words. Was being around me making him too merciful to do his job? What I saw in his expression, Helena did as well. She relaxed, seeing the potential for him to be the Dominic she wanted him to be.

Emoni attempted to quietly slip away but had to get past Helena who only allowed a small space for her to navigate. Anand volunteered to escort Emoni home and to meet them later. She wouldn't drive with the amount of alcohol she'd consumed, but Anand could drive her car home and she wouldn't be without it.

She hesitated on the threshold of the door, giving me an over-the-shoulder look of concern. I offered a nod of assurance and a wide smile, but it didn't put a dent in her worried expression.

16

Anand had joined us at the same building where I'd initially met the Conventicle and negotiated the new terms of operation. At the door, I had a moment of pause. I would agree with Helena very few times in my life, but my presence during this meeting was one time; we were in accord but for completely different reasons. When it came to Peter and me, there were no coincidences. The shades had been freed at the same time I was released from the underworld. It would be easy for the Conventicle to make the connection. The connection might be harder to make without me present. Out of sight, out of mind.

I wasn't naïve or optimistic about Helena's newfound interest in my safety. She didn't want me there because my continued presence with them bound me to the royal trio and offered me some form of protection. People would see me as an extension of the royals, although she claimed I'd be treated with hostility because people would eventually link me with the continued mishaps. It was the protection that she didn't want me to have. Helena wanted them to do her dirty work and get rid of me—leaving her hands clean.

Helena and Areleus believed my death would make things significantly better. As much as I hated to admit it, they weren't wrong.

Entering the building, we were met with speckles of blood at the entrance. Crimson handprints made gruesome patterns on the wall. Violence didn't have a smell, but it had a feel. It created tension and unease in the room. I couldn't keep up with the royals, who left me behind as they raced to the meeting room. When I got there, Helena's hand was pressed against the closed door, a halation of light peeled away from the door, and her lips moved fervently.

When it stopped, her shoulders slumped with fatigue. "It's done," she whispered.

Preparing myself for a gruesome sight, I was relieved that it wasn't as bad as I had imagined, if I ignored the shade's mangled body. I wasn't sure if they breathed normally, but this one clearly wasn't.

At our arrival, Madeline raised her head from the table where she'd been resting and glared at us. The Conventicle's new vampire drew back his lips, exposing stained fangs. A naked man lay face down on the floor. I assumed he was a shifter. Totally comfortable with his naked form being exposed to the world, he lifted his head to look at us, then let it drop back to the floor. The claw mark on his back mended in such a dramatic fashion it looked cinematic. Across from them was another fatigued-looking group who divided their looks of contention between the royals and the shade.

"The other members of the Conventicle," Dominic told me. There were a hundred and twenty members, but I'd only met the representatives.

Dominic took in the room and focused on Nailah and the other Seer who were on the far side of the room, sunk into opposite corners, their bodies in a static state and displaying their peculiar violet eyes and disfiguring grimaces.

"What do you see, Nailah?" Dominic asked.

"The same," she whispered. Death of many people in this room. She eased closer to the dead shade, the bevel of her frown increasing. "If it was alive, I'd be able to read more from their kind." The other Seer moved closer, his unenthusiastic expression unchanged from the first time I'd met him. His t-shirt revealed the brightly colored tats that formed sleeves on his arms. Nailah stopped at the shade. He continued toward me, inspecting me with a haunting interest.

"It's her again," he whispered. "She's the reason we are going to die." With a quick sleight of hand and unexpected flash of movement, he lunged at me with the blade he was suddenly wielding. My hands shot out for protection just as Dominic pushed me out of the way. Unable to get my footing, I stumbled back and fell.

Dominic grabbed the Seer. He wrenched the knife from his hand. The sound of bone breaking and the Seer's wail of pain resounded in the room. The Seer crumpled to a heap on the floor, cradling his arm. A whimper escaped when he saw the fire erupt from Dominic's hands.

"Dominic!" I shrieked. His eyes snapped in my direction, fury blazing in his eyes as his lips drew back into a sneer. Violence was a tinderbox in the room, waiting for him to ignite it and erupt everyone into a storm of violence and magic. I couldn't let that happen. The infighting would surely give Peter the advantage.

"Please," I said, noticing Dominic had returned to his plan of burning the man alive.

I crawled over to the Seer and ignored the anger he directed at me. If he was ever in a position to try again, he would. As much as I wanted to tell Dominic to finish him, my empathy wouldn't let me. I was one person causing a great deal of chaos. The most pragmatic thing to do was to kill me. I wasn't confident that if faced with the same dilemma, I wouldn't try the same.

"Someone help him." I looked to the royals who were defiant in their refusal. Madeline looked hesitant, perhaps from fear of retaliation from the royals, whose cold mien did nothing to dispel that concern.

"It's okay," I soothed, my words holding more confidence than I felt, especially with Helena sneering at me. I gave Dominic an entreating look, and he finally relaxed.

"Heal him," he directed Madeline. "Know this is Luna's wish, not mine. Any more attempts on Luna's life will be severely punished. And I will ignore her unwise requests for mercy."

Areleus and Helena attempted to stand in solidarity with Dominic, but their masks kept breaking, showing their contempt for me. The vampire hadn't missed it as he moved toward the injured Seer.

I eased away as a battle-weary Madeline whispered a spell, her hand hovering over his arm. His pained grimace was replaced with a somnolent look of relief, but he continued to cradle his arm. The Seer's injuries seemed to heal quickly after the vampire knelt next to him and bit into his own arm, breaking the skin and offering it to the Seer's mouth. I allowed my attention to drift over the room in an attempt to keep the bile down at the sight of him drawing blood from the vampire's arm. I wanted out of their world, and despite the benefits of knowing about the supernaturals, part of me wanted to unlearn and unsee everything.

"What have you done?" the harsh voice behind us demanded. The royals, Anand, the vampire, and the shifter didn't seem surprised by the large group of people and six animals spilling into the room. I counted a panther, three wolves, a hyena, and... I couldn't place the other animal.

"A dhole," Anand whispered, startling me. His careful eye on the dhole was a clear sign to pay close attention to the predators who had just sauntered in. My protective instincts pushed me to focus on the menagerie of animals, but because all eyes were on the dhole, I suspected he was the most dangerous of them all. Behind them was another group of people. Madeline glared at them. Magic wielders.

Disabling the shade had taken so much from her that she couldn't put on her mask of arrogance and assurance. Another group of five floated in as if they rode on the wind. Undeniably vampires. Their appearance made me want to retract the many times I'd mocked the Broad Street Creatures of the Night. These stood out. Not just for their otherworldly movements and eyes that were pits of blackness. I tried to place what made them seem to exist in a time where things were very different. Despite being dressed in modern clothing, they seemed liked anachronisms. The royals were immortal; I knew they were older than they looked but it was never revealed in their actions or mannerisms.

Helena, Areleus, and even Dominic swathed themselves in their arrogance like a cocoon. The five vampires possessed the same air of haughtiness. If it were in their power, everyone but them would be wiped out from existence, leaving only a few for food. They bared crimson-tinted fangs, from recent feedings, I suspected.

Hostility swelled in the air. Reading the disdain, I assumed the room had just been taken over by the New Conventicle, the people who wanted to get rid of the existing power and take it for themselves. Adrenaline jetted through me. I wanted to be anywhere but in this room and in their line of sight. Their ferocity and confidence showed they would rule without fear of consequences. Being that inflexible left no room for exceptions—even for me. They had wanted me dead when they learned of my role in releasing the prisoners. From the cold looks that breezed in my direction, things hadn't changed.

To win the game of survival, I needed to know the players

and allies, the reasonable ones, the power players, and the threats. I was trying to figure that out from just looks. Not one member of the New Conventicle looked as if they could be reasoned with. Even the ones who didn't glare at me with fierce disdain might not be reasonable, just deceptively quiet, storms waiting to demolish everything in their path. That was probably why cautious eyes kept going to the dhole. I made sure to put more distance between me and it.

I had met the reps of the Conventicle. Since the New Conventicle wasn't official but a collection of enthusiastic supernaturals waiting to unseat the current group, there wasn't a hierarchy. The differences between the groups were stark. The current Conventicle was politically driven and ruled by appearances. The New Conventicle didn't suffer from such things. There was an off-putting hunger and brutishness to them, qualities that would work in their favor in a coup.

"Why are the shades here?" asked the tall, well-built witch. His pleasing carved features and winged cheeks were distorted by his scowl. Velvet sepia skin and chocolate-brown eyes belied his presence that bellowed he was a force to contend with. Those behind him presented a similar energy.

It was only a matter of time; they would be the new face of the Conventicle.

"They escaped," Dominic said in a crisp tone.

"Samuel." Another witch called to the witch marching in Dominic's direction. Despite her neutral tone, it served as a warning.

His glower softened as he looked over his shoulder at the woman warning him. "He's allowed the worst of our kind to escape, and if the rumors are true, he was imprisoned himself. Shades, whose housing was his domain, are now free in our world. We were attacked by three of them. With all our abilities combined we were only able to destroy one, and we lost seven of our own. I think fearing Dominic is neither warranted nor deserved." He looked directly at Dominic. "Or allowing you to keep your job. You've failed. Why shouldn't you be relieved of it?"

"Are you willing to sacrifice your life to try?" Dominic asked. Samuel kept a distance from him, his eyes sweeping over the room, clearly determining the best way to shield himself while exacting the harm he desperately wanted to inflict.

It didn't go unnoticed by the royals. Claws were exposed and magic hummed. Madeline stood. Her features hardened, her hand moved into a defensive position, and her lips parted in readiness to perform rapid-fire spells. The shifters from the established Conventicle had changed. And I was surprised by the number of Conventicle vampires that I'd missed, who were now baring their fangs. Anand drew two blades that looked more dangerous than the ones I'd previously seen him with.

The Seer came to his feet then retreated toward the wall, his eyes glowing violet. Nailah's eyes sparked violet that then disappeared. Annoyance flitted across her face. Shaking her head, she slowly moved to the center of the room, her comforting gentleness replaced by disdain and frustration. She demonstrated an admirable level of confidence standing in the middle of a barely suppressed violence-lust and brewing war.

"You are all going to die. Some in this fight, others at the hands of the shades and Peter. Lives will be irreparably damaged, and you will be at the mercy of the Awakeners, Peter, and the shades. Fight this out later." Her gaze slid over the royals who maintained their look of impassivity.

"With them at the helm there will always be problems," Samuel asserted.

"Can you put your issues aside until this is over?" Nailah suggested.

"How can we when they refuse to address the problem?" he asked, and everyone in the room turned to look at me. The enigmatic human, the root of the problem. Despite not knowing what I was, they knew I'd attributed to some of it, if not all. They got an A for good insight. The royals gave nothing away. Their solidarity was impressive.

"Give me your word that this *person* isn't the cause of the existing problems," demanded one of the New Conventicle vampires. Her auburn hair was pulled back into a ponytail, drawing attention to her cruel, coal eyes. As a result of a recent feeding, her parchment skin held a rosy color. Her narrow face consisted of sharp points that made the smile she attempted to give Nailah even more unnerving.

Nailah struggled to answer in a way that made me think she was bound to the truth. Lies of omission were her only tools to circumvent it. The room waited while her lips parted and closed several times.

Before she could answer, an explosion of magic hit her in the chest. Sailing across the room, she smashed into the wall and crumpled to the floor as plaster rained down on her. I swallowed my scream before I could make my way to her. Areleus was by her side, his fingers pressed to her neck, looking for signs of life. *Please be alive*, I recited over and over. I needed her to be alive.

The shades swooped in.

Magic streamed into the room with them. Behind the swarm of creatures was Peter, his self-indulgent smile directed at me. I ran, moving out of his line of sight and the shade heading for me. In the sudden chaos, I scrambled toward the exit. Out of my peripheral, I could see Anand at the other side of the room, his spine curved, drawing in his magic—ready to reveal to the others what he was in order to save them. Black illuminated vines fanned from him to inflict their pain and send the shades into a retreat. It didn't happen. It was the vampires who responded to his magic.

Collapsing on the ground, they writhed in pain. Anand quickly retracted his magic, shock skating over his expression. I assumed he'd been unaware of his effect on vampires. Aware that this discovery would make him a target of vampires, I hoped they attributed the assault to Peter. Anand retrieved his blades and ran into the fighting in the center of the room.

Steering around the fighting, I kept shifting my attention from finding safety to looking at Nailah and signs of progress. Several times, I caught Areleus doing the same. There wasn't any noticeable change in her, and Areleus took his rage out on the assailants. The shades' arrival had made allies of the New Conventicle, Conventicle, and royals.

A shade threw a shifter through the air and met the animal on its landing, plunging its clawed hand into the shifter's belly. The dhole proved to be the one to fear. Moving in and out of his animal form to meet his fighting needs, he floated with a swiftness that appeared ethereal.

Areleus lunged at one of the winged shades. His hand pressed into the creature, battering magic into it that made him buck and convulse before collapsing. But his recovery was quick, and he countered with a firestorm at Areleus who was slow to react, shocked that the shade's magic worked on him.

Dominic had enclosed Peter in a diaphanous shield to stop his advance, but Peter destroyed it with a simple touch. Once the shield fell, a tightly coiled ball of magic soared toward Peter from a witch whose face was screwed tight in concentration and effort. Without taking his eyes off his target—Dominic—Peter made a few movements of his fingers, changing the magic's course. In the ball's return route, it expanded, sprouting sharp spikes that slammed into the witch, impaling him and exploding into an opalescent mist that covered him. The witch keeled over, gasping for air, twisting and writhing, lips casting spells that had little effect on the wound in his chest or the convulsions that ravaged him. I risked a glance around the room, looking for a way to get to him or find someone to help. Whatever magic Peter had done had restricted the witch's magic.

The fallen witch got Madeline's attention. She headed toward him, her lips and fingers twisting in unusual ways. The mist appeared to move from the witch but kept returning to its target. The fiery wave Dominic lobbed in Peter's direction engulfed him. For a moment, shock fell over him. I expected the distraction to be enough to destroy the mist that Madeline was struggling to dismantle, but the fire engulfment crystalized then exploded in shards that spread out for several feet, hitting anyone unable to move out of the way in time or put up a protective barrier.

The satisfied smile that curled Peter's lips quickly vanished when Dominic lunged at him. Dominic's punch to Peter's face was delivered so quickly, I realized I hadn't seen the extent of Dominic's abilities. A primitive fury drove their fight as they exchanged blows, alternating between magic and physical strikes. Peter was proving to be the antithesis of the studious awkward person he'd presented for years in the bookstore. Skilled in combat and magic, he may have wanted to damage Dominic, but his main objective was to get to me. Each strike and counter defense brought him closer to me, positioning him to remove any obstructions between us.

One of the shades lurched toward me, only to be stopped by Helena grabbing it by its wing and hurling it back and sending it slamming into a wall. Her face was bright with exhilaration. There wasn't any denying she reveled in the chaos and violence. Scanning the room, she headed to where a vampire and two shifters were losing their battle with a shade. Moments later Helena's body crashing into the table sent splinters of wood flying. I grabbed the broken table legs that skidded a few feet from me. If the shades were supposed to bring me in alive, they hadn't gotten the memo. I battered at the creature who struck with a shot of magic that rammed me in the chest, sending me careening back several feet. Recovering at an impressive speed—well, for a human—I was on my feet and swinging my weapons at the shade, hitting him in his exposed sharp teeth. From either pain or shock it shuffled back a step. Dodging the bodies that were being slung as I ran, I couldn't determine whether they were alive, just that none of them were shades.

I darted out of the door, ignoring the nagging feeling of being considered a coward. What the hell was I supposed to do? Fight people more superior in combat, violence, and magic than I was, to make a point? What would be the point? That I could die easier than suspected?

Weapon in hand, I rushed down some stairs toward the nearest exit from the building, wishing I had something that could do more damage, especially when I found the dhole waiting near the door. My self-preservation alarm was telling me he wasn't there to protect me. When his eyes remained on its target—my neck—I clutched my weapon tighter, prepared to swing it for all its worth. Pepper spray was tucked away in my pocket and I debated if I should risk losing the grip on my weapon to retrieve it. It was no use in my damn pocket. Should have kept it at the ready.

The dhole charged, zigging past me and lunging into the air, soaring as if he'd grown wings. He tore into the man behind me. Magic, meant for the creature it wouldn't effect, hit me. Another person brandished a knife. The dhole slipped out of his animal form into an intimidatingly tall, sleekly muscled man, who was a human embodiment of the animal he shifted into. He grabbed the knife and used it on them, breaking it off at the handle before tossing it aside.

Then he dashed past me, meeting a vampire with short hair and bared fangs with a punch so hard, the man's head snapped back. The vampire delivered several punches to the dhole's face and a strike to his gut, knocking the dhole back into human form, although he recovered from the fall before my eyes could fully grasp the movement. I was becoming unconvinced he was *just* a shifter by his movements that matched the vampire's fluid speed. The vampire grabbed him into a chokehold and wrenched his head to the side, fangs advancing to his neck.

Whipping around, I headed for another exit in the opposite direction. My shirt was grabbed from behind and the wooden leg snatched from me. The human dhole smashed the wood against the wall, giving it a stake-like point.

"Don't you move," he commanded with a thick English accent.

The fuck I'm not. He'd just disabled three Awakeners, who were feared by most of the people upstairs, and he had an English accent. I'm calling it: supervillain.

Retrieving my pepper spray, I didn't risk looking back to see him stake the vampire with his makeshift weapon. My hand was on the door, pepper spray ready, when I was yanked into a firm chest. My height giving me somewhat of an advantage in this instance, I raised my arm, prepared to blindly discharge the spray, when it was forced against my chest and I was bound and whisked away.

When I was released, in my dizziness, I spun and aimed, too unfocused to see the person in front. My arm was grabbed and repositioned.

"Luna!"

Dominic. Relief flooded me at the sound of his voice.

"I have to go," he said.

"Nailah," I managed.

"She's here. My father brought her." He was about to leave then paused, pulled me to him again, and after another dizzying wave, I was in his bedroom. He moved away from me, hurriedly, pulling a strand of hair from my head. With a quick invocation he erected the barrier.

"Nailah should be fine. Don't break this barrier for anyone except me." And then he was gone.

It was the lack of certainty about her well-being that made it so hard to keep to his directive. I wanted to know. Needed to know. But after a long internal debate, I stayed put.

17

After pacing the floor for a while, I tried to distract myself with books. Desperate, again, I attempted spells from any books written in English that I could find. Feeling defenseless was the worst thing ever, and each time I remembered how close the dhole was to me and my belief that he wasn't there to help, fear rampaged through me. There was no way I would have survived. I'd be like everyone who came in contact with him. His presence was a death sentence.

The minutes crawled by. Nothing could distract me. Peter had used me to release the shades and now they were acting as his army to retrieve me. Peter wanted to pull from the well of magic again.

He had a tremendous amount of power, so what did he need me for? To imprison the royals again. What if he could do that without me being in the underworld with them? What would be their chances of release?

Peter now had an army of shades and Awakeners. We had a fractured alliance between the Conventicle and those who wanted to take their position. Could people who wanted your position of power be trusted? After my head started to ache, I switched my thoughts to Nailah. She was somewhere in the house, and I had no idea how she was doing. Flashes of her crumpled body and Areleus's panic-stricken face ran through my mind. He wasn't all cruelty. He cared for her. But the cynic in me had me wondering if his show of compassion was because of her magical skills.

"Luna?" Nailah's strained voice called from the other side of the door. Jetting to the door, I yanked it open and stopped abruptly.

She eyed the illumination of the ward and gave a tight smile to my apologetic look. I trusted her. I was just about to break it when she stopped me.

"Don't. It was put there for a purpose."

Was she warning me against her?

"You wouldn't hurt me," I said with unwavering confidence. Not sure where it came from but regarding Nailah, I had it. Whether magically influenced or not, it was steadfast.

"No. I see you. I know you are an unwilling participant. Unfortunately, you may end up as collateral damage." She winced from pain with the slightest movement. I edged closer to the barrier, wanting to comfort her.

"I'm fine. Broken rib probably. It could have been so much worse."

"This is a war, isn't it?"

She nodded. "One that has been brewing for years. Inevitable, I guess," she whispered. She lowered herself to the floor in front of the door, her face fatigued and worried.

I couldn't let her stay on the floor in pain, when she could rest on the sofa or bed. "Come in, Nailah," Again I moved to cross the threshold.

"No!" she blurted. Then she dropped her voice. "We're not alone here."

The royals were gone but the guards were there. Reading Nailah's expression, I gathered they weren't there to protect me. It made sense why Dominic had rushed me away.

I eased to the floor, too. "I'm tired of my life being in danger." The constant state of panic and fear made being optimistic about this ever ending difficult.

"I know what you are." She said it so softly, I would have missed it if I wasn't so close to her. "Areleus has an idea. Seeing how desperate Peter was to get to you, I suspect the others have come to a similar conclusion."

"I'm not safe, am I?"

Another wince and she held her ribs. Everything in me wanted to comfort her, but there wasn't anything I could do for a rib fracture. Even a visit to the emergency room would be treated with pain meds and rest.

"No. You're not. I wish I had a different answer. I've seen your death too many times and in so many different scenarios," she admitted with a frown. "But at least you're safe for now."

It was a hollow victory because nothing was guaranteed.

"Who's going to win?" I asked.

Her frown deepened. "As of me leaving, Peter will be the victor. I saw humans around them, which mean the supernaturals are no longer living in the shadows."

If Nailah's solemn expression was anything to go by, there wasn't anything I could do. But I refused to do nothing and simply let things happen to me. I just had to figure out what to do. Sitting in contemplative silence, I avoided looking at Nailah whose eyes would flash the violet color every so often—looking at the future I held based on what had happened. Most of the time her expression was blank, but a look of desolation would peek through, letting me know my fate hadn't changed.

"You should be resting." Areleus's voice boomed in the hallway before he came into view. He glared at the barrier but said nothing about it as he helped Nailah stand. He kept hold of her hand while the other one rested on her back. The scent of lilac permeated the barrier and the tension in Nailah's shoulders relaxed.

"Better," he said, pulling her closer to him. She nodded as they headed away. Everything about her seemed better, her gait becoming light and an easy spring in her step.

I could hear part of their conversation as they moved down the hallway, but neither Dominic's nor Helena's name was mentioned. I wanted to believe he would have shown more emotion if they were injured or worse. But who knew? Areleus had proven to be a swarm of contradictions.

The slightest sound at Dominic's bedroom door had me rushing to it. I snatched it open to find Dominic looking pensive. I tried to interpret what it meant. His sister loomed behind him. Both were waiting for me to break the ward but for two entirely different reasons. Stifling the fear her presence caused, I stepped over the barrier and moved aside to let Dominic in.

"Anand?" I asked.

"He's in his room." Dominic's hand moved from its position on his front as he looked over his shoulder at his sister. Helena's keen amber eyes danced with deadly intrigue, her expression set with ominous determination.

"Peter has aligned with the Awakeners. The shades are his new army, and we are at the mercy of two warring sects who will betray to gain more power and benefits." Helena bristled.

"I am aware."

"Are you? Because even with the Conventicle's strongest, we were only able to destroy five shades. The Conventicle doesn't have the ability to manage the chaos that will ensue. It is only a matter of time before keeping the existence of supernaturals will be impossible, and then we won't just be dealing with a civil war but also with humans who will attempt to wrangle some control. The supernaturals will be more than willing to show them that they can't."

She was just voicing everything I was sure Dominic had considered.

"The new Conventicle can't be trusted, and the Awakeners are all tenacity and disorganized ambition. But there are many of them. That needs to be handled if we are to have any chance of getting this under control," Helena cited, deep-seated anger in her words.

"I know," Dominic breathed out, sliding past me and dropping onto the sofa. He ran his hand through his hair, making it as messy as the situation. I took several cautious steps from Helena when she eased in.

"Temporary imprisonment would be best, and once this is handled we need to require a binding agreement that their freedom is contingent upon adhering to the Conventicle's laws."

Helena's brows drew together as disgust twisted her features. "What? No. They are aware they are in violation. There must be swift and deadly reprisal. Nothing else is acceptable. It will serve a dual purpose. It will weaken Peter and make a statement to the New Conventicle that we are not to be challenged. They can't enforce rule the way we can. Let me take care of it."

Take care of it.

"You can't kill them!" I blurted. "What is wrong with you all? Why is violence and death always the first and only answer?"

In a breath of movement, Helena's claws were at my chin and Dominic was on his feet, his own claws extended and glaring at his sister.

Placing her face inches from mine, she sneered. "Because it works and always has. My brother cares about your human sensibilities. I don't." She stepped away from me and glared at Dominic. "Continue showing this one the docile version of you, if you wish. But she will not domesticate this wolf into a poodle."

The insult landed, although I didn't understand why. Nothing he'd shown me was poodle-like or docile. Were they just saying words? Did an underworld dictionary exist that was completely different from the one I knew?

"Helena, I don't disagree with you on this. But if you kill them it won't have the effect you believe. The New Conventicle will rise up because they don't view us as part of them. It will only support their argument that we are savage—"

"As we should be. We aren't human nor should we subscribe to their ways." She shot me a chilly glance. "Don't let your human toy be the anchor to your downfall."

"Luna has nothing to do with my decision."

"She has everything to do with it, and that's the problem, Dominic."

More than she knew.

"Our success today was because we had both the Conventicle and the new," he pointed out.

"We only need them because you have restrained yourself. I don't like this version of you, Dominicus. Your human has caused more damage than just taming you. Whatever she is, I hope it will be worth the harm she has caused." For the first time since I'd met her, she displayed genuine concern for him. Her approach toward him was gentle and assessing. "You've helped me so often. Let me handle this for you. She's in your system and it's blinding you to the problems she's causing. This can't go on for much longer. Let me take the burden."

"You will *not* hurt Luna," he whispered with conviction. Helena looked at me once again before giving a nod of concession. I didn't trust it.

She turned to leave, looking over her shoulder as she tossed out, "Perhaps Emory will offer his assistance since mine was declined. If it weren't for the Awakeners showing up, are you confident he was there to protect your Luna? I'm not so sure."

It was exactly what I thought. The dhole kept me from being abducted by the Awakeners, but it didn't mean his intentions were to keep me alive.

With her departure, I tugged out a strand of my hair and held it out for him. Without a response, he took it from me and made the magical barrier. I wasn't safe in the house with his family, and he knew it as well. I paced for several moments, Dominic watching me from the sofa.

"There are at least forty more shades out there."

He nodded. "The number of Awakeners at Peter's disposal is the wildcard."

"They're emboldened by him. With the type of magic he possesses, I understand why," I said. Under the weight of Dominic's scrutiny, I tried to say what kept going through my mind since his sister's departure. "The chaos and the lives lost is because of me."

"Because of Peter using you," he corrected.

"Semantics. I gave him the opportunity to do it. I'm at his whim and I hate this so much. We need a way to stop me from being used by him."

"I don't know if there is one," he admitted softly.

I had no idea where to begin. The political landscape was a mess. It wasn't just Peter at the root of it, but the dissention, too, and everything in me wanted to find a harmonious solution when there wasn't one. People would die, be betrayed, lose their freedom, and be worse off than before. I didn't cause the fire, but I was fodder for it.

Distracted by my own thoughts, I wasn't aware of Dominic directly in front of me until his fingers were rubbing the creases out of my forehead before kissing me, nothing chaste about it. Heat ran through me, my nipples responding to him stroking against them. I felt grateful for the bra that hid my response to him, but from his mischievous grin, he was aware of it. He'd ruined me. Sex and magic were forever intwined.

He took me in, I'm sure seeing the dejection I felt. I didn't have the ability to hide it.

"You are a wonderful insight into the many parts of humanity that I don't see often. I adore it for its optimism, beauty, empathy, and heart, *but* you are its weakness." The prince had just landed what Emoni and I called a compli-sult. An insult wrapped in a compliment. I was the weakest part of humankind. What the fuck? How the hell was I supposed to take this compli-sult?

Ignoring it, I opened my mouth to redirect the conversation to what I wanted to suggest. Before I could, he held up a hand to stop me.

"You want me to do the spell my grandfather performed to recapture the shades and spare the lives of those who will hunt them. Am I wrong?

"When Callum attacked you against my wishes, he should have been handled without mercy. You stopped that. Your empathy will be seen as weakness and your kindness exploited." Again, he held his hand up to stop a rebuttal. "Nothing you say will make that any less true. I will not sacrifice my magic for that. No matter how many may die. You will see my refusal as cruel, but it is necessary. I will not put myself in a position to be weaker than my father. I need all the power I have because the next attempt on my father will end with his death."

"You couldn't do it before," I pointed out. The complexity and viciousness of their world would never sit well with me, but I felt better knowing he couldn't kill his father.

"You dying when the magic was removed from you is the only reason he is alive. I wasn't aware of the shades' release, but I knew I would need my father to handle Peter and the incipient war. After Peter and the shades are handled, things will need to be stabilized, and the three of us are the ones to do it."

No matter how many times I reminded myself this wasn't my fight, the rules of this game of life were predetermined, and my only goal was to exit it intact, it was hard to blindly accept the ways of their world.

"I can't read you," Dominic whispered, concerned.

The rampant thoughts in my head were concerning, too. "Your sister's right," I blurted.

"Are you petitioning for your death?" Dark intrigue clung to his words.

"No. I just don't understand. You're so pragmatic about everything but—" The words fell away.

"But when it comes to you."

I nodded.

"Well, Little Luna," he drawled against my ear, "since meeting you, I've accepted that some things are beyond our knowledge. I want you around so I can continue to satisfy that curiosity." His breath was warm against my ear. The moment I started leaning into the heat of his body, I startled and took several steps back.

"Stop that. Stay on task," I demanded.

His rumble of laughter did ease some of my tension, but the problems remained.

"Of course. You get some rest. I'll be going out again with the others to hunt."

"For the shades?"

He nodded. "And the Awakeners. They must be taken out of the situation."

"Temporarily imprisoned, right?" I clarified.

I repeated my question when his only response was closing the distance between us, his finger gently gliding along my cheek. Instead of focusing on his touch, I was drawn to the splatter of blood on his clothing.

"That is the initial goal," he offered, leaving no room for

further questioning. He studied me for a long time and made a low rumble. "You will keep my humanity," he said, so softly that it seemed like it was a reminder to himself.

He moved to the door and waited for me to break the barrier to let him out.

"I have dinner with my family at seven tomorrow," I reminded him.

"You'll need to cancel."

"No. I can't cancel or not show up."

"If your family were sources of magic, Peter would have used them."

"You're probably right, but I'd like confirmation *and* I need to see them." My voice broke. There was still a chance I might not make it out of this situation alive and the dinner could be my last time seeing them. It was a morose thought but a very real possibility. I wanted to see my family. I needed to see my family. Blinking caused the tears to spill.

In a heartbeat, Dominic was inches from me, his thumb sweeping gently across my cheek, wiping the tears away. His expression softened to concern. "Of course. I'll be back in time and provide you with a way to determine whether they have magic. But you must come back here. Back to me. Okay?"

I nodded in agreement, squashing the plan I had to talk to Cameron. It would be best to talk to her once things were resolved, anyway.

If things were ever resolved.

18

I was awakened by Dominic knocking at the door. After letting him in, I attempted to drift back to sleep while he stripped off his clothes and headed to the bathroom to shower, but couldn't. When he crawled into the bed, I asked if everyone had returned. He confirmed that they had, but from his smirk, I gathered he knew I was mostly inquiring about Anand—it was hard to be Team Areleus and Helena when they wanted me dead. Enough of the Awakeners had been imprisoned to satisfy both Conventicles and significantly disrupt whatever strategy Peter had in mind.

"Nailah?" I wanted to see her again to make sure she was completely healed, and I was also curious to know if my fate had changed.

I placed my hand over his roaming fingers that were becoming increasingly distracting. Dominic found wicked entertainment in how my body responded to his slightest touch. Light brushes of his finger over the curves of my body caused heat to thrum through me, bringing a devilish smirk to Dominic's lips and his eyes dropping to my nipples as they hardened to peaks.

"Nailah?" I probed.

"I've not seen her since my father took her to the guest house earlier. He assures me that she's well." A worried expression vanished as quickly as it had appeared.

"You don't believe him?"

"I believe she is well. But I know there's a reason he's putting so much effort in keeping me from her," he admitted.

There was definitely something Lord Areleus didn't want revealed.

Despite the marked successes of the previous day, Dominic was uneasy as he watched me dress for dinner with my family. His stoic mask kept falling away to reveal his concern. He didn't want me to go, and the effort not to express it or further debate it was apparent.

Once I was ready, he moved behind me, his arms circling me. He leaned down and whispered in my ear, "Are you ready?" The real question lingered over those words: "Are you sure?"

There were so many uncertainties, but seeing my family and making sure they weren't vessels wasn't any of them.

I nodded. Moments later he'd transported me to the apartment in the city that he shared with his sister. Releasing me, I turned to face him. He handed me a small ragged-shape pearl-color object.

"An Affinity," he informed me as I examined it. After he invoked a spell and blood linked it to me, it hummed with a small vibration. "Similar magic will be pulled to it. Just place it on your parents and brother, and there will be a tug. Like magic drawn to like magic. It will feel like a magnet. Effort will be needed to pull away."

Although I was impressed by it, Dominic wasn't. For him, it was one of the things in their world that was obsolete.

"It must come in direct contact with them," he reminded me as I got into the Range Rover he'd loaned me. Zareb, Dominic's favorite hellhound, jumped into the back seat, and once I drove away, he shimmered and disappeared, the warmth of his body making his continuing presence known.

"It's probably better if you stay outside, because there's no way for me to let you in without it looking suspicious," I told the hellhound as I turned onto my parents' street.

He allowed himself to be visible, intelligent eyes looking at me. Drawing back his teeth was a reminder I was traveling with a hound of the underworld. He snorted, a chastisement for changing Dominic's instructions.

"He said for you to stay with me. If you're outside the door, you're still with me. I can't leave without you and it's not like you can't track me down if I do."

Head tilted to the side, the dog gave me a considering look and another snort before cloaking himself again. I assumed it was his concession.

Seeing me pull into the driveway, my mom rushed out of the house and stood on the porch waving at me. Her presence was going to make it difficult to let Zareb out without it looking weird. Parking the SUV next to my brother's, I hopped out in an overenthusiastic show of wanting to get to her for a hug, leaving the driver's side door open. The display of emotion didn't require a great deal of acting. I was happy to see her. I sank deeper into the hug. Slowly pulling away, I kept enough contact to rub the Affinity over the only place she had bare skin—her hand. My mother was rarely seen without a sweater.

"This is pretty," she said, picking it up from the ground. Swiping the object over her skin hadn't been done as gracefully and covertly as intended.

"I'm thinking of making it into a necklace and wanted Forest to check it out," I lied. Of the many interests my brother had, he'd dabbled in jewelry making but soon lost interest.

"May I?" my father asked, joining my mother. I was grateful when my mother dropped it into his hand, giving me the opportunity to come in contact with him, the object, and me. He seemed less impressed. No tug. No magic in them.

Sure that I'd given Zareb enough time to get out the car, I returned to it to close the door before following my parents into the house.

"Rental?" My mother inquired, the skepticism tight in her voice as she gave the Range Rover another peek over her shoulder. My brother pulled his attention from it long enough to give me a long hug. Despite his sinewy body, he gave the kind of hugs that made the world fall away. They were the embodiment of a security blanket, and I held him tighter and longer than usual. Staggering away, he looked puzzled by my unusual display of affection. I was surprised by it as well. The dysfunction of the royals had given me a new appreciation for him and my family. I wanted to be near him, touch him, and know that if given the ability, he'd never try to claw my face or sic a violent person on me to have his magic returned. I doubted he'd ever give me a reason to take his magic.

"Can you make this into a necklace?" I asked, flashing him a grin that I hoped provided an excuse for my off-putting show of affection.

He examined it, his brows drawing together. "Really?" he asked, returning it to me and giving me another peculiar look when I grasped his hand to take it from him. Another negative result.

Forest's eyes narrowed as he put more distance between us. "What's wrong with you?"

"Can't I just be happy to see you?"

"Yeah, but don't be weird about it. Okay?" He gave my

parents a look which tacitly gave them the same orders. He shoved his fingers through his hair, which was longer than he'd ever worn it. He had a new tattoo on his hand.

"So, what misguided friend of yours gave you access to a ride like that? *He* must be new in your life because he doesn't know you well."

"That's quite presumptuous of you to assume it's a man."

"Your friends are smart and they've seen you drive. And after seeing you park, no one who values their vehicle is going to give you access to something that expensive. Clearly this man's decisions are being influenced," he teased.

I made a face and found myself fussing with his hair before he knocked my hand away. I was being weird and needed to stop. I was being more suspicious than the hellhound could ever be.

"That's what insurance is for," I shot back, putting some distance between us and making an attempt at normal behavior.

"Who's the new man, Luna?" he pressed. I could hear the enthusiasm.

"Just a new friend," I said, making a face that urged him to pursue another line of questioning. My parents looked like meerkats trying to get snippets of my life without being intrusive.

"I wish Emoni had joined you," he said, taking the hint. She'd only come a few times to family dinner and had been offered an open invitation by my parents to return whenever she'd like. My brother enthusiastically cosigned on the offer for an obviously different reason.

"She only likes you for your comfy hugs that you dole out so infrequently. It's our little indulgence," I teased.

"And my charm," he countered. "Don't forget, I'm charming, too."

"Let's discuss this alleged charm over dinner," I suggested, hooking my arm around his waist and moving to the kitchen. "And the new body art," I added.

Sitting at the kitchen table, I looked over the new addition to the multitude of tattoos on his body. "Thinking about getting one?" he asked.

I had never paid as much attention to them before, which caused my parents to stop mid-set up to wait on a response. They wouldn't care that I wanted one, but they didn't seem to be wholly convinced that I was over Jackson, and the addition of body art would only serve to confirm it.

"No, not now. But sometimes I want to cover my birthmark," I admitted.

"Your birthmark is a conversation starter," my mother asserted, placing lasagna and bread on the table.

"What conversation is that? 'What's up with that freaky mark on your back?'"

"It's not freaky, it's adorable. The only thing freaky about it was it got darker instead of fading. By the time you were five, it was noticeable."

"What?" I stumbled out.

She shrugged. "I took you to the pediatrician about it. He said it was odd but never seemed concerned about it. I didn't think you had a birthmark, it went unnoticed for so long. I didn't feel like mother of the year for missing it."

You didn't notice it because it wasn't there. My head flooded with questions that I wasn't sure she would be able to answer twenty-one years later. Was there a seismic event, like me being lost for several hours only to be found and marked, or something as simple as a stranger touching me to give me a compliment, that my mother failed to tell me about in the many recountings of my childhood?

Shoveling salad into my bowl, I reined in the racing questions so that I could probe without causing alarm.

"That's weird. Did Gloria notice it?" Gloria was my mother's friend who watched me when I wasn't at my grandparents.

"No, I thought she'd be the first. She was so attentive to you all." My mother faded into grave nostalgia about Gloria, a woman she'd befriended in the salon. They'd become fast friends and she'd watched me and Forest.

"She was so fascinated by you two. Absolutely adored your curious natures." My mother offered me a tight smile. The many stories of my childhood showed that my parents often saw that curiosity as a blessing and a curse. My mother's reminiscing eclipsed into sadness. Gloria had moved away in my teens. They stayed in touch initially but eventually their daily conversations where she'd call to chat with my mother and wouldn't get off the phone until she'd spoken to us faded. She'd always seemed just as invested in our lives as our parents were. When the calls stopped, my mother wasn't the only one who felt her absence.

Now, I couldn't help but wonder if there was more to Gloria's absence.

"Have you attempted to get in contact with her?" Forest asked. I was grateful that I wasn't the only person asking questions.

"She no longer has the same number. I searched for her on Facebook and Instagram, hoping to reconnect, but no luck."

Hearing the sorrow in my mother's voice, I changed the subject, but the nagging feeling that Gloria's presence in our life wasn't coincidental remained.

"So, Forest, what's your new adventure?" my father asked, swooping in to change the subject and lift my mother's mood. Or at least redirect her because she quickly switched gears to mother mode. Forest grumbled a curse under his breath. He endured the interrogation by keeping his mouth full to avoid answering their questions, winking at me when a different set of questions were cast at me when he wasn't able to answer.

When my father left the table to get dessert, Forest scrolled through his phone while sipping from his wine glass.

"Werewolves are real? What the fuck?" he sputtered, putting his glass down. More curses of disbelief came as he continued to scroll.

Turning his phone, he showed me what was trending on Twitter. Variations of the hashtag and a video of a man clearly changing from an animal to a wolf. Knowledge of the supernatural world wouldn't come in with a whimper but rather a bang. And it had.

Taking out my phone, I scoured my social media account to find variations of hashtags, comments, and posts that werewolves were real. Magic is real was also trending, but that wasn't the first time for that, and when it did trend, it never had anything to do with actual magic. Usually it was a publicity stunt. Except this time, it was about magic. There was a video of two magic wielders fighting in the streets. Another person's lithe graceful movements identifying him as a vampire had taken down one of the witches with a strike, knocking them to their butt then feeding from them.

My breathing came at short inefficient clips before my mother moved closer to see what we were looking at. Just as we were trying to show her, our phones went blank. For several minutes, they cycled through restarting. I didn't share Forest's frustration and was thankful for the manipulating work of techno witches. I hoped this was damage control and not a big reveal.

Forest's phone restarted first and he was frantically scrolling again. Blinking several times. "What the—?" he blew out, flustered. "I know I saw it. You saw it, right?" he asked, turning to me for confirmation. My mother looked at our wine glasses, relieved us of them, and returned to the table with a cloying smile and water.

The rigid creases deepened each time Forest looked at his phone. It served as a reminder of the disconcerting reality of techno magic. It hurt that I couldn't do anything to soothe his anxiety and doubt. His fingers moved quickly over the keyboard. I suspected he was contacting others for confirmation they'd seen it, too. Tomorrow would be filled with speculations, conspiracy theories, and gaslighting as supernaturals initiated their campaign to clean up the mishap.

To distract my brother, I asked about his new endeavor and updates about his life, and we scheduled a date for dinner the following month. That sent a pang through me. I was setting up a normal event when my life was so far from it. There was a very real chance that this may be my last meal with them.

The evening ended with me satisfied that my family had no connection to the supernatural world, and my parents satisfied with my brother's dallying with becoming a web designer. My thoughts remained with Gloria, recounting her interest in me, which I'd attributed to her being my mother's friend, not that she might be responsible for making me a vessel for Dark Caster magic. Was she a Dark Caster herself, or during the times I was in her care simply exposed me to one?

I had so many questions and wasn't sure where to get the answers.

But I needed them.

As we said our goodbyes, I clung to my family tighter as they made gallant efforts not to look at me suspiciously.

Each step toward the SUV felt like I was states away.

I didn't care what I needed to do; this would not be my last time seeing my family.

19

"Be safe, honey, and tell your friend…" my mother called out from the door, letting the latter draw out as she waited for a name so she could start her investigative process.

When I responded with a coy smile only, she returned it with a smirk of annoyance.

Zareb brushed against my leg, letting his presence be known. I opened the door and fumbled with placing my leftovers in the back seat to give him time to jump in.

Once we were at the end of the block, Zareb revealed himself, hopped into the back seat, and helped himself to my food.

"Rude! How did you know that was for you?"

Sharing the arrogance and air of self-entitlement of his owners, he looked me up and down, donned his cloak, and noisily returned to eating. Nothing could convince me it wasn't a taunt.

A turbulent wind hit the SUV so hard, I struggled to keep it centered on the street. The car's steer assist attempted to right the SUV, but it spun out of control and my only option was to bring the car to a stop in front of the nature preserve.

Glowing eyes peered from the thicket of trees and advanced toward me. I expected animal, not Emory—the dhole, in human form—swiftly moving toward me with another person next to him.

He stepped in front of the car. "Hello, Luna." He grinned. Technically we were on the same team, right? Everything about him and his disgruntled partner screamed danger. I wanted to be away from them. The option to force them out of my way was snatched from me when the car shut off.

His partner was a witch. A techno. They were quickly becoming my least favorite magic wielders. The world of technology gave them too much power. We were at the whims of their discretion. Inconspicuously, I slid my hand toward the cup holders where I'd placed the stun gun and pepper spray.

Another man appeared on the back seat, passenger side. Emory's sharp gaze moved from me, and a half smile curled his lips as he pulled a stake from his back pocket. Darting to the right, he collided with a new arrival and with preternatural speed, plunged the stake into the vampire, holding him down until he vanished into dust, denying him the opportunity to feed to survive.

Before Emory could stand, a meaty fist slammed into the passenger window. When I turned my head to avoid the shards, he opened the door. I engaged the pepper spray. Zareb revealed himself and lunged at the person, sending him crashing to the ground and hammering into Zareb, trying to dislodge the grip he had on the man's arm.

I attempted to start the car. Nothing.

Damn. Nothing. I hated techno witches with a passion.

More people revealed themselves. I tried to determine who was friend or foe. Fighting erupted and multiple people were trying to get to the car while others stopped them. I was sure all of them wanted me but for different reasons. The appearance of the royals and Anand was the one assurance that at least two people were on my side: Anand and Dominic.

Emory stopped his attack on what I believe was a witch. With magic at their disposal, witches tended to be lacking in combat skills. He craned his neck to look at the royals, relaxing when Areleus's magic slammed into the witch and with one flash of movement, his claws were at the offending witch. Helena attacked with the same ferocity and indiscrimination, giving Dominic and Anand pause. They were clearly trying to disable only the Awakeners and not anyone from either Conventicle. Three shades swooped in from the sky. One grabbed Emory and soared to the sky with him. A small look of satisfaction moved over Helena's face. Dominic sent a magical spear into the creature. It shuddered and bucked. Dominic struck him in the chest with fire, forcing the shade to drop Emory, who fell too fast. Quick, sharp movements of Dominic's hand slowed his descent. Helena, meeting Emory on the landing, punched him twice, dazing him before her claws slashed over his neck. Dominic had very little time to react, directing his attention to Peter, who had appeared next to Areleus. The dark exchange of camaraderie that passed between Peter and his father brought a snarl to Dominic's face. Darkness loomed, fire blazed in his eyes, magic stifled the air. He slung a rapid fire of rounded magical orbs at his father, who disabled them, with Peter's assistance, while inching in my direction. I looked around. The fighting continued, bodies littered the street, blood stained the ground where someone had disappeared or was taken away. The crowd had thinned. I had no idea where the techno witch was.

I tried to turn on the car. Nothing. Was it disabled or was the witch still around? Surely they had better things to worry about than keeping me confined. A cloud loomed then engulfed Helena and she gasped for breath as it siphoned her oxygen. Peter took notice.

"Find them," he ordered, and a swarm of shades appeared, viciously plowing through any obstacles to their targets with claws and magic, winnowing over the area. Within moments the cloud had receded. Doubled over, Helena hungrily took in breaths. Dominic risked a glimpse in her direction; an innate sibling need to make sure she was okay. It cost him. His father lobbed a fiery ball at him, but Dominic disabled it before it could reach him. The distraction was enough for Helena to get to Dominic. Shock and anger weathered his features as he looked at her claws that she'd shoved into his stomach. His blood spilling over her hand. Acceptance followed his initial shock at her betrayal. When she yanked her hand back, he grabbed the arm, and dropped to his knees, bringing her with him. His claws pierced her skin while his mouth moved slowly. The magic-inhibiting marks started winding over her arms as she fought frantically with her free hand to get away from him. Flailing and jerking, delivering hard blows to force him to release her.

I made another attempt to start the car and nearly wept with relief when it did. I barreled toward Areleus who was moving toward Dominic and Helena. Smashing into Areleus, I sent him back several feet. He might be injured but he wasn't dead. With his extraordinary healing abilities, I had just a matter of minutes.

Hopping out of the car with the stun gun in one hand and pepper spray in another, I blasted Helena. She shrieked at the stun gun touching her skin, her eyes blinking erratically trying to clear them of the pepper spray.

Dominic held on to her, trying to complete the spell. When I knelt next to him, he released her and the markings disappeared from her arm. He took hold of my hand and we stood. He said Anand's name and a word I couldn't make out. A code word, perhaps. I didn't see him anywhere but knew he'd hear it. Dominic pulled me into his arms, and moments later my head was spinning and we were outside the underworld's estate.

He scanned the area, and when Anand emerged from the left, they looked at each other. I tried reading the nonverbal communication. Anand approached. More looks were exchanged. Dominic's brows furrowed together, hesitating before he spoke.

"Things are about to change—probably terrible before better. I won't—"

Anand held up a hand and gave him a withering half smile. "I'll save you the trouble. I'm with you. I always knew there would be eventual fallout. If I'm drawn into it, so be it. I've chosen a side. It's yours."

"I need you to stay away for a few days. I'll find you."

Anand grinned. "No you won't. I'll be found when I want to be."

I don't think there were any truer words stated.

Dominic nodded and they exchanged another look.

"You two can hug," I suggested, prompting identical looks of disapproval. "Fine." I wrapped Anand in a hug. He stiffened, gave me two obligatory pats on the back, and quickly pulled away and was gone.

"Where did he go?"

"He has a safe house. I always thought it was best no one knew of it. I can contact him when he's needed."

"You two just plan for the worst in all cases."

"We plan for the worst because the worst is often inevitable." He drew me to him, cupped the back of my head, pressed a kiss to me, and I was plunged into darkness.

When the dimness cleared, Dominic held me to him while my vision cleared and head settled.

"I'm fine," I croaked. I was far from fine, and I was sure he was, too. There was no fine or okay after witnessing Helena and Areleus betray Dominic. Even if Dominic thought the worst of his father, it was doubtful he considered he was capable of this.

Dominic released me and I stood. We were surrounded by verdant trees so vivid they seemed digitally enhanced. Floral scent inundated the air, and I relaxed into feeling safe. There was something welcoming about it.

Dominic looked down at his wet shirt. The injury had likely healed, but an expression passed over his face showing a wound of betrayal that undoubtedly wouldn't heal.

"I hate that I have irreparably changed your life," I whispered.

He shook his head. "Now it's time to irreparably change theirs."

He stepped forward and pressed his palm to the air, sparking to life a silver undulation. It pulsed back with force. A growl reverberated in his chest. Pushing harder into it, the muscles of his neck distended as the barrier in front of us ripped away to reveal a mirror image of the space we'd left. Flowering trees intermingled with brightly colored poplar trees. Several dirt trails led deeper into the forest. Dominic took my hand and we passed through the entrance. With a few movements of his hand he produced flashes of light that wove together the shimmering barrier.

"Where are we?" I whispered.

"Vita. It's an extension of my home."

"They don't seem to want guests," I pointed out, acknowledging the effort it took to get through the ward.

"It's better that there's some resistance. Gives the visitor time to rethink their decision."

"You have that information and you still decided to enter!" I understood why he sent Anand away, but I was having a hard time figuring out why we were traipsing in places that clearly didn't want guests.

"He did," said a sibilant voice from the trees. A long, jagged tail darted out. Dominic grabbed it before the point of it punctured his face. Using his grip he jerked it, bringing a man into view before Dominic used the tail to swing him and slam him into a tree. The man recovered, turning to display fangs and slitted eyes. He charged at Dominic with black nails sharpened to dagger points and putrid green tips. Dominic moved back, avoiding and blocking the creature, human, or whatever the hell the aggressive man was. His face had a rounded docile appearance with full lips, pudge nose, and wide eyes that became slitted on demand. Dominic's objective seemed to be avoiding being sliced by the man's nails.

"Dominicus, just a little touch," the man taunted.

"I don't have time for your games. Stop it," Dominic demanded, holding the arms and smashing his head until the man-creature's nose bled, then pushing him away. Dominic jumped back in time to miss the man-creature's tail whipping at him. Dominic grabbed it and gave it a jerk, collapsing the man to the ground, then he was on the creature, his claws at its throat.

"Boys, that's enough," a melodic voice commanded, immediately bringing them to their feet.

Her dewy copper skin complemented her jade-color dress with a crisscross neckline. The fit hit the pronounced curves of her body. Thick dark hair was pulled back at the nape of her neck in an elegant low bun. Sharply defined cheeks and jawline made her strikingly beautiful. Her amiable smile reached her erudite amber eyes and should have been comforting, but pleasing looks, gentle smiles, and seemingly affable ways had proven lately to be camouflage for cruel and violent people.

Stopping in front of Dominic, she kissed him lightly on the cheek.

"Hello, son. What has Areleus done to bring you to me?"

20

*H*is mother. The woman Areleus had a transactional relationship with to create his children. Yeah, she was going to be as gentle as kitten cuddles. Right before they claw you. Even with her sweetness to Dominic, I was reluctant to change my opinion.

She gave me a cursory look. I was unable to give her my undivided attention because I was distracted by the unobstructed view of the creature Dominic had fought and the man with the bird-like features who joined him. Set in a humanly round face was a hawkish nose, intense beady eyes, and ears so flat against his head they seemed nonexistent. His silver hair was cut close to the scalp except for a few that were too long and lifted from his head. The avian movement of his head was the most disturbing thing about the man-creature.

"Dragar," she addressed the creature who fought with Dominic, "let the others know that the trespasser is my son. He will be allowed to leave."

"And his guest?" he asked, his words a sibilant hiss.

"I don't know yet. It depends on the reason behind my son's visit."

Yeah, I called it. Without another word, she turned and headed back in the direction she came. Dominic started to follow but stopped when he noticed I wasn't moving.

"Luna?"

"I won't be a prisoner again. She has to let me leave."

"She'll let you leave."

"Her statement seemed to contradict that," I challenged.

He sighed, rubbing his hand over the light shadow on his beard. "Luna, we need her help. I will not let her keep you here."

His mother turned around with a smile so genteel, it urged all my protective defenses to relax. I wasn't falling for it. Weaponless, the only thing I had was distance and the ability to land enough distracting hits before getting the hell out of the garden of creepy creatures. So I was going to keep that advantage.

"Luna." With the same quick eerie movement as her son, she was directly in front of me, offering me another of her enchantingly disarming smiles.

Still not buying it.

"He will not make that decision. I will."

"Mother," he snapped.

"Dominicus, you visit me with the stench of humans and supernaturals on you, and you brought this creature of the unknown." She turned again and continued her walk toward her destination.

I'm a creature of the unknown. This place is the freaking Island of Doctor Moreau and I'm suspect?

Humility. It was a look I wasn't used to seeing on Dominic. He wore it with an aversion and unfamiliarity.

"I had no other place to go," he admitted. His admission stopped her in her tracks.

"What has Areleus done?" she ground out, drawing her lips back in a scowl. The avian creature was showing distress at her display of anger.

Dominic nudged his chin forward, urging her to continue. We navigated along one of the trails to a house that made Dominic's home diminutive in comparison.

A massive and stately white Greek revival home entrance had equally impressive columns greeting us. Beautiful flowering vines wound up the sides of the home. It was an enchanting view until I noticed the vines were in constant sinuous movement and were pulling away from the house and reaching for me. Dominic eased me closer to him.

"Mother."

With a wave of her hand, the vines settled back against the home in the illusion of decoration.

Opening the elaborately decorated iron doors and standing on each side of the entry as sentries was a menagerie of more peculiar creatures.

"Stand down, it's just Dominicus."

"Dominic," he corrected.

She tossed a look in his direction that profoundly rejected his suggestion. The sound of her shoes clicking over the marble floors echoed in the minimally decorated space. No art or a lot of home décor. Walls decorated by ornate wainscoting that I stared at too long, expecting them to do something disturbing.

As she continued to escort us through the house with its distinctive columns and archways, I got glimpses of the peculiar person who occupied it. The evergreen walls looked as if they were made of crushed velvet. What could have easily looked gauche held a level of refinement that embodied his mother. She guided us to a sitting area of four chairs. Dominic sat directly in front of her. I sat next to him, closest to the room's exit.

"Why are you here with your creature?"

I think I preferred the description 'toy' or 'human' that Areleus and Helena used.

"It's Luna," I provided.

She cut her eyes at me and said my name slowly, tasting all the letters and exhibiting the talent her children possessed to make it sound like a curse or defilement.

Moments ticked by as I remained under her cool unyielding assessment.

"I'm Ileana," she eventually provided with a reluctance I didn't understand.

Dominic spilled everything to her, giving freely what he'd held from his father and the others. His mother stayed expressionless throughout the telling. She frowned, seemingly drifting in and out of contemplation.

"He betrayed you for power he already has? It makes no sense."

"It's not power he already has. He wants control of the shades. It would give him a small army with far more capabilities than the one he has. I don't believe he wants the supernaturals to be in the shadows anymore. He wants complete dominance, and the Dark Caster will give him that."

Her gaze trailed over Dominic with a boastful look of pride. "He fears you. You've exhibited something that makes him believe he can't win against you."

Dominic gave her an indolent shrug. The bank of fire that had muted flared in his eyes. He didn't seem to have a problem with their internal battle for power; it was the betrayal that seemed to sting the most. Or was it that he'd never anticipated it? I wondered which betrayal hurt the most, Areleus's or Helena's.

"Easy, son."

Her gentle coaxing words didn't stop his spiral into barely contained anger. Fire pulsed in his eyes, claws embedded in the arms of his chair, and his strong magical energy swirled.

His mother watched him with slight amusement and

concern. "I've always admired and despised Areleus for his power-thirst," she admitted.

"He has no restraint," Dominic said. "The shades are loose, he's aligned himself with the Dark Caster, and he's destroying allies. This will not get him the results he wants."

"The alliance with the Dark Caster will be temporary. Betraying him is imminent, so I'm not sure of the problem."

"I would have agreed, but this Dark Caster is strong, cunning. He has access to more magic, which makes him a force like I haven't seen before. And if he gets to Luna, I'm not sure how to counter him." The unspoken part of his sentence held a complex tapestry of emotions. How did he counter Peter when Helena and Areleus were Peter's allies?

His voice lowered, uneasiness in his admission of someone being stronger than him.

Ileana's brows furrowed as stony eyes gave me a once-over. She clasped her fingers together. The silence stretched and became heavier with each passing moment.

"You want to maintain the status quo," she surmised, showing the same disdain that the royals and the magically inclined held for humans. "They want exposure. Change life. Reveal the existence of magic and its magical creatures. It would allow more procreation and change the power balance of the world. I'm not sure I see the problem."

"At the loss of human autonomy and freedom," I provided.

She frowned at my response, or just the mere fact I spoke. Cool eyes trailed from my feet up to my head. She was clearly annoyed.

"The humans will still have the illusion of autonomy and freedom. Just a change in the hierarchical system. Instead of living alongside each other in separate systems, it will be as one. Survival of the fittest."

"Humans are capable of surviving against supernaturals who possess magic, preternatural speed, strength, and limited weaknesses that can be used to keep them in check?"

She shrugged. "Then they don't survive."

I slumped back in the chair, disillusioned. Trying to appeal to the humanity of people who didn't seem to possess a drop of it was draining.

"No system is perfect but this one is the fairest," Dominic pointed out.

"Fairest." She rolled her eyes.

"Yes. Supernaturals must adhere to established rules and maintain their anonymity. They can't do so at the expense of humans." He glanced at me because that had been insisted upon as a priority when the terms of Dominic's intervention were renegotiated. "When the rules are broken, I handle it."

After a moment of consideration, she said, "Release the prisoners from the Perils. Vadim will cause his typical disruption. He will be an efficient agitator to the shifters and the witches." A shifter immune to silver and with magic was more than just an agitation, he was a menace. "The vampire is the most mercurial of them all. Tell Roman he'll be allowed free rein, but only his line can exist. His ego will convince him that his line is the only one worthy of existing. He'll kill all the other vampires. He's quite good at that. Roman would be the one to cause the most problems."

"His claws are poisonous and mute the magic of anyone they touch," Dominic pointed out.

She dismissed the information with a wave of her hand. "You've encountered him on many occasions, how often have you fallen prey to them? You are a superior fighter. Roman will be of no concern to you."

Dominic appeared agitated by having to remember the times Roman had successfully disabled his magic with his poison. "I felt them enough times to be wary."

"He's dangerous and a threat to all. His release will be an adequate distraction for Peter." She scowled at the name he was going by. "A touch from Roman's claws affects Peter as it does all of us. After he's caused the necessary damage, declaw him. I'm confident you can find a spell that will adequately prevent them healing back. None of his sired have shown to have those abilities. He would be a non-issue. If he remains a concern, once he's served his purpose…" She flicked her wrist. A flippant response to the suggestion of murder. "Celeste is a different story. She's too powerful. I predict the witch will be a problem for you. There will always be someone who wants her free—to curry favor with her. Her extermination will be far more beneficial than preservation of her life."

Dominic seemed to be giving the suggestion consideration. "She spelled herself so that her life is linked to the most powerful witch bloodline. If she dies, they do, too."

I had been reduced to advocating for people who hated me.

"I made an oath to Madeline and her coven that Celeste would be spared until they found a way to break the spell."

She shrugged. "Celeste is the reason Roman is the threat he is," she provided in an effort to coax Dominic into her solution.

Fuck. Helena didn't have a fighting chance of being decent with these people as parents.

"So, your suggestion is to let my world descend into chaos, murder, and dominating the weakest and maybe…just maybe a few humans survive? A magical carpet bomb and then what?" I asked.

Dominic's head rested back on the chair, his eyes fixed on the ceiling. "Then I go in after the wreckage and clean up," he said. "My rules, alliances with those standing, and everything different. New."

"Yes, or you can do nothing. I've always wondered why you all got involved with the humans and supernaturals. Boredom?"

"Someone had to do it." The underworld in all its scariness actually played a vital role in reining in magic wielders.

"So," I drawled in sheer incredulity, "anarchy is the solution we're going with?" My sarcasm irritated Ileana, but at that moment, I didn't give a damn.

Dominic shifted position, studying me for a long time, which prompted his mother to do the same before studying the way he looked at me, her eyes narrowing in scrutiny, her lips twisting into a moue.

When he spoke, he said, "It's been this way for centuries, our level of involvement changing, but we worked as enforcers of the rules. I'd be the first to admit that it teeters in a very delicate balance, but as I stated, it is functional."

"Is functional all you want?" Ileana challenged.

"I believe it better serves my purpose than allowing chaos to reign, sorting through the wreckage, and trying to make something of the tattered alliances, broken promises, and betrayals. Areleus has made quite a mess of things."

Areleus killing the members of the New Conventicle surely led to the existing Conventicle believing Dominic's betrayal was imminent. Further straining their fragile alliance. Whichever effect it had, Areleus and Peter at the helm signified a change in the status quo. Would they fight to keep their presence known or would they fall in line and make taking over human rule their new objective?

"You want things as they were?"

He nodded. "Or close to how they were. I know drastic measures will be necessary to make a point, but not what you are suggesting."

Deep brackets formed along Ileana's face. She inhaled a deep breath through her nose. "If they stop the progression of the new world, what will happen to my Helena?"

Dominic's jaw clenched, her betrayal still raw.

"You know that is Helena's way. She sides with whomever

she believes will be the victor." Ileana preened. That must be mother speak for 'my daughter is a cruel opportunist.'

Weird thing to be proud of? A daughter who was only loyal to the one who wielded the most power and who would allow her malicious ways to go unimpeded with an occasional word of rebuke that she'd ignore. Her violent fits of rage. A fashionable sociopath.

"Dominic?" she said, urging a response.

"How am I to treat her betrayal?" he asked with careful restraint. His expression betrayed his emotions.

"The same as you have in the past. Forgiveness. She has her ways."

"She continues to have these unpredictable ways because she never suffers real consequences. There must be consequences."

"You will not kill my daughter. Do as you will with Areleus. No, not as you will, for it seems you've been more pious as of late." She skewered me with a look, assigning me blame I didn't deserve. I wasn't seeing it. Dominic wasn't as cruel as he could be—as Helena and Areleus were—but he wasn't this lamb they were making him out to be. He was the brutal being he needed to be to exist in this fierce world.

"Have I been clear, son?" she said after minutes ticked by without a response.

"I don't want to kill Helena," Dominic admitted.

"And you won't. Dominicus, you don't seem to want my advice, so why are you here?"

He explained about me temporarily dying in response to the magic being removed, then added, "I need to destroy any chance of Peter using Luna's magic and the possibility that he has magic that outmatches mine."

"Ah." She nodded over her steepled hands. She may have understood what he was asking but I had no clue. My eyes bounced between the two of them, trying to figure it out.

A slow smile curled her lips, excitement bright in her eyes. "You want me to recreate your creature?"

"No the hell he doesn't," I blurted at the same time as Dominic nodded. Nothing about that statement seemed like something I wanted to be a part of. Recreate? No thank you. Standing, I put necessary distance between me and Dominic.

The expansive room seemed too small, and panic made my body too warm and breathing too difficult. Each short-clipped breath I took did nothing to ease the rush of emotions.

"Luna," Dominic eased out in a strained voice, inching toward me as if he feared I'd scurry away. He wasn't far off. But where would I go? Outside to hang out with the other creatures I presumed his mother had created? Fondle those weird vines winding up the house, probably also her creations or 'recreations'?

"This is the best choice. A way to save your life and give you magic, too."

"At what cost!?" I snapped. I stayed put as he removed the distance between us.

"Not one greater than your life."

It was becoming increasingly uncomfortable to be under his mother's scrutiny. We seemed to be a source of entertainment that she was thoroughly enjoying. Sensing my discomfort, he extended his hand to mine. I hesitated.

"Luna, come with me."

Holding my hand, he navigated me through the massive home, walking past beautifully decorated rooms where I slowed to get a look at the people inside. People, there were actual people. The sight of them gave me an unexpected and welcome ease. Then one of the occupant's snake-slitted eyes met mine. My startled response brought a wide, fanged smile to his face. A woman walked across the sitting room, giving me a view of a tail. An older man walked toward me and flashed a smile when I noticed that his beard looked very similar to that seen on a goat and that there were small horns peeking from the mass of wavy salt and pepper hair. I stumbled back into Dominic, unable to hide my unease at the sight of all these peculiar beings. He caressed me to him and directed me into an apartment.

"Would you like something to drink?" he asked, waving to the coffee and tea bar at one end and an actual bar at the other. I was already on edge; coffee would have just added to that. Not wanting to dampen my anxiety, which was a healthy response to the idea of being 'recreated,' I declined herbal tea or alcohol.

Dominic poured a measure from the bottle of bourbon. The wafting scent had me reconsidering. Nope, I needed to keep a clear head.

"What should I call your mother?" I asked, causing Dominic to stop mid-drink from surprise.

It was the most innocuous of the many questions that flooded my mind, but at that moment it seemed oddly important. I needed to know more about her other than her being Dominic's mother, a woman who'd had a transactional relationship with Areleus in order to procreate, was a strict adherent to the tenet of survival of the fittest, considered the carpet bomb approach to ending strife, and could create unique creatures. Overwhelmed, I needed to know something simple about her.

"Ileana is fine," he said.

"Is she a queen or some nobility? Lady?"

"This is her domain, and she has been the queen of other domains in the past. Not by birth or marriage but conquest."

"Of course, conquest. I want this space, so I'll annihilate anyone in my way and take it. Please and thank you," I snipped back. I worked at easing the frown off my face but gave up.

"Everyone who lives here is one of her creations. She's their god. She won't take offense if you simply call her by her name as long as it's not accompanied by disrespect. Those who wish to curry favor will refer to her as Lady Ileana," he explained.

"What is this place, her retirement home?"

"She's had such a tumultuous history that when she travels, she is always met with apprehension. She visits us and other places very seldom."

What a charming and diplomatic way of saying his mother moved through the dimensions of the underworld causing havoc to the point that her presence bred suspicion. I got a clearer picture of why Areleus chose her as their mother.

"Her distaste for 'humans' supernaturals.'" That was a hell of a misnomer. How could they be ours when we lived unaware of their existence and were subjected to their magic when they failed to maintain their anonymity?

"They have weaker magic. She's unable to appreciate their ability to navigate the human world unnoticed."

"You've done it." There was an otherness to them. Enough to take notice of their presence in any space.

"Not effortlessly. I don't go as unnoticed as I should." He studied me for a long moment as he took a sip from his glass. "Those aren't the questions you want to ask, are they?"

"Of course not. You asked her to 'recreate' me. How can she do that? What is she?"

"She's a dark deity with the ability to create life."

"Is that the main reason your father wanted children with her?"

"They chose each other. My father is powerful in his own right, but he'd hoped we'd be gifted with the ability to create life as well. There's always the risk of dilution of the magic when the parents are not the same. That happened with us."

"You can't do 'recreation' or 'create'?"

"I believe I can have children. That is a form of creation."

"You know what I mean. Like your mother."

"No one can. She's quite powerful. My magic is strong because of her, and I was able to create my hellhounds."

Snapping my gaping mouth shut, I blinked several times. They might not be humanlike, but they were intelligent creatures. And Dominic created them.

"I'm not sure what my recreation would even be but I'm pretty damn sure it's something you should have discussed with me first."

Dominic's solemn look of introspection was a clear indicator that he didn't agree. A recreation needed to be done, so it would be done. The world needed to be righted, so he'd do what was needed to make it happen without consult from those involved.

I dropped onto the sofa. "Give me details of what you asked of your mother."

"You exist as a vessel of magic. Technically you aren't alive. You're, for lack of a better word, an inanimate object. The magic can exist without you—you can't without it. I need her to recreate you into a living being that exists alongside the magic. My hope is that you will emerge as the person you are now but with access to that magic. Not just an object that lives because of it."

The explanation sounded worse.

"Dragar was once a snake."

"And she made him into the thing that likes to greet people by attacking them?"

"Just me. He was playing with me. Others aren't treated as kindly."

"You want your mother to play Doctor Moreau with me?"

He shook his head. "What he is was my mother's choice. They all are. She will make you Luna—Luna with magic."

Catching the morose hitch in his last words, I studied him.

"You don't want this, do you?"

He sighed. Placing the drink on the table next to the sofa,

he sat down, pulling me to him and positioning me until I straddled him. I'd become so comfortable being around blood that I barely noticed the stains on his shirt from his sister's assault. My fingers languidly traced the contours of his jaw. Closing his eyes, he moved into my touch. He took my hand in his and kissed it.

"I don't like making decisions out of a desperate circumstance. The way things are, you will die at someone's hands, either by Peter when he takes away all your magic, or someone else will kill you because you've been linked too many times to the misfortunes that have occurred. I'd do everything in my power to stop it. I don't have my father and sister at my side. They're killing those I could turn to as allies. All they know is that Peter wants you. His persistence in going after you will not go unnoticed. If your recreation is the success I think it will be, you wouldn't be a source of magic for the Dark Caster. You'll have your own magic and be a force in your own right. That, I look forward to seeing."

Pulling my hands from his, my fingers ran over his face, rubbing out the furrow in his brow. "Tell your face that," I teased. "But?" The unresolved question hung in the air. A burden too difficult for him to bear.

"I've grown to find comfort in you. You're very *human*." I could tell that in the past such distinction didn't hold the same value. "As much as a recreation is needed to keep you safe, I fear that you won't be Luna, my Luna, when it's done," he admitted.

A slight flush moved over the pronounced lines of his cheeks. Gently, I ran my fingers over them, the heat of his body warming my fingers.

"I find more than just comfort in you. I'll take a world I don't understand, because you're in it," I admitted.

He kissed me deeply, his tongue exploring my mouth, hands roving over me before caressing me to his body. "Good. I'm finding it very difficult imagining my life without you. There's a wholeness when you are around. And you have this surreal way of making me feel grounded. I don't want to lose that. I *can't* lose that. Or you."

"I'll always be your Luna."

They were supposed to be words of comfort and assurance. But they felt like an oath and acceptance of me being his and he being mine. Despite hating the world he lived in, I wanted Dominic. Every intention I had to stay away from him and this world seemed to fall away. This world was the baggage he came with.

I stayed, pressed against him. Despite the warm security of his arms around me, I couldn't dismiss what I'd discovered about my sitter, Gloria. So, I relayed everything that occurred during dinner with my family, including the werewolf that was trending along with people discovering magic. I wasn't the least surprised that Dominic knew about it and took part in it being handled.

"Could Gloria have been a Dark Caster? Don't you find it peculiar that she just conveniently disappeared from our lives?"

"What did she look like?" he asked.

I described her and he seemed to be trying to remember if he'd encountered her.

"She was probably an emissary or follower. Despite supernaturals in your world living in the shadows, it is impossible to be completely unnoticed in any world. There's always a group of people who know of their existence, are followers or acolytes." He gave me a tight smile. "And that is another issue humans will have to deal with if there is ever a reckoning between humans and the supernatural world. Humans will have defectors." It was a reminder how important it was to maintain the system we had. It just needed to be enforced better, with protections extended to humans. "I'm not sure if she was a Dark Caster or someone who worked for one, but how does this information change anything, Luna?"

"If we find her, maybe she could reverse what was done to me," I suggested. "Recreation seems like such an extreme option," I added when he seemed unmoved by my proposal.

"The most extreme is your death. And that's what they want, Luna. You dead."

Knowing this fate was disheartening. Whether or not I'd performed the spell that released the prisoners from the Perils, I would have been swept into this world because of what I am.

Dominic cradled my face. "You're a tool for Peter and you're at his whim. You know how I feel about this situation. I wish there was an alternative, but there isn't. Understand, this is the best way to save your life. Will you do it?"

I nodded. He sighed, pulling me closer to him.

"Now we must hope my mother agrees."

"What? You think she wouldn't?" I pulled from his hold to look at him.

"My mother is very protective and ungenerous with her magic," he said.

"Not even at your request."

"She'd give it more consideration, but my mother has never had feelings of maternal obligation. If it is a sound decision, it will be granted."

"She was very insistent that you not kill your sister."

"Yes, she values our lives as an extension of who she is. If she doesn't feel that my retaliation toward Helena is satisfactory, she'll exact her own because Helena attempted to kill me. No one kills my mother's creations without retaliation."

"Well, hopefully she'll be equally invested in my life."

"She won't have to, because I will."

Dominic decided to seek his mother's answer the next day and took me to the shower, where we attempted to wash away the savagery of the day, his touches a desperate need as they slid over me. He was ravenous. No matter how many times he found some satisfaction in me, he remained unsated. Curled up in bed, in the apartment he'd either claimed for the night or was his own since he showed a great familiarity with it, Dominic held me. Last thing I heard was "My Luna," before I drifted off. I was okay with being his Luna, but I was left with a vestige of apprehension that I wasn't going to be the same Luna any longer.

But if his mother agreed, I would do it.

21

Ileana's stony eyes took me in, running them over the slip-on ballet shoes I had on from the day before and the billowy yellow dress Dominic had given me that morning to wear. My face was a vibrant glow from the endless night of sex. He had been a lustful distraction, but it was only a matter of time before the sex would be interrupted by my stomach growling. It was. The apartment had a meager supply of food. I ate a bagel and fruit and then we searched for his mother. He was greeted with a kiss on the cheek, me with a look of apprehension. When asked if she'd considered his request, the seconds of silence stretched to minutes.

"Will you do this for me?" he asked.

She frowned. I was treated to more scrutiny.

I was hyperaware of her every movement and the tension-laden silence as she stood and headed for the door.

"Luna, come."

Dominic shot me a warning look, urging me not to suggest she ask me to follow rather than demand. I met the challenge and followed her.

She led me into a garden. Passing the beautiful gold-color

lilies, black-and-white dotted roses, striped tiger lilies, and an array of florals I'd never seen before, we approached a small cottage suite where we were greeted by a man. Or rather another one of her man-like. A combination of panther and human, he stretched to a height close to seven feet. Silky black fur and taut muscles covered his anthropomorphic form. My eyes were drawn to his arm where I saw fur-covered digits instead of a paw. He wore shoes, so I assumed he had feet. It was like standing face to face with a panther.

"Hello, Luna."

I responded with a start, surprised by his clear, deep, euphonious voice. He smiled.

"Expecting me to roar?" he asked, airy laughter in his tone.

"I don't know what I was expecting," I admitted.

"That's understandable."

Okay, Luna, be normal. Don't try to scratch the panther-man behind his ears. And you damn sure better not rub his belly.

Forcing a tight smile on my face, I tried not to be weird, but it was a task. Chatting with a panther-man was nowhere on my life's bingo card.

"It was nice meeting you, Luna," he said, gracefully moving past us after giving Ileana a reverential bow.

Food was set out: an assortment of berries, grapes, cheeses, chocolates, and bread. After seeing flowers move, anthropomorphic animals, and all the oddities of Ileana's world, I wasn't in a rush to try the oversized strawberries that looked like they were staged for a commercial. Blueberries plumper than I'd ever seen. Large, bright green grapes. The strong scent of chocolates that looked as delectable as they smelled.

It wasn't until Ileana started eating the strawberries that I took one, chomping at it with caution. Ileana remained standing, so I did. She roamed around the suite, slowly eating the strawberry, carefully watching me.

"You intrigue me," she said. Demonstrating the same eerie grace of movement as the others, she devoured the distance between us in a breath of movement. Would I share similar abilities once I was recreated? Peter moved normally. But then, I'd only seen the version of him that he wanted me to see.

"What is it about you that draws my son?"

Dominic's admission yesterday felt intimate. A confession meant for my ears only. Among those like him, it could be perceived as a weakness. He wanted to be grounded to a humanity he didn't possess. For me to be the voice of reason and anchor him to humankind. Refusing to reveal our tacit secret, I remained silent under her continued inspection.

"This problem could be resolved by destroying the vessel and killing the Dark Caster, as he did with the others."

"He kept him for questioning to find out if there were others."

"When dealing with the likes of them, death is the answer. No questioning needed."

My eyeroll was automatic. Tired of death and violence being the only answer, I wanted one person to believe in an alternative. But it was foolish of me to expect it to be the person Areleus chose to make his children. Nothing she'd said since our meeting had proven otherwise. Somehow, I remained optimistic and hopeful.

"He's not human," she asserted.

"I know."

More of her narrow-eyed assessment. "Do you? He may be drawn to you for some unknown reason. He is my son. To perform his job, he needs to be cruel. Savage. Feared. People with great power and magic need a reason to abide by the rules." She inched closer to me, studying me. "What you may perceive as unnecessary, is essential, I can assure you."

"I am familiar with the way this world works." Familiar enough to be saddened by the harshness of it.

"So young," she whispered, and I knew my expression had betrayed me. As perceptive as Ileana seemed, I might as well have screamed my thoughts.

"My son will not be sacrificed to appease your need for civility," she said, returning to the table and snatching up another strawberry. As she ate it, nothing about her seemed to signify she was a terror. A woman so feared and who harbored so much disdain for other magic wielders. Another strawberry devoured, she bit thoughtfully on a chocolate. Again, space was swallowed in a blink of an eye. She looped a strand of my hair around her finger and stared at it.

"You are pretty and you have a satisfactory body. And based on the reports from his apartment, you two find great satisfaction in one another. Hours of satisfaction."

Why was this freaky family so open about discussing sex? Did I come from a family of prudes? How had I lived twenty-six years without my parents so brazenly discussing my sex life?

"Dominicus is no stranger to finding satisfaction in many ways with many others." She made a face. "Human and your betters alike. But it's the human that captures him." The last part she mused as if she was trying to make sense of a complex riddle.

The room was fraught with a discord that needed a release.

"I'm witty."

It spilled out as a joke, hoping to add some much-needed levity to the conversation.

Head canted, her brows drew together. "I don't see that as being true."

Ouch.

"Perhaps I'll never understand the draw. But I accept that it exists. I question whether you will be a strength or weakness for my son. Know that if you are the fall of Dominicus, you will not survive the day."

"Of course, because you can't simply say, take care of my son the way I believe he will take care of you."

The sensible part of me wished I'd held my tongue. As each minute ticked by, I scolded myself. When she started to speak, I expected her to respond with venom or more threats, but she didn't. She made a choked sound I assumed was a laugh. Rusty from lack of use.

"You are a funny little creature. I see that you've mistaken it as wit." She shrugged it off. "Very well."

I wanted to debate it, but I wasn't very funny and my wit was debatable. But I was good for a smile or two.

"Will you?" she inquired, returning to my comment about taking care of him.

"I want to," I fumbled out, the words spilling so freely from me it felt mystical. This should have been said to him first. My feelings and intentions should have been voiced to him before sharing them with his mother. This world made everything ass backward.

"Helena betrayed him," she acknowledged in a whisper, compassion and anger flooding her eyes along with the verdant green that eclipsed her amber eyes. A green that was then drowned by charcoal black. She was life and death. A creator of the peculiar beings that occupied her land. Through all her emotions, she seemed resigned to that being the way of her daughter. Another of her creations.

She frowned and stood. "They've had their share of quarrels. This one should resolve." Her hand covered mine, confirming my assumption that this wasn't an observation but a request for me to somehow intervene. I had no idea how I could help because I was firmly in Make-Helena-Pay-Camp. Theirs wasn't a typical sibling quarrel. She'd stabbed her brother in the gut with every intention of stopping him permanently or hurting him to the point that he wouldn't be an obstacle to their plans. Remembering his sorrowful look of betrayal made me resolute. I didn't want her to die, but if he removed her magic and never returned it or made sure her remaining days were spent imprisoned in the Perils, she was deserving of it.

Ileana's gaze moved over me in accusation, assigning blame to me for their conflict. With a forced smile she stood and headed for the exit in the opposite direction.

"Tell Dominicus that he and his creature are to meet me in my chambers at seven."

"Luna's fine," I called after her. 'His human' was bad enough, but 'creature' seemed like a different level of disrespect.

Ileana made no indication that she'd heard me. Things had gone downhill fast and I had no idea how.

When I exited the suite, the panther hybrid was waiting. He flashed a grin at my handful of chocolates and me desperately trying to eat the ones I'd shoved in my mouth so I could speak.

"Hi—" I waited for a name.

"Sabin," he offered. "I'll escort you to the house. Dominic put up a flare when he closed the ward here and the others are a little upset. I don't want them to take it out on you," he told me. "They would never hurt you," he quickly added, "but they wouldn't think twice about using you to show their discontent."

"Flare?"

"Yes, the ward should be sufficient, but he put up a flare as a secondary warning, giving those who choose to enter an opportunity to rethink. The queen doesn't like visitors and it is made known." His tone led me to believe that when you entered unindicated, you didn't leave, and if you did, you would definitely not be in the same condition.

I was trying not to be rude and stare at the peculiar creature, but it was nearly impossible. A mishmash of human and animal was intriguing. Shifters seemed boring in comparison. He stopped walking. Smiling, he extended his arms out slowly and made a complete turn, giving me a full view of him. I took it all in, trying not to gape.

"You're lovely," I said. A lovely freak of nature but lovely nonetheless.

He preened. "I am." It was apparent I wasn't the first to give him that compliment.

"What is it like?" I asked. "Being created like this?"

"I don't know of any other way."

I was asking the wrong questions but had no idea which ones were right. All the information whirled in my head.

"You want to know what the recreation will be like?" he asked.

I nodded.

"Your situation is different. We were made from nothing. Your question is equivalent to you asking me to recall your birth and all that you felt. I was created like this. Not from another animal. Just a creation of her imagination. I believe you will be her first recreation. First human recreation."

So he wasn't formally a panther given humanoid characteristics. Panic overtook me. She'd never recreated a person. It had to be different. Taking slow measured breaths was the only thing keeping me from spiraling into a full-on panic attack. Had I agreed to be an experiment? Was Dominic overconfident in his mother's abilities and her ego wouldn't let her decline?

A heavy hand on my shoulder offered some comfort as the heat from it suffused through me. I hadn't realized how cold I'd become.

"The queen would never agree to something she'd fail at. There are some benefits to dealing with people with egos of her magnitude." His easy smile caused me to relax. Returning it, I started to walk again, desperate to find Dominic.

Sabin redirected me from the bedroom, where I'd

assumed Dominic would be, to a library nicer than the one in his home. Floor-to-ceiling books on mahogany shelves embellished with molding at the top and the odd, animated flowers and vines that slithered along them provided a haunting decorative flair.

Dominic, seated in a black tuxedo chair, looked up from his book. I divided my attention between him and the fantastical range of creatures milling about and reading. Some were as beautifully intriguing as Sabin, and others were disturbing. Beauty being subjective, what I found horrifying may have intrigued others. Two people who were the human embodiment of butterflies walked by. Honey-color skin, coltish bodies, oblong faces, wings tapestries of pastels. Some of my apprehension dissipated. If I came out on the other side with cute wings, I was fine with that. Dominic's gentle kiss to my neck drew my attention back to him.

After intensely studying me, he turned a pointed look on Sabin.

"Oh, get off and stop being so overprotective. I didn't say anything to your Luna that would scare her away from here." Sabin narrowed his eyes on Dominic and gave him an impish look. "Or you. So don't be giving me any looks." Sabin bristled with a dramatic wave of his arm. "I preferred broody and cynical rather than this infuriating overprotectiveness."

Dominic glared. "She's nervous about the recreation. I just wanted to ensure that the talking panther didn't make her more so."

He looked smug when he turned. "Myelinated jaguar, not panther," he corrected. "I'm always correcting them."

"You don't have to. You choose to," Dominic said, his expression mirroring Sabin's.

"I live to educate," he shot back. "There's no such thing as a panther," he muttered under his breath as he left with long, confident strides. Thinking that we had inadvertently offended him, I was relieved when he flashed me a grin.

Sabin was odd. Marooned in the world of peculiar creatures, I couldn't help but be amused that the thing he was finicky about was not being half panther.

"How was your meeting with my mother?"

I shrugged. "She very much belongs in your world."

"And you don't think you do?"

"I belong with you. I'm not sure about this world," I admitted. He looked away, a flush creeping up his cheek. I preened. Inching closer to me, he leaned down and placed his hand on my side.

"You are very adaptable, Little Luna," he growled as he moved his hand slightly, his thumb stroking over my breast. My nipple responded to his touch. I quickly scuttled back and glared at him. The prince didn't like losing any control, and this was his way of wrangling a little back. Now I was the one blushing from his intimate touch in a library full of kind-of-humans. Pseudo-animals. Or whatever. "You belong wherever I am."

The heat of his body laced around me. His lips covered mine in a deep sultry kiss.

"Your mother wants us to meet her at seven," I breathed out when the kiss ended.

He nibbled at my ear. "Then we have time." Taking my hand, he led me back to the apartment. As soon as we were in the room, his hand teasingly ran over my body, a delicious distraction that I refused to succumb to. I took his hand in mine and led him to the sofa where I urged him to sit.

"Helena sided with your father. That has to hurt and I'm sorry that happened." More so because his refusal to kill me was likely the root of it. I laced my fingers with his.

A stern frown settled on his face before it unfolded into poorly restrained anger and frustration.

"There must be a reckoning for her, but my mother's wishes will be honored."

Helena's life would be preserved. The flames that erupted

in his eyes made it clear that only her life would be spared. The punishment would be harsh.

"Punishment or not, it has to hurt," I said. Ileana's words, although convoluted as hell, stuck with me. I needed to take care of Dominic in my way. Even if that was in no other way than allowing him to vent his anger about the betrayal.

"It's not that she chose my father's side. It is Helena's nature to choose the side of strength." He pressed his lips together, unable to voice what it meant. She saw a weakness in him that led her to believe that siding with her father to disrupt and destroy what Dominic had built was the winning side. After the sacrifices and accommodations Dominic made in service to her, to protect her and make sure she didn't suffer any severe consequences for her many malicious acts, this was how she repaid him.

My lips swept lightly over his skin before making their way to his ear. "I want you to do what needs to be done to reestablish a world that will protect humans and hold supernaturals accountable if they violate the rules. I want fairness for both, and I think you do as well. Most of all, I want you to be Lord of the Underworld. By any means. I will be your anchor to make sure you never become your father, that you don't lose yourself."

Concessions would have to be made on both our parts. I had to accept that the world he occupied was darker, more turbulent, and handled with a ferocity that I wasn't accustomed to. Dominic would have to see that his way may not always be the answer, but I had a feeling he'd listen and try.

I let out a sharp gasp when I found myself on my back, Dominic's hips cradled between my legs. "Little Luna," he rumbled against my ear, "you turned out to be an unexpected treat."

"Maybe I'll get some height with the recreation," I teased. "Maybe a boost to five five, five six. Or a total giant at five seven."

His roar of laughter possessed a lightness I wasn't aware was possible in him. Whether it was for the moment or entirely, he had shrugged off the heaviness and tenebrous mood. "Like I said before, I want—need—you to come out of this as Luna, my Luna. I want you just the way you are."

But I wouldn't be just the way I was.

I'd have magic.

22

Ileana's chamber didn't display the regal, unique beauty of the other rooms. Textured pewter-color walls, thick heavy drapes covering a floor-to-ceiling window, and a somber peach glow from the lantern sconces gave the room a grim appearance. There was a bookshelf on one side of the room, filled with books, jars, and on a shelf by itself, a dagger with markings.

Ileana gave Dominic's and my clasped hands a look of cool regard, her lips forming a tight moue before her gaze trailed over Dominic's face, studying it with an intensity that would have made me uncomfortable but had no effect on him. Her low-cut white flowy maxi dress exposed toned arms and legs with each step she made toward us. Her hair pulled back in a braid gave us a full view of her features that seemed harsher under the unflattering lights.

Extending her hand to me, she gave me an expectant look, cuing me to take it. I did, and a small smile eased over her lips.

"Dominicus, she's mine now."

So, there's not a less creepy way to say that?

He nodded but hesitated, definitely sensing my unease

that I couldn't seem to marshal. After several long, measured breaths, I assured him it was okay. Or as okay as it could be, given the circumstances.

Once he was gone, with a wave of her hand, the ajar door closed completely. My attention snapped to it. Bronze illumination locks formed along it, followed by a wall of lively vines. Moments later the lights dimmed until she was just shadows of movement circling me. Following each step, I focused on the glint of the knife in her hand. Risking a glance, I looked at the shelf where the knife had been. It was gone.

"He's never been one to take the easy way out," she mused in a low, sorrow-laden voice. "Nor have I fully understood him."

With each revolution, she got closer and closer. Finally, she was directly in front of me, her eyes pensive and full of curiosity. "He chooses entropy over your destruction. I don't truly understand. You are quite lovely, but are you worth it?"

Taking her question as rhetorical, I tried to breathe normally while preparing to ward off a knife attack that I wasn't likely to survive.

"I could save him from himself and make this situation markedly better," she continued.

"But you won't," I asserted with an assurance that surprised me.

"No, I won't." A trace of sadness was in her admission. "I may not understand the plays he makes, but they have always proven to have long-term benefits. He wants you alive. I don't believe it will serve any other benefit than to make him happy. And that matters to me. Extend your arms."

Ignoring the feeling of dread that washed over me, I thought of her words. Ending my life would hurt her son. Despite her odd sensibilities and apathy to chaos or the well-being of anyone who wasn't a creation of hers, she loved her children. It was warped in its nature, but it was intrinsic in its execution.

My arms shook as I held them out. The room flooded with energy as I felt the caress of the magic around me, providing an analgesic effect that left me numb and my body lethargic. I struggled to keep my eyes open. There were some quick slashes of the knife. I saw the crimson liquid run down my arms but didn't feel a thing as Ileana lowered me to the ground. Fading in and out, I heard Ileana speaking in a rapid clip. Words rushed over me and a noticeably different magic began to slink around me. A mist floated over me as my eyelids flickered to stay open. It moved closer, spreading over me and tugging at my body. I gave in to the darkness, falling away from it and life.

Ileana's voice was a low melodic entreaty that felt so far away. She asked me to respond but I couldn't muster the energy to do so. Feeling weighted down with a boulder, I tried to push past it and through the murkiness that had consumed me. It didn't feel right. Dark, dank, and draconian. I felt misplaced. Ileana's voice became more pleading and laced with a deep sorrow. Consumed by an emptiness that I couldn't escape, desperation and fear settled in.

Ileana said my name, but my mouth couldn't form words to answer. My body wouldn't cooperate enough to give her a sign that I could hear her. That I was alive. But I wasn't alive. I didn't think I was. There was too much emptiness. I was a hollow husk. I could feel more magic tugging at my body, energy winding around it. A flare of light. I attempted to reach for it with arms that previously wouldn't cooperate. But now they floated with featherlight weight toward it, dragging the rest of me with it. I emerged from the darkness. My restricted movement was a result of being wrapped in Ileana's arms. When I squirmed, she released me with a smile of relief that made her face brighten as much as the room.

"That's you," she told me.

With each breath I took, the lights brightened like a heartbeat. Squinting at the brightness, I asked, "How do I get it to stop?"

"You tell it to and then force it to your will."

It couldn't be that easy. And it wasn't.

"Stop," I whispered.

Nothing. As the light violently pulsed, my body whirred. It was nothing like when I borrowed magic from Madeline. Everything about it was painful and wrong. A rejection of magic that wasn't mine. It was a strange dichotomy, a soothing harmonious hum and an energetic burst of adrenaline. I had no idea what to do with it.

Closing my eyes, I took in a deep breath, trying to reconcile the two opposing energies in me. Control them. Make peace with this being the new me. The new Luna. And when I opened my eyes again, the room was a muted glow around me and Ileana was standing against the wall with a smile.

"I think you will be a quick learner," she said. It was the first time there wasn't a tightness of apprehension in her voice. "You can come in," she whispered.

The vines curled away and disappeared, the bronze locks vanished, and Dominic was quickly at my side, his eyes roving slowly over me with an expectant look. Inconspicuously, I ran my hand through my hair—no horns. There wasn't a way to check my back for wings and butt for a tail.

From Dominic's smirk, it was apparent he knew what I was looking for. He stood next to me—my height hadn't changed, either.

"Luna, the same Luna," he whispered against my lips before kissing me in a wholly inappropriate manner in front of his mother. I abruptly ended the kiss and put a few inches between us, shooting a look at his mother, who was unbothered. I'd never get used to their family.

"Now it's time to teach you how to use your magic," Dominic asserted.

23

Dominic whisked me away to a large room that could only be described as minimalist. A table against the wall held a stack of spellbooks, a small metal bowl, and a tray with an array of bottles filled with various colored ingredients. One I was sure was salt. An oversized lounge chair was placed in the corner. Weapons: a sword, dagger, and sai stowed on the wall. In the middle of the room, a large rug with sigils burning in it. I could see specks of a rust-color powder on it.

"A containment circle," he said, breezily responding to the careful attention I paid to the strange rug. "Sometimes visitors require *encouragement* to answer my mother's questions. In the circle, magic is restricted so they are at my mother's mercy."

"A torture rug," I clarified.

His shrug was dismissive. "I've never been in the circle. I'm not sure of its capabilities."

"I don't need protection from the truth."

"Not quite a torture rug, but it is capable of causing a great deal of pain if you find yourself enclosed in it."

I nodded and gave an Oscar-worthy performance at seeming unbothered by the confirmation.

"People are intrigued by my mother and her magic. As you've seen, it is quite extraordinary. There are some who wish to have access to it, by diplomacy or force. Diplomacy is used initially, and when that fails…" He let the rest linger in the air as if he didn't want to remind me of the world we were in. "And she has made it abundantly clear she wishes to be left alone. Very few people know how to negotiate the barriers she has in place. When they are breached, she likes to know the source of such information."

"You added a flare to give them a chance to rethink such a stupid endeavor."

"Not just for their sake, but hers. The more you torture and murder, the less bothered you become by it. Even thirst for it. It is better that she doesn't revisit the violence she enjoyed before. Her creatures seem to fulfill her. It is better for everyone that they continue to do so."

We were in agreement on that.

"The first and most important thing you need to learn is a protective barrier."

"So I can hide."

"No, so you can protect yourself and live to fight another day."

He instructed me on how he did his, and after several failed attempts it became obvious there were distinct differences to our magic. I quickly learned that as with all magic, there were some commonalities: a protective barrier was a protective barrier. It was the execution of the wielder's magic that was the difference. Tenebras Obducit magic seemed to go a step darker than even Dominic's.

It was offensive and aggressive in nature. Everything I gathered from Dominic and the others who'd dealt with that magic led me to believe it was strong, powerful, and minacious. The same qualities were attributed to the practitioner, but I couldn't help but wonder if it was the magic that made them that way.

Dominic urged me to erect the protective barrier. Instead of urging the magic to protect me, I willed it to push Dominic away. Crowd him out. Thrash him. It managed to form a diaphanous shell around me. Dominic smiled, directing magic at it. It wavered but never fell.

"Drop it," he instructed. That was more difficult than willing it to go away. Chaotic energy burst from me, slamming into it and dissolving it.

"I had to think of hurting you," I explained, frowning. "It's very aggressive magic. Be careful."

He snorted, suppressing a laugh.

"Excuse you. I have bad-ass magic now. I'm to be feared." I extended my hands in quick jerks of movements.

"What are you doing?" Amusement coursed through his words.

"Making claws." A great deal of effort was put into my unsuccessful attempt to cosplay Wolverine.

His rumble of laughter filled the room. Erasing all the distance between us, he was next to me, his claws grazing lightly over my skin, sending shivers through me at the sensuous touch and his control of them. Like his nails crawling over my skin. Then they slid over the front of my dress, from the top to my belly. I shrugged the material off, giving him a full view of me in my panties. He hadn't brought a bra as part of my wardrobe and I went with it. He kissed my lips, then laved his tongue and light nips over my jaw, neck, collarbone, and shoulder while his hands kneaded into my back, sliding over my butt before caressing me into his hardness. Putting some space between us, he continued to stroke my body until he came to my breasts. Palming them, his thumbs teased the nipples until they hardened. His fingers twined through my hair as he pulled me into a kiss. I quickly kicked away the torn dress as he lifted me into his arms. A breath later, he'd pinned me against the wall, letting me settle against his hardness. A frenetic energy raced through me, like nothing I'd experienced. It needed to be sated. The need so commanding and intense I clawed at his shirt. Magic stirred and mingled with my desire. I willed it, and it happened. His shirt shredded with a simple touch.

Dominic glanced down at the missing shirt and pulled away. "Luna," he drawled, pride in his voice despite me using magic to disrobe him. It was going to be damn near impossible not to conflate magic with sex as his mouth covered mine. My legs circled his hips. He inched away, giving himself just enough space to unbuckle his pants. His cock pressed against me, and I accepted him with a deep moan that was silenced by his lips covering mine. My fingers curled into his back, meeting the frenzied rhythm of his hips with each thrust and my back pounding into the wall. The blaze between us erupted into hard, hungry kisses. Pants and groans filled the room. I yearned for more—we yearned for more. Deeper and hungrier, our bodies connecting devolved into something primal. A cumulation of magic, need, and lust exploded into intense satisfaction.

Dominic rested his head against my chest before easing me to the floor. I turned, following his eyes to the damage we did to the wall.

"That was intense," I acknowledged with his nose nuzzling against my cheek.

Sex, magic, and Dominic's sensual touches were no longer conflated as I glared at him. He'd gone from the sexy Dark Prince of the Underworld to a taskmaster urgently trying to teach me a lifetime of magic in just a few days because Dominic—no, *we*—needed to return to the situation we'd left and start damage control and repair the shambles. The multitude of problems we were going to return to were distracting, so I pushed them aside.

After our intense sex session, he'd left and returned with more clothing. Then for the next two hours, it had been nonstop magic practice.

"Again, Luna," he instructed, giving me a devilish smirk at the sharp glare I'd fixed him with. The first hour, I perfected the barrier, erecting it with an ease and speed that satisfied Dominic enough to move on to other things. It was easier to transfer an object from one spot to another. Even easier to lob it at someone.

Performing my version of the ictus spell on a vase, I looked around with a dichotomic feeling of pride and fear at the pieces of the vase I'd exploded. I didn't want to do that to anyone. It was a very good spell to have in my quiver against the worst of the worst, but I dreaded doing it accidentally.

"A person, even a human, won't respond like that. People with magic are even less fragile. It will be a powerful blow and one that would protect you, but you wouldn't be surrounded by body parts," he assured me. "Do it to me."

"I will not."

"Luna, I'll be fine."

'Fine' was being generous as I watched his jaw clench so hard the pressure could make diamonds from coal. As the pain abated, his short sharp breaths leveled out.

"See?" he said. "A tinge of pain and it was over."

Tinge, my ass. I saw his face. Well, maybe that was a tinge to him. What was his pain tolerance like? Dismissing those thoughts, I moved on to the other spells and tasks he had for me. As the lessons ticked by, some things came easily to me. Learning to heal myself was a challenge I mastered, coming up with several variations of spells and offensive magic that could work to heal me. My string of successes led to a moment of hubris until Dominic enclosed me in his flames.

"Get out of there, Luna," he directed me. The flames were

far enough for them not to be a threat; Dominic had impeccable control, but I felt the heat, which drove my desire to defeat it. To do something similar to what Peter had done, crystalizing it and blasting it away. Nothing. It was a reminder that I was still a novice. No matter how strong the magic, it was still limited by the skill of the wielder.

Feeling a little defeated by a string of failures, I was staring at the floor when Dominic's finger lifted my chin. He listed all the things I'd learned in the ten hours of practice: protective fields that only another Dark Caster could break, performing offensive and defensive magic, and a general understanding of the differences between my magic and Dominic's. The latter was something we were discovering together because he'd never had such intimate proximity to Dark Caster magic to understand it other than in an adversarial manner. The hunter to the hunted. Now he had the opportunity to explore it through me.

24

Three days had passed, and I had shown remarkable improvement, but concern had taken up residence on Dominic's face. I awoke to him watching me with a pensive look.

"What?"

"Stay here with my mother until things are handled."

"No." He'd given me a statement and his tone left no indication for feedback, but I had plenty to give. "I have magic and I'm able to protect myself and perform magic. I can help, and you'll need it."

"You can't fight, and you're still a novice," he pointed out. We'd discovered I didn't have preternatural strength or speed, either. No spells had successfully improved that. And despite my constant efforts, I couldn't produce claws.

"But I've proven myself," I said, sitting up in the bed, shocked by his request. He sat up, holding my gaze. The gentleness in them had been missing during the days of training. Several times I'd commented that he was treating me like the enemy and his response simply had been, "The cruelest thing I could do is leave you unprepared."

I was grateful for it. I felt ready, strong, and capable, and him wanting me to be hidden away and guarded by his mother was insulting, and I let him know.

"This isn't wholly about your capabilities. I think my mother was right—"

"No, she wasn't right about any of it. A scorched earth approach isn't going to work. Let chaos reign and clean up the mess afterward? You realize how many humans will be hurt by this? I'm sure there are supernaturals who just want to exist, and not deal with the civil war and the devastation it will cause. I can help. You'll need all the allies you can get. I'm your ally."

A smile curled his lips. "You are tenacious, aren't you?" he said with a sigh.

"Not if you're making it an insult," I snarked back, and though there was admiration in his voice, there were hints of irritation as well. I thought the matter was settled. I should have known it had ended too easily.

I awoke to him gone. In a panic, I dressed and frantically searched the house. My heart clenched with anger and anxiety when I couldn't find him.

"Luna." Sabin's voice pulled me out of my spiral and I turned to find his head canted, his feline eyes assessing me and definitely judging. So much judgment.

"Dominic. I'm looking for him."

He made a choked sound. "A few hours from him and this is how you react? You two have gone from interesting to annoying. He's with his mother." He was really judge-y as I started to explain myself while he guided me to Dominic, who was with his mother in a room I'd never have found. I figured that was the point. Like their home in the underworld, it was a hallway that I'd missed or had been cloaked from my view.

The gothic-looking room had deep garnet-color walls, dark furniture, and floor-to-ceiling storage that held an array of objects, ingredients, and books. The crystal chandelier added some vitality to the ominous room, and the only thing light in the somber space were the stylish cream baroque high-back chairs around the marble table.

Dominic offered me a faint smile. His mother's lips spread wide in an ebullient greeting.

"Luna, I'm so happy you've joined us."

Dominic clearly wasn't, shooting daggers in Sabin's direction that he chose to ignore.

"Perhaps you should leave Luna an itinerary the next time," he teased, pressing a gentle hand to my arm and giving me a well-meaning beam. Attempting to return it, I became distracted by the weathered vellum and the object similar to the Affinity I'd used on my family.

Easing into the room, I stood instead of taking the seat that Ileana indicated, dividing my attention between Dominic, his mother, and the items on the table.

"She doesn't need to be here," Dominic opined.

"I disagree. This is exactly where she needs to be." Again she directed me to a seat, and with a wave of her hand, I received a magic nudge. I returned it, forcing a surprised gasp out of her that grew into an appreciative curl of her lips.

"Is her command of magic better than you've led me to believe?" She directed her question to Dominic, but I got the impression she wanted me to answer, too.

"I've made no such claims. I admitted her spell casting is impressive for the time she's had to learn, along with her rudimentary defensive and offensive skills. I said it was too big a risk for her to use the Garon and I stand by that."

"It is not your place to stand. It is a reasonable solution."

"No, it isn't," he snapped, coming to his feet and pressing his hand against my back to urge me out the door.

The room rattled with her unfettered power and uncontrolled emotions. "Dominicus, get back here. Now." The lashing ice of her tone lingered. But her expression displayed a surprising look of compassion and distress. Compassion.

When he turned, his jaw lifted. Not in defiance or the conflict of love and hate that he'd shown with his father. It was a plea for understanding. Locking gazes, the mélange of unspoken emotions, misplaced hostility, and indecision was thick in the air.

"When you came to me, I helped you because you wanted it. I see that you care for her in a manner that is quite surprising. I honor that."

That was a lie and she made no attempt at making it sound convincing. There was a hint of rebuke as if she was saying "What the hell? *This* creature?"

"Your desire to protect her is blinding you to what is necessary to succeed with your goals. I'm your eyes, son, because you can't see past the emotions. She's capable and this will increase your probability of success with little risk to you."

"And all the risks falling on Luna. It is unfair to ask that of her."

I'd been dropped into the middle of a debate and worked to make sense of it.

"Will you all stop talking as if I'm not here?"

Dominic inhaled a deep breath and with effort, returned to his seat. He steepled his fingers, settling into his disapproval but seemingly accepting that his mother was going to inform me about the discussion he clearly wanted me excluded from.

"The Garon will do to the Dark Caster what was done to *your Luna*. Quite fitting, don't you think? It will pull his magic from him and transfer it to Luna, leaving him a shell and her with insurmountable magic."

"He won't die, will he?" I asked.

She shook her head. "But he'd be magicless."

"You'd have to be close enough to use it against him. Essentially have to bait him to you."

I wasn't a fan of this plan, but a magicless Peter would

destabilize things enough to give us the advantage. How was this not a good idea? We had been gone for five days and had no idea how things were.

"Tell her the rest of your plan," he urged.

"Then you perform." She pushed the paper to me. I read the unfamiliar language on the paper. I had no idea what the words meant, but they looked easy enough to sound out.

My eyes bounced between the two. "What will this do?"

"Return the shades to the underworld," Dominic offered.

"Good."

"Without me suffering a loss of magic. But you will."

"She didn't have magic in the first place but with help of the Garon, she will possess a great deal of magic. It's not a great sacrifice for Luna. But the future Lord of the Underworld *can not* have vulnerabilities. *My* son can not have vulnerabilities." Her eyes slid in my direction, clearly seeing the dilemma as an acceptable vulnerability with conditions. I'd keep her son from losing his magic.

I agreed with her.

He ruminated, his gaze moving between the two of us. "I know it's the right thing to do, but Luna holds the most risk."

"I'm willing to do it. I want me alive as much as you do. I don't care about my magic being diminished or losing it all together." I placed a hand on his arm. "This is bigger than me and it needs to be done. I appreciate you being selfless and wanting to protect me, but I want to do this. I need to do this," I whispered, wanting the conversation to be for his ears only, but under his mother's intense scrutiny it was doubtful she missed any of it.

He grunted a mirthless sound. "Actually, it's not selfless. It is quite selfish. I don't want to risk you."

The understanding made me smile. "I'm okay with doing this."

Dominic's agreement was reluctant and with the dark, calculating look I caught on his face I was confident that he was doing a risk assessment of Ileana's previous suggestion of dealing with the situation. As I neared the Garon, I expected to feel something. A whirr of ominous energy or diablerie or something. But there wasn't anything. A bland object with a powerful use. It was heavier than I expected.

"What do I do with it?" I directed my question to Ileana as Dominic didn't seem fully on board. She recited the spell and I repeated it and the object came to life. I was startled by the Garon pricking my fingers. When the blood swelled, my hands illuminated. Fingerlike tendrils looped and extended from the object in search of similar magic. The glow died when it didn't find any.

"That wasn't difficult," I admitted in surprise.

"The spell is easy, but what will be Peter's response? He will try to reverse it or make you pay," Dominic said.

"You won't let that happen," Ileana asserted. We all knew that.

"I guess this is the plan," he said.

I slipped the Garon in my pocket, and he took the spell to recapture the shades. We both turned our gazes on it. It was *a* plan. But I was convinced it wasn't *the* plan he intended. I'd never get the chance to use it because he'd get to Peter first. I caught his eye and held it. We just stared at each other, seemingly making a tacit agreement for this to be the last resort.

25

I wished we had the luxury of more time to practice my magic. But we stayed in Vita long enough for me to be able to recite the spell for the Garon efficiently. Before returning to my world, we made a detour to the underworld.

We stood in their garden with the morbid black flowers of his sister's making. Dominic's fingers ran over the leaves of bat orchids before a flame erupted over them. He did the same to a few more before he whisked me away to the apartment he shared with Helena.

"Your act of arson, was there a point or were you being petty?" I asked as he knelt on the floor, his claws gouging markings in the floor similar to the ones I saw on the rug at his mother's. With a wave of his fingers over each sigil they disappeared.

"I wanted to get her attention," he said. "I need to talk to her."

"Phone call or text would've been nice, or a note."

Eyeing where he'd placed the sigils, I got the impression he would be doing most of the talking. It wouldn't be a conversation but an interrogation. Turning in the room, I looked at the framed art on the wall, the only one with a black frame.

"TV?"

He nodded and opened one of the decorative boxes on the table and handed me the remote.

I turned it on, going through the news channels, trying to figure out the state of the world. Were the supernatural out? Had there been more sightings? Were the Conventicles able to contain things?

He left the room and returned with a phone, his fingers tapping across them.

"Contacting Anand," he said, answering my questioning look. When he was finished, I asked to borrow it. My phone had been left in his car the day of the attack.

Scrolling all the main social media, I was surprised not to see anything. Reports of fights, sighting of shifters, recent hashtags of magic being real. I deduced that at least some of the witches were still alive and managing the damage control.

"You have my attention, Dominic."

My eyes snapped up from the phone to Helena standing at the door, keeping the several feet they had from each other.

"You betrayed me for a Tenebras Obducit?" he pushed out through gritted teeth.

"No, I was showing you the errors of your ways. And you still haven't learned." She looked in my direction and the sphere of magic she lobbed at me hit the protective barrier I'd erected with little effort. The attack still caused my heart to squeeze and a soft pant escaped. We had practiced it at least a hundred times, but with Dominic and not against someone who wished me harm. Admittedly, a part of me worried about the efficacy. But it held, and I was safe.

Helena's wide-eyed shock at me having magic cost her precious seconds. In a flash of movement, Dominic's magic forced her into the air and landed her on her butt in the middle of the cloaked sigil circle. He evoked the spells, and shimmering crystals formed around her. Confusion warped her expression as she attempted to make sense of the situation. I had magic.

"You betrayed me for a Tenebras Obducit." It wasn't just the betrayal but who he'd been betrayed for. Would her siding with their father have hurt less? His lips moved slowly. Helena's body jerked and tensed. She collapsed to the floor with a shriek of pain.

Pressing her hand against the enclosure, her face strained as she attempted to use her magic to break it. Nothing. With more effort, her face folded into a grimace.

He lowered himself to the ground so they were face to face. Eye to eye. Glare to glare. If there were any fragments of sibling love, it was hidden well.

"You don't have magic in there. If I wish it to be so, I can give you so much pain you'd beg for death to end it."

Arrogance drained from her face, leaving a look so docile and repentant that if I hadn't witnessed all the things she was capable of, I'd be begging for leniency for her.

"I'm sorry," she whispered. Yeah, there's more honesty and sincerity in the emails I get from a prince offering me thousands of dollars. "If you want someone to blame for me turning on you, look in the mirror." She turned a look in my direction with the same curiosity. Magic. I had magic. "She has magic now. You didn't make things better, brother. You made it worse."

Anand's appearance lifted the look of desolation on her face. There was hope of him changing her situation. He looked around at the captured Helena, Dominic kneeling near her, and me in the protective barrier. Not an ounce of surprise showed on his face when I dropped it. He stared for a little longer before a frown settled on his face. I couldn't figure out the target of his disapproval. My acquired magic,

Dominic's response to his sister's betrayal, or some disaster we weren't aware of.

"Some members of the New Conventicle have defected. Be aware that not all who were once allies are still—"

The room vibrated and the door exploded into flying splinters of wood.

A cadre of vampires moving at an imperceptible speed entered. Helena stood, watching the scene with interest as they were met with a force of magic that blasted them back against the wall. Before one could recover, Anand had a stake inches from his heart and was about to plunge it in when Dominic called out to stop him.

Dominic had plucked another vampire from the group and had him secured against him by the neck with his claws at the vampire's throat. The others he kept secured against the floor with his magic. Anger plastered his face as he took in the vampires and looked for the magical threat that caused the disruption. The assailant remained in the shadows.

"Enemy or ally?" Dominic asked the vampire he held.

He responded with silence and a piercing look. At a slight nod of Dominic's head, Anand finished the job with the other vampire.

"If you are my enemy, no mercy will be given."

I bit my tongue and gave myself the same internal speech that this violence was necessary for there to be peace. I needed to believe it.

"Answer my question," Dominic demanded. Although their silence seemed like an indicator of their position, Dominic wanted more. Claws pressed into the vampire's throat that he was holding, the vampire's blood turning Dominic's shirt crimson as it spilled over it.

"Speak."

He didn't, meeting his fate with defiance along with the others. Dominic stood in silence, taking in the remnants of dust from the dead vampires. Tension filled the room as he waited in anticipation of more attacks.

"You don't have any allies, brother," Helena said. "We never really did. There were those who saw our ways as a benefit to them and abided by the rules, and those who were biding their time until things got fucked up. That's where we are now. Kill Luna, weaken Peter, and reclaim your rule."

"You sided with Peter!"

"I sided with the victor." She said it as if that would temper the betrayal. "One who wouldn't let a human derail everything." There was a hint of questioning in her voice over the word 'human.' I had magic and was different. Human was a misnomer. Formerly human? Not quite human? Posing as human?

Dominic moved toward the confinement, a hard set in his jaw, fixing his sister with a glare. Flashes of hurt shadowed his face. It was so difficult understanding how her betrayal was unexpected to him. Perhaps because it was to Peter, a Dark Caster. Magic that rivaled his.

"You chose wrong. Things will return to the way they were. Helena, you'll answer to all that I sheltered you from. Areleus will not be in a position to request leniency on your behalf."

She winced. Before, there had been the question of whether he'd commit patricide. There wasn't any question about it now. Whatever weakness she'd seen in Dominic had no hints of having ever existed. Color drained from her face.

They held each other's gaze, breaking only when magic flooded into the room and three unfamiliar witches walked in. One made her way toward me, the other sending pellets of magic in rapid fire toward Dominic. With a swipe of his hand he returned them to her as he attempted to weave around them. At the witch's approach, I created my barrier, protecting myself my primary goal, while the other witch attempted to release Helena, whose alliance with Peter gave her alliance with the Awakeners who were now fully committed to Peter.

Her hands against the magical prison did nothing. The battle between the witch and Dominic ended badly for the witch. He watched the witch with a satisfied smile as she examined the revealed markings in the floor, then he whispered a spell, the shimmer of it fell, and with a nudge of magic, he pushed the witch in with Helena. Then he invoked the spell to keep them enclosed and another that made them writhe in pain. They folded over into ragged pants when the onslaught stopped. Dominic pulled his attention from them to the witch who was attempting to break down my barrier, dividing her attention between Dominic and her surroundings as if she was looking for the source of my magical barrier.

The window exploded into shards of glass, some hitting Anand in the arm he used to protect himself. Three shades who spilled in expanded their wings, obscuring most of the room. One soared toward Anand, grabbing him with his clawed hand and tossing him to the other side of the room like a doll. He crashed into the wall and hit the floor with a thud. Dominic was in a battle with the other two shades. As the witch continued to barrel her magic into my barrier, her face ruddy with frustration, I concentrated. Timing my action for the best chance of success, I dropped my barrier, placing us just a few inches from each other. Pushing magic into her chest, I sent her clamoring back a few feet and into a fall. My mistake was not wanting the same thing that happened to the vase to happen to her, despite Dominic's claims that it wouldn't. But it was enough. Her shock that I had magic delayed her response. I didn't hold back with my next assault. The magic smashing into her sent her slamming into the shade. His body, as resilient as a wall, left him standing and her on the ground wincing in pain.

Erecting my barrier again, I looked for more openings as

the chaos erupted and more people spilled into the room. Some were familiar and some I believed were part of both Conventicles with the sole purpose of containing and disabling the Awakeners and their allies. I couldn't be sure because of Anand's warning. It was the periodic attempts they made to get to me that made me assume they were enemies.

My heart pounded when a shade advanced toward me. Choosing physical violence over magic, he clawed at the barrier with no success. Drawing back his lips, his mouth moved without the smooth mechanics of someone used to speaking frequently.

The barrier rippled, undulated, pushed in, but held. He put more effort into it, and I could see Dominic out of my periphery trying to get to me. I didn't have a weapon. I should always have a weapon. Briefly, I considered dropping my barrier, making a grab for the discarded blade to my right, and erecting the barrier again, but my attempt to walk with the barrier up failed. Shades moved fast and had built-in weapons of claws. The fact that Peter wanted me alive didn't seem like an advantage, because nothing about the shades gave me the impression they cared about rules. Chaos maybe. Violence definitely. My demise would give them what they wanted.

Too much fighting and magic in the room made thinking clearly difficult. Just surviving wasn't enough. I looked for vulnerabilities. Eyes. I could get to his eyes, claw, poke, or whatever I could do. Nose was another. Heel of my hand needed to smash into it. I crouched a little to give myself the leverage to put all my weight into it.

I started to lunge, when out of the side of my eye, Areleus came into view. Before I could execute my plan, the prison around his daughter fell. The two turned their energies to Dominic, my barrier fell without me releasing it, and I was pulled against a sinewy body.

I smashed my head back, trying to hit a nose or anything hard of whoever had wrapped me in a bear hug.

"There, there, it's just you and me," Peter cooed. Then the world of chaos disappeared as Dominic growling my name was clipped into silence.

Head spinning, I closed my eyes to get my bearings and gave no care as to who was on the receiving end of my indiscriminate magic. I blasted and heard a hard thump of a body hitting the wall. Glass crashing and items falling. When I focused, Peter was coming to stand, a dark smirk of satisfaction on his face as he quickly moved toward me. The room had many objects, and I sent them all careening at him. Coffee grinder lobbed at him, he swiped away with a wave of his hand. Books, dishes, home décor, and cups were hurled in his direction while he used his protective barrier as a shield. I continued to pummel whatever items I could get to into the shield, hoping for an opening or a waver in it.

I assumed he lost his patience or no longer wanted to flaunt his magical acumen. He returned offensive magic. It felt like he slammed a weighted ball into my chest. I smashed into the wall hard and then crumpled into a heap on the floor. We were face to face as I panted for breath. A gleam of satisfaction moved over his face, brightening the cast of darkness that fell over his features and chased away any hint of the studious man who spent his time giving unsolicited history.

"Luna," he drawled. "I will give it to the prince, he's managed to succeed in what I spent years trying to discover. He made you one of us. Where there was just one, now there are two."

He seemed excited, as if my presence was the implied alliance.

"No, there aren't two. I have no intention of helping you."

A slow deviant smile curled his lips. "Then this will be a battle of will." His eyes eclipsed to coal. Magic wrapped around me, stealing my breath. I could feel the full presence of his power. An indicator of why he was feared. And the chaos, violence, and destruction he could cause. He inched closer to me.

"The question is, dear Luna, what will it take to break you?"

I allowed my hand to slide over my pocket where the Garon was hidden.

I had no intention of being broken.

26

Peter moved to the far side of the room, cloaked in an insidious intent as his eyes casually swept over what I had left in ruins. His dismissive look at the wreckage hit at my confidence but not my drive to take his magic and leave him magicless and unable to cause more destruction.

"For so long, I thought you were just a rumor. A well of magic that could give us the ability to destroy the ruthless trio." His eyes hardened, anger drawing him taller. Agitation forming a rough scowl on his face.

"And you're not ruthless?" I challenged.

"Not nearly to their degree," he ground out, baring his teeth. For a moment, I expected to see fangs. I didn't discard the possibility that he had them and chose to keep them a secret.

"Dominic hunted and killed all the Casters. I'm the only one left." His eyes brightened. "*We* are the only ones left."

"There's no we," I shot back.

His mirthless laughter filled the room with an ominous threat. "You've heard his version of reality, so your response is understandable. I'm not the monster you've been led to believe and Dominicus isn't the lamb he's presented to you."

Everyone was using words so wrong. Lamb? Dominic had never given me the impression he was a lamb. Didn't give me the impression he was decent a hundred percent of the time. Never denied that his morals sat firmly in the gray area. He wore the armor of a ruthless monster when needed. I waited for Peter to continue. As he inched closer, his arms crossed over his chest, hair disheveled, t-shirt molded to his sinewy chest, and loose-fitted jeans, I got glimpses of the deceptively bookish-looking man who hung out at Books and Brew.

My attention stayed on the wide-rimmed prop glasses he clearly didn't need. Noticing where my eyes had landed, he removed them, and with a quick whisper they vanished in a cloud of smoke.

"We are powerful and never subscribed to their rules or leadership. Why should we? Magic like ours give us the privilege to shape the world in the manner we see fit." He inched closer. Closer was better. The closer he was, the easier it would be to use the Garon. "Why should we be held to inferior rules? Dominicus, Helena, and Areleus aren't. We should be extended the same privileges."

"They work with the supernatural community to protect humans."

He snorted. "What lies has he fed you?" he asked. "They seek to control the supernaturals. Humans being provided some modicum of safety is just a byproduct. We'd do the same, but under our terms."

"What would be our terms?" I asked.

The question eased some of his reticence as he swallowed up more of the distance between us.

"You have no idea how powerful you are. Now we have the shades, who will do our bidding so long as it satisfies their needs."

"Their need for violence and chaos," I pointed out.

He dismissed it with a wave of his hand. "Do you want a docile army or one that is feared?"

As the moments ticked by and his question went unanswered, he said, "It would be foolish to believe there won't be any violence. Even the humans haven't managed such a feat." Disdain raveled around the word 'human.' "I've established an alliance with them that is mutually beneficial. They will be controlled."

"Okay, we have an army. What next?"

Peter's smile widened and he moved until he was in front of me. He extended a hand to me. "Let's sit on the sofa. Me speaking to you while you're splayed on the floor seems… uncivilized. We are equals."

Me sitting on the floor never meant anything more to me than just that—me sitting on the floor. Everything about this world had a meaning, a demonstration of a person's role and position.

I eyed his extended hand, debating whether to smack it away or give him the finger. I did neither, taking it and allowing him to help me to my feet, hoping the small show of acceptance would cause him to lower his guard. I made sure to take the left side of the sofa, so that when I positioned my body toward Peter, I'd have quick access to the leg with the Garon. My casual seat, one leg crossed on the sofa, appeared to put him at ease. Sitting closer to him, I could feel the thrum of his powerful magic. It was undeniable. How had I never noticed it and how off his energy was?

"Here you are," he whispered. "The Casters were all looking for you. I'd given up hope. There was no way you were just a tale of a sacrifice of one to give others the power they need to deal with Dominic. Then I happened to walk into Books and Brew. The description of what to look for had been skewed so much over the retellings. But the hair. The moment I laid eyes on you, I was sure. But I needed to be certain." I ran a self-conscious hand through my auburn waves. "Discovering how curious you were made confirming you were the right person easy. That particular spell wouldn't have worked on anyone else. It only would have worked with an affinity magic." A dark smile curled his lips, his eyes slowly traveling over me as if he were getting thoughts of us being some awful dark-magic power couple. His head canted as he scrutinized me.

"You're not human," he said as a reminder.

"I know." My chest squeezed. It felt like a betrayal. Despite knowing it, there was a part of me that felt a loyalty to humanity. To protecting humanity because that was all I'd known myself to be.

"Dominic, Helena, and Areleus are wrong and you're right?" I inquired, needing more information and for him to be more comfortable with me. Needing him to be relaxed to the point he wouldn't expect me to take his magic.

His eyes drifted to the window behind me. "What is in place is fine. Humans should know of our existence. And we should have a place at the table in society. No, we should be at the head. Entirely running things."

"We?"

"You and I, of course. Do you understand the power I wield? With one spell, I could kill everyone on this block. I could unleash the shades with a word. I could bring most of the supernaturals to their knees with a well-crafted spell."

"You against hundreds of magic wielders, shifters who are immune to magic, and vampires who move like lightning?" My words dripped with a skepticism that I made no effort to hide. He was a monster and an arrogant one, too.

"There's a spell that will end the shifters' immunity. The two of us can do it. I have no intention of allowing them to maintain that advantage. Too many vampires currently exist in this world. I will be pruning the population—"

"Pruning sounds a great deal like genocide," I countered,

surprised at my ability to keep my voice neutral despite his admissions. I saw his easy reveals for what it was. My fate. He offered the information freely because he was confident I wasn't going to leave. Whether my position with him was voluntary was up to me. Everything about his ominous smirk showed that.

"Our hands will remain perfectly clean. Roman will be released from the Perils and allowed to curate the vampires. I suspect he'll only want his bloodline to remain. Which would be advantageous. They would be an asset and our goals would easily align. Vadim will also be a good addition. The spell would cause him to lose his immunity to magic as well. I'll decide later if he'll be allowed to keep his magical ability, based on how much of an asset he proves to be. Unfortunately, Celeste and her bloodline needs to end. That bloodline of witches has proved to be too powerful. Too obstinate. There are other skilled witches who'd be better."

It didn't go unnoticed how freely he had claimed the union between us. Having Vadim as an ally would ensure Peter could use him against Dominic, Helena, and Areleus.

From his appraising satisfied expression, I gathered he'd taken my silence as acceptance and not the same disdain and incredulity that raced through me when Ileana offered a similar plan. *What the fuck was wrong with these people? Did great magic lead to being so malevolent and amoral?*

"We'll carefully sieve through those that remain. This is a good strategy. I thought I'd just have your magic to pull from, but now I have you. A far better situation, and I have the prince to thank for that." Once again, I found myself under his unwavering inspection as he leaned forward.

"How did he do it?" he whispered.

"Do what?"

He wasn't fooled. With a swipe of his hand, I was hoisted in the air, magic coiling and tightening around me, making breathing difficult. It continued its winding to my throat, cutting off all breathing. Panic seized me and a tear slid down my face.

He inched closer until his face was just out of reach. I closed my eyes and concentrated. Trying to break the bonds. Pulling at its strands. Trying to force my magic to destroy it. This magic was all about destruction and violence. Why wouldn't it break the bonds?

"I've had this magic for hundreds of years. Honed it to perfection. Do you believe your days with use of it will match mine, Luna?"

I had a body, but I'd never questioned if I could die. As my head grew lighter, there was a clear answer. I could. I would. What would happen to my magic upon my death?

"I'll ask you again, how did he do it?"

Was Dominic's mother unknown to most?

A strangled sound escaped from me and he relaxed the magic.

"He had someone do it," I choked out.

"Who?"

After a long stretch of silence, he gave me a few more inches of space. The hold of magic lessened enough for me to get some oxygen, but I was fully aware that just a flick of his wrist or an invocation of a spell could return the stranglehold.

"Release me and I'll tell you."

"You'll tell me because I asked." He was directly in front of me, trying to catch my eyes. Seeking eye contact reminded me that vampires required the same to compel someone. I wasn't sure what Peter was going to do, but I knew me looking at him was essential. I closed my eyes. There was a tug at them, like fingers were being used to open them. I didn't feel a body close to me or shadow from a body or an extremity near me. He was doing it with magic. He barked out a dark, cold laugh and pain surged through me.

I can do this. Luna, you can do this. Forcing all my will into my command, the coils loosened and a surge of power exploded from me. There was a loud thud and I opened my eyes to Peter coming to a stand, an appreciative look spreading over his face.

"Strong untrained magic. I can work with that." Approaching me, he released his magic and I fell on my butt. Even through my attack, he was able to maintain his magic. I wasn't a challenge to him. I needed more practice.

"There won't be need for Dominic, Helena, or Areleus anymore. Killing them will be difficult. If I don't succeed, *we* will secure them in the underworld, where they won't be able to intervene where they aren't needed."

My expression betrayed me. His lips formed a dramatic pout. "Aw. Have you grown fond of that dreadful family? Or just Dominic?" His last comment a sheer mockery. I had no issue with him locking Helena and Areleus in the underworld. But not Dominic.

"Who did this to you, Luna?" he asked again.

"What? Abused me with magic? That would be you," I hissed.

"Who are you protecting, Luna?"

It wasn't protection. He wanted the information for a reason, and not a good one. I was doing what I could to limit his acquisition of power. I wasn't completely confident he couldn't get to Ileana, but based on Dominic's stories, maybe they should meet. He might not walk away from that encounter. My gut was telling me not to give him the information, so I pressed my lips tightly together.

"I'd like to have you as a companion in this. It will be a lonely venture, but I'm quite capable of doing it by myself. All I need is your magic. I can take it with a spell, or I can use that gauche Garon in your pocket you've been trying so hard not to draw attention to."

Shit. I shot into action. Snatching the Garon from my pocket, I launched at him and held on like a koala to their momma. Instead of being latched to his back, I held on to his torso. Any painful magic he inflicted on me, he'd feel himself. I evoked the spell. The magical object took its claim on my hand, drawing blood.

I couldn't see if the Garon illuminated or if the black tendrils branched out in search of similar magic. But I could feel a different magic sweeping over me—over Peter. He croaked a sharp sound of surprise. A hum of words emitted from him, but the magic continued to suffuse. Thick and heavy, there was something dank and different about it. I no longer had a koala hold on Peter; it was the new magic securing us to each other.

A gray haze formed in front of us, a larger replication of the tendrils formed during my practice with the Garon. Coolness swept the room. Blinking several times, I took in the figure before it disappeared, leaving behind traces of the ominous magic.

The front door blasted open, raining splinters of wood everywhere.

"Luna," Dominic called out, his light footfalls nearing us. I risked a look in his direction to see the horrid expression on his face. Rushing over, he reached me and hissed in pain but continued, ripping me from Peter. Dominic didn't give Peter a moment to respond. He tossed Peter feet away, then sent a glowing sphere of magic into his chest that crashed him into the wall across the room. Peter slumped to the floor but attempted to return fire. His eyes widened and filled with panic when nothing happened. He made several more fruitless attempts, his breathing increasingly short and raspy. Fear and confusion washed over his face.

"Where's the Garon?" Dominic asked.

Preoccupied with keeping contact with Peter and successfully performing the spell, with the influx of the new peculiar magic, I'd lost track of it. I looked around the immediate area for it. Gone.

"I don't know." Standing, we both searched the surrounding area. Peter remained frozen in stunned disbelief, unable to reconcile with the new knowledge that his magic didn't counter the Garon and that his magic was gone. Dominic's mask of anger fell when he looked at me.

"Perform magic, Luna," he instructed.

I tried to erect a protective spell. Nothing. I attempted a spell. Nothing. Swiping my hand over the room in effort to clear things from my path had no results.

In a flash of movement, Dominic was on Peter, a hold around his neck, claws at the pulse of it.

"What did you do?" Dominic demanded.

The shrewd confidence exhibited earlier had vanished. Peter looked just as confused as I felt. Without his magic, he was at a terrible disadvantage with Dominic. Despite it, he managed a glare in Dominic's direction.

"Why would I take my own magic?" he barked.

There was a long moment of consideration before Dominic drew back his hand, the unbridled viciousness and mercilessness shown in his sneer. The same look I'd seen when he fought.

"No!" I blurted. He stopped with his claws just a half an inch or so from Peter's neck. He snapped in my direction.

"The Garon is gone and so is our magic. Someone took it." I explained the figure with the tendrils that resembled the tendrils I'd seen during practice with the Garon. How I had been secured to Peter and the off-putting magic that mingled with ours. "If someone took it, we may need Peter to get it back."

"We won't. We'll find another way," Dominic asserted.

The blaze in his eyes made my approach to him cautious. Driven by fury, he wasn't taking everything into consideration. Recounting Peter's plans, a number of scenarios went through my mind of what could be done with both of our magic and none of them were good. I wasn't spiraling into a full-on anxiety attack because it wasn't another Dark Caster who took the magic. Peter was the only one. *We* were the only ones. The unthinkable level of destruction the thief could cause if they learned to harness it, scared me. Dominic was looking for a way to use the magic—what if someone had beaten him to it?

"Please," I whispered. Dragging his eyes from Peter, his gaze was gentle as he looked at me.

"Remember what I told you," he said softly. He'd warned: "Your empathy will be seen as weakness and your kindness exploited."

"This isn't about kindness or weakness. Our magic is gone. Peter has access to spells and magic that you aren't aware of. Killing him will take away an advantage."

He released his hold on Peter but used magic to keep him pinned against the wall. Taking hold of my arm, he moved me to the other side of the room, out of Peter's earshot.

"My mother gave us the Garon," he said in a pained voice. I heard the implications in his tone. He thought it was his mother. He'd been betrayed so often by his family, he could no longer extend the benefit of the doubt. "Peter took you. That can't go unpunished."

Gently, I touched his hand, aware of the scrutiny of our audience. "Make sure it's her before you do anything with him. Please." If it was, I had no intention of appealing for mercy for anyone. Accepting another betrayal wasn't in me, either. It was hard to see Ileana betraying her children, but her suggestions and Peter's plans were aligned.

"Ask her," I urged again.

Shooting another spiteful glare in Peter's direction, without a word, Dominic pulled me to him, plunging me into darkness as we quickly went to the underworld and then to Vita. Standing in front of the ward, he made the silver undulation come to life. Running across it were streaks of crimson waves that pushed us back. His upgrade to the barrier. It wasn't just a magic flare, it was a stop sign. An urging to just keep moving. A few rote movements of his hand and a spell, it fell and we moved through it.

Dragar stepped into view, a miscreant look on his face, tail whipping behind him playfully. "Dominicus," he drawled, the smile dropping from his face, the playfulness draining as he looked at Dominic. Wrathful and murderous looking, Dominic stalked past him toward his mother's estate.

Meeting us at the pathway to her house, concern swept over Ileana's face at Dominic's state. A mixture of emotions that he didn't bother to mask.

"Dominicus, what's wrong?" The soft maternal request was a direct contrast of what she'd ever shown.

"The Garon is gone and so is Luna's magic," he said.

Her brows drew together, and her breath whooshed out the question. "What do you mean?"

"It's gone." Although his voice remained strained, there was notable relief. His mother wasn't responsible. She was given all the information I gave Dominic. By the end, Ileana's breaths were short and ragged.

"Peter's magic is gone, too?"

We nodded. Her gaze swept from me to Dominic.

"You know what this means, Dominic?" How could they not. An unknown person had just acquired an insurmountable amount of magic that would give them the ability to do everything Peter had planned, including locking the royals in the underworld.

He nodded. "No one is safe, including us."

Luna and Dominic's adventure continues in A Taste of Magic (Magic of the Damned Book 3). Available for preorder.

MESSAGE TO THE READER

Thank you for choosing *A Hint of Darkness* from the many titles available to you. My goal is to create an engaging world, compelling characters, and an interesting experience for you. I hope I've accomplished that. Reviews are very important to authors and help other readers discover our books. Please take a moment to leave a review. I'd love to know your thoughts about the book.

For notifications about new releases, *exclusive* contests and giveaways, and cover reveals, please sign up for my mailing list at McKenzieHunter.com.

McKenzieHunter.com
McKenzieHunter@McKenzieHunter.com

Printed in Great Britain
by Amazon